MESSIAH

By

Tom E Shelby

Text Copyright 2019

Tom E Shelby

Acknowledgements

Book cover by **Tom E Shelby** . Pictures from Deposit photos.

I would like to thank Nico Maeckelberghe and Claire Lawrence for making some coherent sense out of my ramblings. Also for pointing out any plot flaws or timeline glitches. These are the sorts of things that are invaluable to an author and things that we miss. I couldn't ask for a better pair of beta readers.

To all the indie world for having supported me since I switched genres to erotica, you are all amazing.

A big thank you to my Street Team **Tom E Shelby's Sassy Sirens** for promoting my work under this new pen name. It is not easy starting to write under a new name after creating a following under another. I know that they use a lot of their personal free time to promote not just myself but other Indie Authors. They are the unsung heroes of the book world. Without them our words would not reach as many people as they do and we should and are all eternally grateful.

CHAPTER ONE - MILLIE

"Come now, and let us reason together, saith the Lord; though your sins be as scarlet, they shall be as white as snow; though they be red like crimson, they shall be as wool. If ye be willing and obedient, ye shall eat the good of the land."

*"But if ye refuse and rebel, ye shall be devoured with the sword: for the mouth of the Lord hath spoken it." **(Isaiah— Chapter 1, Verses 18 and 19)***

That was the mantra my grandmother lived by and she brought up her children to abide by the Scriptures. She was raised a Protestant and Baptist, believing that girls were to cheerfully obey their parents and the Bible. As an active member of the Nazarene Baptist church, girls were expected to live by the rules known as the "big five". Going to the cinema, dancing, interacting with the opposite sex, swearing and drinking alcohol were totally forbidden. Acts such as these were clearly sinful and to be avoided at all costs.

It was a huge disappointment for her when my mother complained that she wasn't allowed to have any fun. Surely the church and Sunday school provided the unparalleled joy of worship. What more did a young teenage girl need? In time, she might meet and marry a good Christian boy. She was to be sorely saddened in this respect.

The nearby town of Ingleton was a hot bed of sin and my mother was intrigued by its lure. Having been warned about sin all her life, she wanted the opportunity to observe some of it first-hand. She would sneak out at night and visit the vibrant clubs where the music was loud and prospective dance partners were plentiful. At eighteen, she believed she wasn't a child anymore and wanted to get to know the ways of the world. It was at one of these clubs that she met a young soldier who was some eight years her senior. He was a strapping, handsome young fellow and my mother fell for him immediately.

He was a man that was wise in the ways of the world and his silvery tongue soon captured her heart. She was the perfect prey for his smarmy charm. She was flattered to receive the attentions of an older man and would regularly visit the club and meet with him. This went on for about six months, until one day she discovered she was pregnant. When she delivered the news to the young man, he informed her that he was to be posted a few weeks later, but would return.

It was after several months, and no sign of him, that my mother realised that he would not return, let alone do the right thing by her. She didn't keep the unborn child a secret from my grandmother, and not surprisingly she went into a blinding rage. How dare she bring shame on the family name? There was a condition to not being disowned and she was to put aside her sinful ways and live strictly according to the Scriptures.

In the first few months of her confinement, she clung to the hope that the young man would return and rescue her from the hell of living under my grandmother's puritanical rules. Of course, this never happened and as the baby began to kick, her rage began to swell. How dare he abandon her alone with a child to raise! Although she disagreed with my grandmother, one thing she wanted most of all was to have a man to guard and protect her. To provide for her and her unborn child, just as her father had done. She was determined to find a man and to show that bastard who had abandoned her, that she was a survivor.

She knew exactly which man would be her prey. He was also a regular at the club and had shown a keen interest in her in the time she was dating that other fucker! He was unlike the other; small in stature, but with a kind, caring nature. His name was Henry Stewart and he was also a former soldier who had settled in the area once he completed his time. Working now as a garage mechanic in the town, he would often frequent the bar. There was an instant connection between them and within three months they were married. As she was not yet of age she lied on the marriage certificate and was listed as being twenty one. This was so her mother's permission would not be required. So, at last she had a husband and was happy.

It wasn't long before the shine wore off the marriage. My mother began to get itchy feet. Although devoted to her young child, at eighteen her hormones and rebellious nature returned with a vengeance. She would often go out without her husband and at times would show up at her mother's or Aunt Glenda's house, babe-in-arms. She would disappear for days at a time, sometimes in the company of her elder brother, Marcus. Both her mother and aunt were concerned about the child being left with unsuitable babysitters, whilst my mother was out living life to the full.

It wasn't long before my grandmother became concerned at rumours circulating about her daughters activities. The news in the neighbourhood was that my mother would entice men in bars with sexual favours. Once they were outside of the premises, her brother Marcus would beat them up and relieve them of their hard-earned money. None of these facts were substantiated, but my grandmother was sure that anyone who went against the Scriptures was capable of anything. She confined my mother to the house, but she would often sneak out without her knowing. On more than one occasion she would beat my mother to try and drive whatever demon had possessed her. Daily, if not twice or three times daily, trips to the church to cast out the spirit that had taken over her little girl. This was, of course, ludicrous. My mother was just like any normal girl of that age whose hormones were raging.

Henry Stewart was a quiet, patient and caring husband. Even with such a nature, they were only two years into the marriage and he could not take it anymore. No longer could he endure his wife's drunken exploits and infidelity. Not to mention her abandonment of a child that wasn't even his. He had given his name to the child on the birth certificate, even though it belonged to another man. He filed for divorce, which was not contested by my mother. She was probably in some drug or alcohol-induced state at the time of the hearing and he was granted the divorce.

He also claimed that he was not the biological father of the child and after a DNA test, this was confirmed. That being the case, he was not legally obligated to pay a penny in support and all I got from the sordid affair, was his last name.

Left with no money or support of any kind, except for emotional support from my grandmother, she immediately went about searching for my biological father. As she still frequented the bars in Ingleton, it didn't take her very long before she tracked him down. One of his former colleagues mentioned that he had left the service and settled in the nearby county. Armed with this information, my mother brought a bastardy case against him. She no longer held her erstwhile lover in the same starry-eyed worship as when they first met and wanted him to take some financial responsibility for his actions.

My father was no pillow biter, that's for sure, and attempted to fight the case. The fact that he did not deny he was my father, sealed the case and the court ruled in my mother's favour. I even recall him coming to see me when I was a toddler. He held me in his arms and I remember that look in his eyes. It was not love, more a look of malice. It was as if I was to blame for his, now, financial situation. He didn't give off the same feelings that a doting father does to his child. A willingness to give everything he could to see that I would grow up to be a fully functioning and rounded member of society.

After that first visit and his initial financial contribution, he reneged on the agreement and my mother never saw another penny. She was livid and asked that the court deduct the amount from his wages. This was never implemented, as at that time, the courts were not obliged to issue such a demand. That would turn out to be the least of my mother's worries.

Over the next year we lived between my grandmother and her Aunt Glenda's place. The place was overcrowded as Marcus often stayed there with his girlfriend, as my grandmother would not allow such a thing under her roof. Glenda and her husband, Tom, were good, hard working, Christian people. They were not as straight-laced and fanatical as my grandmother when it came to the Scriptures, but attended their church regularly. They would often take me along with them after my mother had disappeared on one of her Saturday night excursions into town.

As I allowed the words of the preacher to infiltrate my innocent, impressionable ears, I was captivated. At the tender age of just over two years old, I was still learning the meaning of words. That did not seem to matter as there was a confidence and a positivity about the man who stood in front of us. He exuded a belief in what he was saying and the congregation hung on his every word and syllable that dripped from his lips. That was my first recollections of Christianity, but due to circumstance, it would not be my last.

By the time I was five, my mother had become disillusioned and wanted something better from life. She was no longer a naïve young girl who wanted to go out to dance and have fun. In desperate need for cash, she entered into something that would define my life from that fateful moment on.

In the summer of that year, Sharon, the girlfriend of my uncle Marcus, and my mother were out having drinks in Ingleton. During the course of the evening, they made the acquaintance of a friendly guy called Steve. His rather naïve attitude immediately drew my mother's attention. Like most men, she quickly worked out what he was after. As the drinks flowed between the three of them, my mother noticed the roll of cash that he was carrying in his back pocket. She made an excuse to leave the table and motioned for Sharon to join her in the restroom. They both made their excuses that they were going to freshen up, with a wink to the unwitting middle-aged man.

"Have you seen how much money he has on him? No one should have that much money!" My mother blurted out as soon as the door closed behind them.

"I know, right!" Sharon was of the same mind, her eyes wide from the drugs that she had taken earlier in the evening.

"Well, let's make sure we relieve him of some or all of it!" Sharon passed over some white powder and my mother took a huge sniff and it disappeared up her nostril.

"Let's do it!" The buzz from the drug was immediate and she shook her head as she opened the door and the pair returned to the table and their waiting victim.

She explained to me about that fateful night a year later, when I was taken to visit her. She said that Steve was just a sexual predator and deserved everything that was coming to him. It was apparent as soon as they returned to the table, that he had designs on the pair of them. Even though Sharon told him that she was in a relationship, it did not deter him and he suggested that they carry on at a nearby motel.

Sharon and my mother explained that they didn't have the money for that, but he assured them it was his treat. They both hid their smiles as the plan began to form in their minds.

"I know a place just out of town. The Ranch Motel, do you know it?" Steve began to fidget as he seemed eager to be off.

"Yes, we know it." My mother answered for both of them, a salacious grin affirming that she was up for it.

"It sounds like it could be fun." Sharon backed up my mother's enthusiasm with a little of her own.

He was quite a strong-looking guy and two females would find it impossible to relieve him of his cash. They were going to need help. So Sharon made an excuse to leave the table to use the pay phone, saying she would have to explain to her boyfriend that she was staying over at a friend's.

While Sharon was making the call to Marcus, with what was going on and the location of the motel, my mother toyed with her victim. She slid her hand under the table and ran her fingers along his thigh. This brought a huge grin to his face and he shifted forward in his seat so that his erection was touching her fingertips. Before things could go any further, and much to Steve's consternation, Sharon returns.

"All sorted. Shall we go then?" Sharon reach over and took her bag from the seat and threw it over her shoulder.

"You bet, baby doll!" Steve jumped up from his seat and Sharon's eyes were at once drawn to his raging hard on.

"I can see you are definitely up for this." She whispered in his ear and surreptitiously fondled his throbbing cock.

"Like you wouldn't believe, babe." In return he squeezed her buttock with one gigantic hand. She squirmed and giggled, going along with the game.

On leaving the bar, Steve hailed a passing cab. They could have walked the mile or so to the outskirts of town, but he was obviously excited to get on with the fun. All three of them jumped into the back seat and after being given the destination, the driver pulled away from the sidewalk. The drive to the outskirts of town and the motel took only a few minutes. Sharon and my mother continued to keep up Steve's interest by stroking his inner thigh, lingering around his balls and now rock-hard dick. The light-coloured pants he was wearing were stained from his arousal and the hook was definitely taken.

When they reached the motel, Steve handed over a dollar bill from his roll of notes. Both my mother and Sharon winked at each other behind his back. On stepping out of the vehicle, he asked the girls to wait while he went to see if a room was available. Of course they complied with his wishes and Sharon checked her watch to see how long it would be before Marcus showed. It was only a fifteen to twenty minute drive from where he was, so they would not have to continue the sham for too long.

Steve returned within a couple of minutes. He had a set of keys in his hands and a smile as wide as the fender of a Cadillac. He jingled the keys tantalizingly in front of the two girls, who giggled as he opened the door to the room that, by chance, they were stood outside. Throwing open the door he invited them inside, slapping my mother's ass cheeks for good measure. She feigned mock surprise and wiggled her butt, which obviously excited him even more.

On entering the room, the two of them immediately began to undress. Once they were down to their underwear, *they began to kiss and fondle each other. Of course, Steve thought he had died and gone to heaven. Who the fuck does not appreciate a good lesbian floor show? He began to fumble with his belt, trying to unbuckle himself in haste. Sharon glanced at her watch once more as his attention was diverted. Marcus should be arriving anytime now, she mused, and thought it expedient to get Steve out of the way.*

"I hope that thing is clean?" She pointed at Steve's cock, hidden beneath the shorts he was wearing.

"Of course it is, you cheeky fucker!" He sounded hurt as he cast his pants and shirt aside and stood there now bare-chested, only in his shorts.

"Well, why don't you give that lovely cock of yours a good wash? We want to taste that luscious piece of meat, don't we, babe?" It was my mother's turn to speak, immediately picking up the vibe that Sharon was giving.

"Okay, I have no problem with that." Steve turned to make his way to the bathroom and as he disappeared, the sound of tyres crunching on the dirt outside heralded the arrival of Marcus.

They couldn't have timed it any better and Sharon slipped from the room and went outside to explain the situation. She knew she didn't have long and they both arrived moments later. Marcus was carrying a baseball bat and my mother indicated the bathroom where the hapless sap was washing the cock he would never get to use. At least not on these two wayward fillies. They could have just rifled his pants and relieved him of the money, but they weren't sure if they had time for that. Marcus took up a position at the side of the door to the bathroom.

"Well, lookie here at this piece of prime, Texas meat just for you two lucky ladies!" Steve wanders into the room holding his impressive looking cock in his hand. He does not notice Marcus standing just behind the door frame.

He steps further into the room and advances towards my mother and Sharon. Step by step he draws closer to them, all the while stroking his cock. The veins are raised around the shaft as the blood fills them to capacity. The look on the two young women is not the reaction he was looking for. Their eyes seem to be looking past him over his shoulder. As he turns his head to look back towards the other side of the room, Marcus brings the baseball bat up between his outstretched legs. The blow catches him squarely on the testicles and he retches on the already stained carpet.

"Now that's not the sort of action you thought you were getting, is it you piece of shit?" Marcus sneers in his ear as the unfortunate guy doubles up in excruciating pain. There is a muffled thud as the bat is brought down at the base of his neck.

His body falls unceremoniously to the floor, as if he was a tree felled by a lumberjack's axe. He twitches for a moment and murmurs something unintelligible before lying still. The three of them look at each other in fear that Marcus may have gone too far.

"Grab the money! We better get out of here quick!" My mother needed no second invitation and she quickly rummaged through his rear pocket and stuffed the roll of bills into her blouse.

Without another word, the three of them fled from the room and into the car that Marcus had parked directly outside. In a screeching of tyres and a cloud of dust, they exited the motel parking area, causing the guy on reception to poke his head out of the door. They sped off down the highway in the direction of their aunt's house. My mother was in the front of the vehicle, hastily counting the bundle of money they had taken. It came to just under $100 and it was more money than she had ever seen in her lifetime.

It was only hours later, that two police cars, with sirens wailing and lights flashing, pulled up outside the house of my mother's Aunt Glenda and Uncle Tom. They had no idea what was going on, but were soon put in the picture as Marcus, Sharon and my mother were arrested for robbery and assault. My uncle Marcus tried to defend the two women saying it was all his idea; but when they were interviewed, the two of them admitted to their part in the assault and robbery. This was to be the first of many spells in jails around the country for my mother.

On hearing the news, my grandmother was distraught. Even though she knew what her children were like, it did not stop her fearing what might become of them in prison. The prisons were notorious for being hard and brutal. How would they cope under such conditions? More to the point, what was to become of her grandson? How would this effect her poor innocent Curtis? With no father in his life and now no mother, she vowed to herself she would raise me as best she could with the help of her sister and brother-in-law.

CHAPTER TWO - CURTIS

I remember my grandmother taking me to one side and explaining that my mother had to go away for a while. We never really formed the bond that was normal between a mother and child. Yes, she did dote on me and tried her best to raise me; it was just that she wanted so much more out of life and I was not her number one priority. My grandmother told me that although I may be able to visit her from time to time, I would not live with her for almost five years. To a child, that seems like an eternity, but I took it with a pinch of salt.

The prison where she was to be incarcerated was in a neighbouring state and at least a four hour drive. This was another dilemma for my grandmother. Fate would have it that her sister and brother-in-law were due to move for Tom's work. So, the decision was made that I would move in with both of them, as the prison was only fifteen miles from the town they were relocating to. It was heart-wrenching for my grandmother, as she wanted to bring me up according to the Scriptures. It would turn out that I would take that path on my own terms.

The small town of Barnard with a population of approximately six thousand, was a blue collar, lower-middle class sort of place. Everyone was either employed at the steelworks, like Tom, or in the mines that were dotted around the area. One side of town was bordered by a river and was covered with trees like maple, sycamore and birch. The other side of town was at the foot of a range of hills, thick with forests and studded with mineworks.

It was the kind of place that you could safely leave your door open during the day and some often did. Each family was headed by a father who ruled the roost, so to speak. He was the main breadwinner and the womenfolk stayed at home and raised the children. Very few of the residents owned cars, as all amenities were provided in the town. Grocery stores, small department stores, a dentist and a doctors surgery. The nearest hospital was only a half hour drive by bus, which was also provided.

There were almost a dozen churches within the city limits of all denominations. They boasted more about this than the number of bars that equalled the churches. The hardworking men of the town would often blow off steam at the local hostelries and Tom was no exception to this. His drinking got to such a stage that before long, it became a problem. He took a long, hard look at himself and cut down on it, as it was affecting his family life.

The setting was idyllic. A perfect environment to raise good Christian children without the influences of the wicked outside world. In fact, the townsfolk cared little about what happened outside their self-contained bubble. Glenda kept house and was active in church life, as were my cousin Sarah and I. Both Sarah and I went to the same school, the one for Protestant kids. The Catholics had their own and everyone got along with everyone. Then they added me to the mix!

Beyond my grandmother, I heard it said that I was a disagreeable child who had nothing to admire except my smouldering looks. People would remark how my dimpled cheeks could light up a room, but my eyes were dark and expressive. My saving grace was they pitied me because of my mother's forced imprisonment. The good Christian people could not hold that against a child, even if he was a little different.

I used this sympathy as an excuse to lie and to generally get into trouble on a daily basis. All Glenda, Tom, and my cousin Sarah were already aware that I could be a handful and a little irritating at times. They had grown accustomed to it and I was sure the locals of Barnard would also. I think my guardians thought that now I was in a stable environment my behaviour might improve.

Sarah, who was three years my senior, was given the onerous task of chaperoning me. She was to accompany me to school and anywhere else I went in town. Her remit of being my "older sister" was to see that I was protected from bullies and to keep me out of trouble as much as she was able. I can tell you now it was not a job she relished, as I made as much trouble as I thought I could get away with. Tom and Glenda said I was an attention-seeker and that, in part, may have had a slight truth to it.

There were two things Glenda and Tom expected of me. One was to go to school as soon as possible and the other was to visit my mother. I can seriously say neither of the experiences went well.

As we drove the short distance to the prison, there was a storm brewing on the cold horizon. The noon darkness and damp-smelling air threatened to choke me as I hung my head out of the open window.

"Curtis, wind that window back up, you stupid boy!" Tom gave me a sharp reminder of who was in charge in this household. I felt like telling him to fuck off.

"Yes, Sir!" I sarcastically replied, with the obligatory sign of respect.

I cast my eyes to the charcoal sky; my attention was held by a golden streak, a crack in the cloud layer where the sun streamed through, as fast as water through a cracked dam. The rain was forecast and the wind was already unleashed and the trees swayed under its force. Thunder rumbled in the distance and a bolt of lightning cracked the dark noon sky in two. A lot of children would be scared of nature's fury. Not me, I revelled in it. Jagged flashes of pure light cast a glow against the monochromatic background. I sat and marvelled at its beauty and was disappointed when the prison came into view.

It was nothing like I imagined. The walls of the Penitentiary rose up some twenty feet from the ground. It was more like some dark, foreboding medieval castle than a prison. Not the kind out of fairy tales with some maiden trapped within its walls, waiting for her shiny knight on his white charger to rescue her. I estimated the outer stone walls to be about four feet thick, with watchtowers interspersed around its circumference. Each tower contained an armed guard complete with sunglasses and rifle. I remember thinking to myself, why the fuck were they wearing eye protection on a day like today?

We pass through a security checkpoint and the guard inspects our identity and our business there before lifting the barrier. As we pass under it and drive towards the main façade, I could imagine tortured souls screaming in the subterranean dungeons. When I grew older, I heard stories about those prisoners locked up for the worst crimes imaginable. They would be dragged to punishment rooms, stripped naked and bent over a low platform. Their feet and hands were tied to rings on the floor so they were unable to move. A guard would strip their flesh with a water soaked leather whip until he could not lift his arms any more, or the prisoners passed out from the beating.

This particular prison was almost three times the capacity it was built to accommodate. Men often shared three to a small, dingy cell. The women fared a little better as they were housed on the top floor of the main administration building. It was the first time I encountered race discrimination. Black and whites were totally segregated. In several places there were black and *white lines painted on the floor to indicate where each ethnicity was to walk. Never the twain should meet, even in the cramped dining hall.*

They were not left to languish in their cells during the fulfilment of their sentences. The men would be hired out to local farmers and businesses at a rate that was almost modern day slavery. There were no regulations regarding how the prisoners were treated by their temporary bosses and they were fed or not fed by them. If any stepped out of line, then a report would get back to the governor and punishment sessions were enforced. It was a hard life, but so it should be, I thought. I would later reassess my opinion on this.

The female inmates were not left idle either. Most were employed in the sewing factory, where they would attach collar and cuffs to the coarse material prison garb. The unlucky ones spent the day mopping floors that were often puddled with sweat, urine, vomit and blood. Others were involved in the production of items that would be sold to the public by the state. All of the proceeds went into the Penitentiary coffers and not a cent went to the inmates. They even had a prison vegetable garden and the produce was also sold at a local market and what was not good enough for sale, went to the prison kitchen. It was a harsh regime and one that I myself would experience too many times in my young life.

"Listen to me, Curtis; there will be no snivelling like a girl when you see your mother." Tom reminded me that boys did not do that sort of thing, as we wait at the reception.

"Yes, Sir!" I humbly submit to his request and take a deep breath.

He gives our names to the stern-looking official at the reception desk and fills out some paperwork. As soon as the formalities are complete, we are collected by one of the prison guards. I have never seen a man of such a gigantic stature. He towers above Tom, and I have to crane my neck to see his face. It looks like it is chiselled out of granite. A strong, square jaw with a dimple in the centre of his chin. From his wrist, on a leather strap swings a baton. It's black, highly polished surface reflected in the reception room lighting.

"Follow me." His voice is deep and gravelly and he turns his back on us and leads us down a corridor to our left.

We turn left through a door and enter a dimly lit room. I am pushed toward a wooden, slatted bench and ordered to sit down. In front of me is a clear glass panel. A black telephone sits on the counter on the other side. It is replicated on my side of the glass. I reach out to touch it but my hand is slapped away by Tom. I look at him venomously, just long enough to convey my anger. Then, as he gives me that "who is in charge" look, I drop my eyes.

A muffled sound causes me to raise my head. The sight of my mother, in her dreary prison overalls, is heart-breaking. She looks so tired and haggard. It has only been a few months and she looks like she has aged a number of years. There are dark rings around her eyes and her look seems vacant. A brief smile crosses her lips as she takes a seat facing me through the glass. She points to the telephone that is to my left and picks up the handset of the one on her side. I do the same and hear a crackling sound.

"Hey, you. I hope you are being good for Glenda and Tom?" The familiarity of her voice is disguised, somewhat, by the static interference from the phone.

"Yes, Mommy, I am." Tom knows this is not entirely true, but keeps his peace.

"That's my good boy. Mommy is going to be here for some time, you know that don't you? I think about you every day, in my prayers, before I go to sleep. Will you say a prayer for me every night, my darling?" Her words are almost pleading and a tear begins to form at the corner of her eye.

"Yes, Mommy, I will." There is a croak to my voice as I fight to hold back the tears that threaten to flow. The words of Tom are still ringing in my ears. It is unbearable and I drop the telephone and flee from the room.

That was to be the first of my ordeals, the second was to come on my first day at school.

Being a new kid at school is a frightening experience, even for people who can generally fit in. So many questions run through my mind as I try to sleep. What's the new school going to be like? Will the kids like me? Will I be accepted? Will I like the teachers? Will they like me? I try and avoid thinking about it, but it is an impossible task.

The inevitable first day comes around too quickly and I depart the house with Tom for the short walk to my new centre of learning. I tried to delay our departure but it would have only made things worse if I arrived late. It would make me more visible, but with Sarah holding my hand, I feel a little more at ease. That first day was to be one of the most memorable moments of my life.

We enter the school grounds and we are immediately stared at by some of the kids. Hushed whispers behind covered mouths and looks of sympathy by some. It is as if I have been given a lengthy prison sentence, just like my mother. My heart is pounding in my chest and all I want to do is turn and run. As we enter the building, Sarah says her goodbyes and heads to her class.

After going through the registration process, I am led to the Principal's office. She welcomes me with a wary eye, obviously knowing of my background. In a small town, nothing is secret. Once I have been given a few do's and don'ts, she leads me by the hand to my class. My mouth is dry and I feel like I'm going to vomit. The perspiration builds on my brow as the door is open and we step over the threshold.

Every head and pair of eyes in the room swivel in my direction. I shuffle uneasily from one foot to the other under their scrutiny.

"Mrs. Meachem, I have a new pupil for you. This is Curtis." The principal lets go of my hand and I turn to face my new teacher, whose name was foretold to me by my cousin.

Apparently she was a legend within the school, from present and past pupils. Not one person had a good word to say about her. Sarah told me that she was well-known for how awful she was to her students. She ran her class like a military unit. The desks were set up in four rows of four. Each were perfectly aligned with the one next to it. The same for each column, all neatly squared away. The first row was for the clever kids and teacher's favourite. The second for the less academic and likeable students and so it went. The last row was reserved for the least promising pupils and those that would get the rough edge of Mrs. Meachem's acid tongue.

She gives me a look of disdain, weighing up my small stature compared to others in the class. I must have looked like I was easy prey for a bitch like her. She was attempting to see if I had any insecurities that she could exploit. I knew from that very first moment, we would not get along. This was quickly confirmed as the Principal left the room and I was ordered to take a seat in the fourth row, closest to the window. The student who already occupied it grinned at me as he moved his stuff to the adjacent desk. He must be thrilled to have a new boy to take the heat off him. I take the seat and settle in, my heart rate begins to return to normal.

During the course of the day, Mrs. Meachem took every opportunity to exploit the apparent many defects to my character. The fact that my mother and uncle were imprisoned for some heinous crimes, was obviously my fault. She made sure it was brought up more than a few times that day. Also, the fact that I would never amount to anything and had a hopeless future set before me. I took everything she had to throw at me and bit my lip.

At the end of the day, I picked up my things, placed them in my bag and ran the entire way home. Tears streamed down my cheeks as soon as I left the school premises. My vision was impaired as I fled home, but my outburst did not go unnoticed. Tom was picking up some supplies from town as I careered past him. He called after me, but I ignored him. I would be reminded that men do not cry in public.

At that time, parents rarely questioned a teacher's treatment of a child. If they were given a beating or a tongue-lashing, they must have done something to deserve it. Even the viper, who was Mrs. Meachem, was never questioned, even though her reputation was well known. I burst into the house and went straight to my room. I threw myself on my bed and buried my head in the pillows, staining the cotton with my sobs. Glenda entered the room and tried to calm me down, but I cried uncontrollably.

Not twenty minutes later, Tom entered the house and I could hear his heavy footfall on the stairs as he bounded up them. The door flies open and rebounds off the wall. Tom is stood there, his face glowing red with fury.

"What in God's name is going on here? How dare you embarrass me by running through the town crying like a girl!" He immediately begins to berate me for showing my emotions in public. A boy should stoically accept the punishments he is given.

Tom had very little patience with whiners and here I was living under his roof. Not only that, I had fled school acting like a weepy girl, bringing shame on his good name. I wasn't his son, but that made little or no difference at all. The damage was done.

He was a self-made man and took pride about that. He had taken what life had dished out to him and still managed to succeed. It takes guts and resilience to get by in life, nothing is handed to you on a plate. He genuinely believed that although my mother and uncle were bad apples, with his guidance he could make a man out of me. He slowly began to calm down and I thought it was all over.

The next morning before I had woken, I could hear a commotion coming from Sarah's room. I couldn't make out what was being said, but I could clearly hear Tom's voice. Just a few minutes later, he appeared at my bedside and threw one of Sarah's dresses on the sheets.

"If you want to act like a little girl, you can dress like one. Put that on!" His eyes were wide and I could tell that he had thought the whole night about this.

I reluctantly pull back the bed sheets and clamber out of bed. I remove my pyjamas and put on the brightly coloured dress. Sarah is a couple of years older than me and a great deal taller. The material hangs loosely off my body, like a potato sack. Tom orders me to go and get washed and have breakfast. I do as I'm told and after breakfast, he marches me back to school.

When I enter the classroom, it is already full and Mrs Meachem is doing the roll call. The room explodes in raucous laughter as I stand there in my cousin's dress. A smirk crosses Meachem's face and she nods to Tom as he hands me over to her. She is fucking loving this, the heartless bitch! I walk to the back of the class to the sound of tittering and whispers and take my seat. I spend the whole day dressed like that and it is something I will never forget for the rest of my life.

CHAPTER THREE – MILLIE & CURTIS

I was almost nine years old when my mother was released from prison. She kept her nose to the grindstone and managed to stay out of trouble. That couldn't be said for my uncle Marcus. He was involved in a series of minor offences during his first three years which culminated in him breaking out. Just like the ill-fated robbery it did not go to plan and he was caught after only two days on the run. Any chance of a reprieve and shortening of his sentence was lost and he would serve the full ten years he was originally given. On the other hand, my mother was released two years early, serving only three years out of the five. Those three years with Glenda and Tom were the most miserable of my young life.

Grandma and my mother were not on very good terms so moving back with her wasn't an option. All my mother wanted was a quiet life with her son. The last thing she wanted was to be under her own mother's thumb once again, so she decided we would setup on our own. Those first few weeks with my mother were probably the happiest times of my life. But that was soon to change.

At first my mother managed to get us an apartment in Barnard and quickly got a job in a local bar as a barmaid. The people of the town were used to inmates settling in the area. The good Christian folk that they were, meant they preached and practiced forgiveness. Her employer was willing to give her a second chance for which she was thankful for. It wasn't long, though, before she became unsettled. Perhaps it was the close proximity to the prison and the fact that her brother was still serving his sentence. Whatever the reason, it was only six weeks before we moved to a town just over the border.

The small town of Newtonards was almost a mirror reflection of Barnard, like a lot of towns in that area. My mother immediately put herself to the task of finding meaningful employment. Within the first week of us arriving, she had secured a job at a local grocery store. The wages were not great, but it provided a roof over our heads and the stability she needed to get her life back on track. Her boss, Ike Harvey, was a kind and generous employer and did everything in his power to help her adjust to normal society. I think he felt sorry for her and the fact she was struggling to bring up a kid on her own. He knew that our extended family lived some distance away so he would invite us to dinner with his family.

People have remarked that I was always a disruptive and badly behaved child. I was never very good at making friends and maybe that was the reason for my bad behaviour. My mother said that I just wanted to be the centre of attention all of the time. That was probably because I was never given attention as a young child.

Shortly after I enrolled in the local elementary school, I began to miss lessons. I would spend my time wandering around or hanging about the grocery store where my mother worked. I would beg money off local passers-by and spend it in the shop. This infuriated my mother but what could she do? She had to work and couldn't stand guard on my classroom door to prevent me from playing hooky! She accused me of being manipulative, getting total strangers to give me money. That has been my curse, I suppose. As I grew older, I found that I could make people do what I wanted them to. As if I exuded some magical power over their minds. This would become even more noticeable in my later years when it came to women.

I was the least of my mother's concerns. She still loved to dance and drink and the appeal was more than looking after her wayward son. The lure of the local night life outweighed her maternal instincts. I was left with a series of questionable baby-sitters and I could tell my mother was not happy about it, but she did it anyway. Gone were the romantic beliefs that she would find a man and fall in love. All she wanted was a husband to provide for her and her son.

Her bubbly outward going personality still attracted men, and being in her mid-twenties now there were no lack of offers. She shared her bed with a number of different suiters, but none of them were ready to marry her and take on a young child. It wasn't long before she fell into old habits and was arrested for grand larceny. I don't remember the details as she never told me. The charges were dropped and she was free to go. She continued to seek solace at the bottom of a bottle but continued in her search for that allusive husband.

It was almost a year since my mother's release and she drifted from one job to the next. My behaviour became even more erratic and aggressive. I was removed from school for a number of weeks for an attack on a fellow classmate. I don't recall how the fight started, only that I saw red. The last thing I remember is the boy's head between my legs as I pummelled his face to a pulp. It was difficult for my mother to curb my outbursts as she couldn't deal with her own issues. So she let me fester and things only got worse.

Is it so wrong to want time with your mother? To have her undivided attention? My mother was the most important thing in my life and I should have been hers. I have no brothers or sisters to detract from that one-to-one time I crave. A simple thing like taking a walk together in the park would have sufficed. Just some demonstration of how important I was in her life. No, I always came second best to a whisky bottle. It wasn't long before my mother realised she had a problem and took the courageous step on joining alcoholics anonymous.

It was during her time in the group that she met her next husband. He, being an alcoholic with anger issues, was not the perfect father material in my eyes. I guess that my mother thought that a bit of male influence in my life might get my behaviour under control. His name was Jerry and it wasn't long before he moved into our cramped apartment. He was amiable enough towards me, but I resented the fact that my mother gave him more attention than myself.

In a matter of the months the pair were married. My mother invited my Grandmother, Tom and Glenda and my cousin Sarah. It was an attempt to try and bury the hatchet. She no longer wanted or expected a fantasy romance. All she craved was to be married and live a normal life. However, because of her new husband and myself she didn't get one.

Jerry promised her that he would provide and protect her and her son. After only being married a few weeks my mother quickly worked out that he did not have the slightest intention to honours these promises. While she managed to get her drinking under control, he did not. Jerry actually caused my mother more problems than I did. With his excessive drinking and the inability to hold down a permanent job meant that she had to continue to work to provide for us.

Whatever his intentions and promises were prior to the marriage, he did not believe it was his job to raise her son. He had no interest or patience with me saying it was my mother's job to make me behave. What a fucking cock sucker he was. Once more, my mother picked another fucking loser! But, for all his faults, the fact that he wanted to be with her was enough. Perhaps she thought that was all you could expect from men and decided to stick the marriage out. That, of course, was going to bring its own problems. What was she going to do about me?

At that time, my behaviour only got worse. I would steal small items from stores at first or anything of value I could find around the house. A psychiatrist may say that it was a cry for help. That's bullshit! I did it because I wanted to. I would give my mother the excuse that she didn't give me enough so that is why I resorted to stealing. This of course didn't go down well with her and my new father. The fucker was always yelling at me for things I hadn't done so I may as well do something that was worthy of his chastisement.

I continued to play hooky from school and every truant officer knew my name. I was threatened and bribed, but it made little difference. So concerned was my mother that she determined to put aside her difference with my grandmother. I was taken to see her, and she invoked the scriptures that every child should be obedient and honour their parents. I was never rude to my grandmother, but her lecturing did little to improve my behaviour.

Even though my mother managed to change her own ways, she did not persuade me to do the same. At times I would fly into an uncontrollable temper. This would scare my mother and she remarked that my wild eyes were that of a mad man. I was the devil incarnate! A personal insult which I was later to take to heart. I believed I was made for a higher purpose in this world. I just didn't know what that was yet.

My dear mother was at a loss with what to do with me. She began asking around what could be done. She learned that foster homes and schools could help wayward boys. She didn't want to do it, but it was the last roll of the dice. Her train of thought was that maybe if I was out of the way, she could concentrate her efforts on Jerry and perhaps get him back on track. It was just another thing on the long list I was building up of being rejected.

It was agreed that I would go into foster care on a temporary basis. This was to see if my outbursts and attention seeking could be brought under control. Also a chance for my mother to give more time to Jerry and with me out of the picture to frustrate and annoy him he would also improve. Even my Grandmother thought it might be the best for all of us.

My mother searched high and low for schools in the state, but none that she found were suitable. No appropriate foster care homes had openings, so she began to search further away. Finally after a long search, she found a place in the next state. It was called Upton Abbey and was run by a group of Benedictine monks. The place was a hundred years old and was started to give a rounded education to Catholic boys. It was not totally for just Catholics, other applicants were considered. It boasted to offer a positive learning environment for male delinquents. It provided places at that time for a maximum of one hundred and thirty students. My mother somehow pleaded her case and I was accepted into their fold.

It was not just wayward kids they took in. Pupils from a multitude of different circumstances, including those from overseas, those looking for military schools and of course, those in search of a traditional Catholic boarding school. It was the monk's mission to share the same Benedictine values, with an aim to be a bright light and inspiration for their pupils' development and learning. All of this done with Christ at the heart of all they did. The monks lived a very simple existence devoted to God. They divided their time between prayer and work around the Abbey.

Although all of the students did not have to be Catholic, everyone was expected to receive a religious education. To attend daily religious services and classes. A typical day would comprise of prayer six times a day for monks and students alike. The first was at 6am and was known as Vigils. Second, closely after at 7am, which was called Lauds. Then after breakfast it was mass. The daily routine of classes and sports and other character building pastimes took up the rest of the morning. Then, it was midday prayer at 12:30pm followed by Vespers at 6pm. The day ended with Compline, the Night Prayer, at 8pm. After that, the boys were given one hour free time before the lights were switched off for the night.

I thought I would have rebelled against this system, but I was strangely drawn into it. In the past my Grandmothers fanatical study and following of the scriptures was alien to me. I could not understand how so many of the world were compelled to live their lives by words written down by unknown hands almost two thousand years in the past. It was only during my time at Upton Abbey where it all began to make sense. I would study the Bible fervently in my free time. I wanted to understand its meaning and message. The characters within its pages drew me in. None held my interest more than Jesus of Nazareth. He *was adored and loved by many, hated and despised by others. He was different, a little bit like myself really. That holy book was never far away from me and a force within me began to burn brightly.*

In the beginning, I changed my ways and lived strictly by the commandments and the holy book. I was still socially awkward and found it hard to make friends. To live your life as a good Christian did not mean following rules and regulations. Nor did it mean that you needed to attend church regularly. This is what I worked out in my first year at the abbey. It's about a friendship - a friendship with Jesus Christ. Jesus said that knowing Him is the doorway to a special relationship with God. That was good enough for me and I didn't require other friendship. We begin such a special relationship with God by committing ourselves to follow Him.

The one thing that fascinated me was the advice that Jesus offers in the Bible. He made it understandable to the common man, sometimes using stories or symbols, but always keeping His message simple, straightforward and practical. He covers many aspects of human life, but the one that was most significant to me was the need for love. His focus was not just on the love for our friends and family, but something much more challenging, a love that tests every nerve and sinew. This was what was missing in my life and I grasped the concept with both hands.

He spoke of a love for those who we want to hate, a love for those who already hate us. This love requires effort, and strain, and every ounce of self-command that man can summon up. It was one of the most challenging aspects for me to get my head around. I had so much hate in my heart that I thought I would never let it go. It is easy to hate and let that fester and grow inside you. That hate can feel justified and spark a need for revenge. In reality it leads to dark, unadulterated hate and a spiral of destruction.

So, I learned another major lesson and that was forgiveness. Once we have understood what we have done wrong, we can ask for forgiveness, and then make a serious effort to correct our mistakes. It is only when we do this that we can truly be a follower of God. My thoughts turned to my mother and to look at the sort of person I had become in her eyes. The reason why she saw fit to banish her own flesh and blood from the bosom of her love. Some people who are self-righteous and confident look down on others. As I turn the pages I find a passage that describes how Jesus explain this.

"Two men went up to the temple to pray, one a Pharisee and the other a tax collector. The Pharisee stood up and prayed about himself: 'God, I thank you that I am not like other men, robbers, evildoers, adulterers or even like this tax collector. I fast twice a week and give a tenth of all I get."

"But the tax collector stood at a distance. He would not even look up to heaven, but beat his breast and said, 'God, have mercy on me, a sinner."

*"I tell you that this man, rather than the other, went home justified before God. For everyone who exalts himself will be humbled, and he who humbles himself will be exalted." **(Luke 18:9-14)***

After reading this passage, I understood the forgiveness of our sins is not without a cost because when we break laws, whether they be civil or divine, we should expect to face some consequences. I can sympathise with my mother for sending me to that place and in that moment I forgave her. We must humble ourselves in a way that allows us to truly understand what we have done, what we deserve, and what Jesus gave up so that we could be free. The meaning of His words resonates deeply within me and I close the book before the lights are extinguished.

A muffled sound wakes me from my slumber. Whispered voices from the bed that is only a few feet away. A hunched black figure stoops over the small form huddled beneath the bed sheets. The slight figure rises and the dark silhouette assists him to rise. He leads him by the hand out of the dormitory of sleeping adolescents. They move silently across the highly polished surface of the room. I can tell by the body movements of the smaller figure that he is resisting. As soon as they disappear from sight, my curiosity gets the better of me and I throw back the sheets. I sit upright and swing my legs over the side of the bed until my feet make contact with the cold floor.

I tip toe past the lines of sleeping students, who seem oblivious to my presence as I draw closer to the exit to the dormitory. As I pull on the handle, the light from the corridor blinds me causing me to blink. Once my eyes are adjusted, I take tentative steps away from the room. A door to the washrooms is ajar and I can hear muffled voices coming from within. I creep closer and push open the door a little further so I can peer inside.

One of the monks has his back to a wash basin. He is wearing his dark robes as they all did no matter what time of day. The golden crucifix attached to a string of black beads hangs loosely low below his chest. The other monks wear silver ones so even with his hood raised I know that this is the Abbott of the Abbey. The small figure that he had led from the dormitory is kneeling between his robes. These have been lifted and the Abbott holds them up high revealing pale skin that has never seen sunlight.

The young man, I estimate to be around twelve years old, has his head buried deep in the Abbotts groin. A stifled slurping sound echoes around the wash room. His head bobs back and forth ably assisted by one hand of the Abbott. It was the first time I had experienced or witnessed a sexual act and my mind was in turmoil trying to make sense of it all. As I tried to process the images and information, the groans from the Abbott grew louder his head tilted back and his cowl dropped revealing his silver hair with shaven circle at the crown. His hips seemed to shudder as the boys movements increased in speed. I inadvertently push against the door and the creak it makes draws the Abbotts attention to my presence. His eyes burn into mine for that split second before I turn and flee.

The dawn came around too quickly and I did not want to face the day ahead. The whole of the morning I was dreading the call to go to the Abbotts office. The call never came. The next few days past into weeks without further incident. Then one day I was late for Vespers. I was so engrossed in a passage from the Bible that I lost track of time. I rushed to the chapel, only to be caught by the Abbott. I still remember that sardonic grin on his face as he shook his head in dissatisfaction.

After Vespers I was ordered to go to the main hall. When I arrived, the whole school were already assembled. On entering the space I noticed the wooden trestle that was used for administering punishments. The Abbott stood up on a dais watching over the students. I was beckoned forward by the next senior monk of the Abbey. He held in his hand a wooden paddle the size of two table tennis paddles. My heart sank when I realised I was singled out for corporal punishment due to my lateness at Vespers. This was not normally a punishable offence, but I was not about to argue. I knew if I did, it would only make things worse for myself.

I stepped forward confidently and took up my position in front of the trestle. One of the monks took a pace forward and bent me at the waist so that I was draped over the implement. My wrists were bound by leather thongs which were tie to metal rings secured in the stone floor. Once my hands were secured and I could not move my legs were strapped to the legs of the bench. The next sensation was that of hands fumbling at the waistband of my pants. Rough fingers pulled at the material and the cool air of the hall circulated around my now naked buttocks.

I felt the first blow before it even arrived, the air being pushed before it hit my ass a split second before the paddle. I lurched forward to ride the sting and pain but the restraints did their job and kept me secure. As was the rule another two followed in quick succession. My ass was on fire. The surface of the paddle totally covered my small ass cheeks. A tear welled up in my eye, but I remember Tom's words. Men in this family do not cry like little girls. I held the tears back as I was untied from the bench and floor. I rose until I was fully erect and was looking straight into the demonic eyes of the Abbott. He smirked as I pulled up my pants and hiding my shame, and without a word, turned and left the hall.

That was it. I made an enemy of the wrong man. I witnessed an act that was to go on again and again. I was never approached or subject to the same. From that moment on I would never again mention the sights I saw. I kept to my studies and the bible with my head down. Maybe something in me broke over those years. I was punished on numerous occasions and felt the warmth of the paddle time and time again. Of course, they were for indiscretions I never committed. Just a constant reminder of what would happen if I opened my mouth. It seems so long ago now since I entered onto my own path of righteousness.

CHAPTER FOUR – NANCY

It's as if the slowly changing tone touches different parts, a sort of auditory massage for my mind. Nature provides the same sensations, a light wind flowing over you cooling your cheeks. That is what music does for me. It is an invitation for slowness and to feel the presence of myself, the ever patient version of me who waits to be spoken to. Music fills the air without effort, like the waves filling holes in beach sand, the sound rushing in and around every person in the room. Some react to the rhythm and the beat, tapping their feet in time to it. Others chat between themselves, an excited look in their eyes at this new act.

The tones emanating from the heavy satin wood acoustic guitar are rich and full. My eyes are drawn to the strong fingers that dance effortlessly along the frets on the neck. The ordinary looking wooden instrument seems to come alive in the hands of its master. He makes it much more than ordinary, it is extraordinary. I am a slave to the music and he is my master.

His voice is coarse, like fragmented rocks in a hessian sack, moving and grinding against each other. Somehow it compliments his dark complexion and the raised veins in his bull-like neck. As his fingers run across the strings on the upstroke, he wipes away the dark hair covering his forehead. He fixes us with the darkest eyes I have ever seen. There is a seriousness to them, a hint of danger. At the same time, they are eyes I could happily stare into forever. The denim shirt he is wearing clings tight to his well-proportioned, muscular arms. His faded denim jeans flare a little at the bottom, hiding a pair of perfectly formed thighs. A pair of light-brown suede boots finish off his rather casual, but sexy look.

The lyrics of the song drift around the room, reverberating off the walls. They are of peace, love, forgiveness and all that is good in the world. His words are full of sincerity and hope and sung in a way that you know they come from deep within his very soul. He has a quality and delivery that makes every female in the room sigh under their breath. I notice a few of them adjusting their clothing so that a little more cleavage than normal is on show. Just as in nature, using their assets to tempt the opposite sex. I cannot help feeling jealous that I was not as blessed as some of them in that department.

Then the mysterious, gorgeous, if not slightly dangerous-looking guy, looks up from his guitar and his eyes catch mine. He ignores the big-breasted girls who are wriggling in their seats trying to grab his attention. His gaze seems like I am the only person in the room, but maybe that is my perception. This guy is a total enigma, but I can't tell why. His words are captivating as they roll effortlessly from his very kissable lips. A dark covering of stubble where he hasn't shaven for a few days, only lends to his sexy, rough look. A bit of a bad boy but with just a hint of a loving, caring nature. He seems like he hasn't a care in the world. He appears stress-free and relaxed, as if he was the type of person that wouldn't hold a grudge.

Just being in close proximity to him, is like taking a vacation from any worries I may have, but he's no open book. He is new to the club and the music scene in the city. He appeared out of nowhere already fully-formed, as if he always had been here. There is not one person that I know of who knows where he came from, what his childhood was like or if he had any siblings. He was a complete enigma, but one that I am fascinated with. No man who seeks to be mysterious can truly be, there's something about wanting the attention that gives them away. Truly mysterious men have no such desire, their motives remain hidden and hence the allure.

As human beings, we are programmed to size one another up quickly. Our first impressions of each other are influenced by different things, such as facial shape, someone's voice, attractiveness, and general emotional state. This first impression of a person is often a gut feeling and you immediately form an opinion. Once that opinion is formed in your mind, it is difficult to change it, even if you have evidence that disproves your original thought process. This all happened in those first moments as he stared into my eyes.

His voice trails off as his eyes still stare into mine. His hands cease strumming the strings of the guitar and there is a brief moment of silence. Then, a tidal wave of applause, slow at first and gaining in tempo and volume. It is accompanied by the members of the club, one by one getting to their feet and saluting the mysterious minstrel. The seriousness of his face is wiped clean as a perfect set of straight, white teeth emerge from between his parted lips. He nods and gives a slight bow to the onlookers and makes his way down the steps from the stage. My heart is beating like a drum as he makes towards me.

It is like everything has gone into slow motion. I swear I can hear every footstep as his heels strike the floor of the club. His arms swing confidently as he strides in my direction. His hips move with a seductive grace of a model. I am captivated by every movement of his body. The spell is only broken as he changes his course and heads over to the area that is reserved for VIP's.

In a darkened corner of the room sits the legend that is Milton Rogers. He is surrounded by the usual entourage of flunkies and groupies, each of them fawning over him. Not just females, but males alike. I guess when you are one of the country's most famous modern-day folk singers, you will receive attention such as this. A rather scruffy individual with long, wavy, dark hair rises from the group. As the mysterious newcomer reaches the group, he is met with a handshake from this guy. A few words are spoken between them before the curly-haired one moves to leave. As he emerges from the darkness walking towards the exit, I see it is none other than Bob Dylan. I have to prevent myself from hyperventilating. He has been my idol over the past few years. He is a regular at the club but I have never had the good fortune of meeting him in person.

So, how does this stranger know Bob Dylan? In fact, why is he in the company of Milton Rogers? This only lends more fuel to his enigma. The assembled group make room for the stranger and Milton hands him a drink. I can tell from the body language that they are obviously good friends and the sound of raucous laughter fills the room. The stranger who I know is called Curtis, purely from the posters that were displayed on the entrance to the club, is immediately surrounded by young girls. Milton does not seem to mind that his friend has diverted the attention from himself. A girl sits on the newcomer's lap, her arms draped around his neck. She is a pretty little thing, although a little too young to be in a place like this. Perhaps that was just jealousy, I don't know. What I do know is that I have a yearning to get to know this man.

I sip on my bourbon and coke, making small talk with my friends who have accompanied me for the evening. The talk is all about the new act who has just performed. So, it is not just me who felt that same animal magnetism that he seemed to exude. I try and concentrate on the conversation, but my eyes constantly wander over to the corner of the room. The stranger moves his head around the young girl and stares directly at me.

There is a twinkle in his eye as he notices me looking at him. The same smile that he gave after his performance greets me once more. I avert my gaze, the heat from my embarrassment burning my cheeks. I have never really been shy, but he seems to stir up emotions in me that are alien.

To my horror, he moves the girl from his lap and gets up from his seated position. He exchanges words with Milton before heading once more towards the stage. It is only now that I notice the ink that covers his hands and the breastbone which is exposed from his open-necked shirt. I cannot make out exactly the images that are depicted, but his skin is barely visible. To my surprise, he stops in his tracks when he reaches our table. His head inclines towards me and only me, not giving my friends a second glance. I let his eyes slide over my body, as he makes his examination. The mere act of doing that has my clit throbbing in my panties. My skin feels dry and I am breathless.

"I was wondering if you would like to join us at our table?" That same husky voice which filled the room earlier, is directed at me.

"I would love to!" There is no chance of me even reconsidering his offer and I am out of my seat before I know it.

He takes me by the hand and moves so close I can feel his breath on my face. There is a dancing spark of excitement in me as he leads me back towards the VIP area. Through the gloom, I can see that all eyes are directed at me as we near the seating area. I feel a little awkward with a celebrity such as Milton sat only ten feet from me. The looks on the girl's faces are a picture of false emotions.

"Guy and gals can I introduce…" He pauses when he realises that he hasn't even asked me my name.

"Nancy, I'm Nancy. It's fantastic to meet you." My reply is to Milton, not the other celebrity cock-hungry sluts who are draped all over him and his friends.

"Hey, baby, take a seat. Chill out take a smoke!" He passes me a joint, one of many he has probably smoked that night. The air is sickly-sweet from the pungent weed.

"Hey, thanks man. I will." The summer of love has lasted almost a decade now and recreational drugs are the big thing.

I take the joint from his outstretched hand and Curtis makes room for me in the semi-circular booth. Milton grabs the attention of a passing waiter and orders a couple of bottles of champagne. I can't really say I have drunk champagne before, but I'm not ready to admit that in front of these fucking bimbos.

As I take my seat next to Curtis, I can feel the warmth that radiates out from his skin under the denim material of his shirt. That is not the warmth I feel from the looks I am getting from the groupies seated around the booth. Women can be, at times, very territorial. I, myself, am not easily given over to jealousy. With females, jealousy can rise to the surface for a number of reasons. I have found that the biggest factor is that of comparison and competition. It's usually emotional jealousy rather than sexual. From the vibe that I am getting from these particular groupies, it is a mixture of both. The fact that I have encroached on something which they believe they have already "claimed" is enough for the green eyed-monster to emerge.

Unlike most men, Curtis has picked up on this and he immediately puts me at ease. He places his hand in a tender fashion on the back of mine. It is now that I can see the ink is of a biblical nature. There is very little natural skin on show as the artwork covers almost all of his hand. His eyes meet mine as I shuffle nervously in my seat.

"Now, now girls, let's play nice. Nancy is my guest and you will give her the respect she deserves." His words, although spoken softly, have a magnetism about them. The groupie's attitude immediately changes.

"Hi there, Nancy; I'm Cassie." One of the girls leans over and offers me her hand. An olive branch has been extended and I take it gratefully.

"Nice to meet you, Cassie." One by one, the others introduce themselves. It was then that I knew there was something special about this man. He held an invisible power over these women.

The champagne arrives and for the next hour or more, we consumed bottle after bottle. The mixture of pot and alcohol was beginning to make my head spin. I was totally relaxed and seemed to be accepted by the group now. It was strange how even though Curtis was not really known on the music scene, he received more attention than Milton. The folk singer did not mind having the attention diverted from him. I guess it was a change not to be in the spotlight for once. It was a peculiar pairing between Curtis and Milton. Yes, they were both in the music business, but they appeared to be different sides of a coin. Curtis was charismatic, where Milton was more subdued and did not exude that particular quality that draws people to him. One thing they both had in common, was the use of drugs.

Almost every drug imaginable was available in the booth. Magic mushrooms were being passed around as if they were candy. The air was heavy with the sweet smell of cannabis, and lines of white powder covered the table. Not for very long, as it was snorted through rolled up bank notes. I stuck to the cannabis and a couple of 'shrooms. That was enough for me and I was already feeling the effects. The room became a kaleidoscope of colours as the hallucinogenic began to course through my system.

"What say we party back at mine?" Milton's words were slow and slurred. His eyes were misted over and he could not focus properly. He grinned like a cat that just got the cream.

"Fuck yeah man! Let's blow this joint!" Curtis was more lucid, but I could tell the narcotics were fuelling his excitement.

The complete entourage began to drain their drinks and get up from the table. As I stood, I swayed from the drugs and alcohol. A strong arm wrapped around my waist and Curtis prevents my fall. I could smell the muskiness of his manly odour, it was more intoxicating than any drug.

"Hold onto me, my child." His voice whispers in my ear and I feel the warmth of his breath. I clench my legs together as the tingle begins between my legs.

We move as one, stumbling our way through the crowd of club members. One of Milton's security personnel makes a path for us to follow on behind him. We emerge into the night air and I feel faint once more. The arm that is holding me around my waist squeezes a little tighter as I feel my knees give way. He pulls me up once more and I rest my head on his shoulder. We do not have to wait long for a ride. Milton's private car is already waiting for us and Curtis helps me inside. We manage to get six people inside and the rest have to wait for passing cabs.

We travel from the centre of Los Angeles into the leafy suburbs of Brentwood. I have very rarely visited this part of town as it is exclusively for the rich and famous. Brentwood has been home to notable residents like Marilyn Monroe. It is a quieter area than the glitzy Beverly Hills, Bel Air, and some of the more notable areas of Los Angeles. With huge mansions and a beachy, laid-back vibe, it is where Milton's mansion is located.

We enter through some wrought iron gates that swing silently open on our approach. The frontal edifice of the house is akin to that of the White House. Six white alabaster Doric columns rise up to the second floor. A perfectly manicured lawn glistens with water from the sprinkler that is disseminating the liquid evenly over its surface. A series of shuttered windows with blue Spanish blinds, are spaced evenly along its width. A black double set of doors with golden locks are set into the wooden frame. To the right of the doorway on a pole, hangs the Stars and Stripes. The car draws silently up to the entrance and we stumble out of the interior.

Milton invites us inside, and as I am still a little unsteady on my feet, Curtis aids me through the door. The inside is as lavish as the exterior. This is the first time in my life I have witnessed such luxury and even in my stupefied state, I am in awe of its opulence. The lights are activated as we enter the hallway and I am standing on a black and white chequered stone floor. It resembles a massive chessboard. It's highly polished surface is like a mirror and I can see the reflection of my panties in the glossy material.

"It's party time! Who wants to take a swim?" Milton turns to face us, just as the rest of the group burst excitedly through the open door.

His announcement is met by cheers and squeals from the groupies. I count them and there are eight of them. Nine females and only three guys. The other man who has accompanied us was also sat in the booth. I never gave him much attention as he seemed to be zoned out on whatever narcotics he had taken. Not now though. His eyes were wide at the thought of a pool party. I could see the rising erection in his faded jeans and his hand wandered over the material, just to highlight the fact. One by one, the girls rush past me and Curtis. They obviously knew the way to the pool and were stripping off their clothes as they ran. I feel a little uncomfortable at first, but the drugs and alcohol have lessened my inhibitions somewhat.

Curtis walks me through the living room and the sound of music fills the air, as Milton turns on the music system. He has already removed his shirt and jeans and is standing in his boxer shorts. Just like his friend, he is sporting a rather impressive looking hard-on. I can feel my temperature rising as we walk through the patio doors into the yard. The azure blue pool is illuminated by lights surrounding its edge. We are not overlooked by any property on any side. The girls have discarded their clothing and jump naked into the cool water.

"Come in, Nancy, the water is beautiful!" Cassie calls out to me, her voluptuous breasts breaking the surface of the water.

I was brought up a strict Catholic and this age of decadence is a little frightening for me. I have always been shy of my own body and a little self-critical. The move to California from the Bible belt, was so I could cast off my religious upbringing and be myself. I was still not fully emerged in the culture of free love, as yet, although it is what I crave. In fact, it is what I need.

"There's no need to be frightened, my child. We should not be afraid of the gifts that God has bestowed upon us." His gentle voice and captivated stare has me rooted to the spot.

"Of course not." I reply meekly looking down at my feet.

"We can go into the house if you like and you can undress there." Before I have time to answer, he takes me by the hand and leads me back inside.

I can hear the squeals and laughter from the other girls and look back over my shoulder as Milton and his friend, now naked, dive into the pool. They are immediately surrounded by the groupies and it is a swirling mass of naked flesh. If I wasn't turned on before, I definitely am now. Curtis could quite have easily have undressed me by the pool, but I believe he has an ulterior motive. He sits me down on a couch and takes up a seat next to me. He unbuttons my blouse, while all the time staring deep into my eyes. I feel my skin prickle, raising in anticipation.

The thin material slips easily from my shoulders and I thrust my 34C breasts instinctively forward. He requires no second invitation and his tattooed hands envelops them in seconds. He massages them gently, his thumbs circling the areola. I squirm in my seat as he begins to rub the nipples in tandem. They are taut and his touch sends a spark of electricity from my chest deep down south. I moan out loud as his wet lips surround the left one and his tongue flickers over the surface of the bud, teasing it out even more. I am in heaven and a murmur escapes my lips.

My murmurs and moans only encourage him and it isn't long before he has removed my skirt and panties. The secretions from my pussy are running freely down my inner thigh. What a slut he must think I am, as I involuntarily raise my hips, offering myself to him. First one finger slides effortlessly inside my opening, testing how wet I am. It is rapidly joined by a second and I have to bite down on my lips from the sensations they are providing. In slow, well-practiced movements, he pleasures me. With his free hand, he pulls off his shirt and I fumble on the waistband of his pants. In a see-saw motion, I manage to get them down over his muscular thighs.

He pauses for a moment and I open my eyes. The sight that greets me causes me to catch my breath. I am staring into the face of Jesus Christ. His crown of thorns surrounding His head, which is inclined to the side. His arms are outstretched and hands nailed to the cross, which is emblazoned across Curtis' chest. The word MESSIAH, in Coptic script, is captured just above the figure of our Lord. The artwork is of beautiful quality and I can only imagine the hours of painful work that went into its creation.

He leans forward, his lips meeting mine and our tongues seek out each other in the caverns of our respective mouths. He is not forceful, but the pressure is enough for me to respond in kind. His hands cup my face as he smothers my cheek, neck and shoulders with his gentle kisses. I reach around his neck, drawing him close and running my fingers down the length of his muscular back. His body is just as I expected under that tight-fitting denim clothing. Not one inch of fat, only sinew of carved muscle. As my hands descend down his back, the tips of my fingers are raised and lowered. It is a strange feeling, but I am too aroused to give it much thought.

Curtis removes his hands from my jaw and continues to probe my pussy with his fingers. I raise and lower myself to his ministrations as he brings me close to climax. I reach out and find what I am looking for. The shaft of his penis is thick and pulses under my grip. I slide my hand around the girth before running it along its length, then returning to the head. The action causes him to exhale and inhale rapidly as the pleasure takes hold. The sticky fluid from his arousal aids my fingers as they glide up and down his cock. His own fingers increase in tempo and intensity, as we both seek to bring each other to a satisfying end.

Our moans and heavy breathing become more audible and I fear we will be overheard from the pool. The screams of pleasure and laughter dispels my concerns as I look through the open door. Milton has climbed from the pool and has three girls lined up, their asses facing him. His dick is buried balls-deep in one of the girls, as his fingers fondle the pussies of the other two. They are all three are squirming under his onslaught and the sight of it brings me over the edge. At the same time, I feel Curtis jerk as he spurts his seminal fluid all over my stomach, some of it landing on the floor.

I look up at him and there is a satisfied look on his face which turns to a scowl. My heart sinks as I rack my brain to work out what I have done to displease him. I don't have to wait long to find out his change in mood.

"I hope you are not going to let the nectar of heaven go to waste, my child." The scowl has turned into a leer, but a playful one.

"Of course not, babe." At once I understand his cryptic message, as he stares down at the pool of liquid which is warming my body.

I use my fingers to scoop up the semen which contrasts against my golden skin. I seductively suck on my fingers, drinking every last bit of Curtis' sweet cum. When I think I have finished, and with a smug look on my face, I lean back.

"You haven't finished yet, my sweet child." He motions with his eyes to the pool of jizz on the wooden floor.

I do not know what has come over me, but without questioning, I push myself up from the couch. I scramble down onto my hands and knees and begin to lick up his cum from the floor. I must appear like some animal, but I am unusually aroused by my actions. I hear a grunt of approval from Curtis and observe his feet as they move around behind me. With my ass high up in the air, I am open to his examination. The next thing I feel is his hot breath once more on the back of my neck and his fingers probing my pussy. He coats the digits in my ejaculation and then rubs the wet tip around my ass bud.

I lift my head from the floor and peer around over my shoulder. His eyes are fixated on my rear as he forces a finger tentatively inside me. At first, I clench my ass cheeks to prevent his entry into my sacred hole. I have never in my life been violated in that place. Just one look from those dark eyes is enough and I relax. His first finger is joined by a second and he thrusts them in and out of my butt. I give myself over to the pleasure that they instil in me, my stomach flutters and I sigh openly. It isn't long before the juices in my ass are as abundant as in my pussy. All of a sudden he stops and withdraws his fingers.

"I think we should continue this in private, my sweet thing." He moves around so that he is in front of me and extends his hand.

I reach up and grasp it, feeling the strength in those fingers. He tenses his tight thighs and the sinews and muscles in his arms tighten visibly. I am hauled from the floor like a rag doll. He turns his back on me and guides me from the room. It is then, that I see the whole of his back depicts the scene of the last supper, with Jesus and His disciples. The colours are vivid and dance, even under the room's meagre lighting. The figures seem to move as he strides from the room, every muscle in his back flexing. My mouth drops agape when I see the scars that form a lattice on his back, breaking up the picture in places. So much pain and hurt and I fight back the tears when I try to imagine how he came by them.

CHAPTER FIVE - CURTIS

Mankind is such a mix of social creatures. There is so much self-deception at all levels, from the single man to how society is structured. It has always been a patriarchal dominance which shaped how we think and behave. This gave the patriarch's control over those who they saw as beneath them, or not on their level. An advantage of this way of thinking and living, means that the dominant class will always avoid the more difficult tasks in life. When it comes to the role of women in society, the traditional role was that of bearing and raising the young. An important role in any civilized species, it was combined with undertaking many single tasks throughout the day, at the same time as maintaining emotional intelligence and endurance. Most men avoid these tasks in favour of something that is not as stressful and which they can have some level of control.

So humankind is really based on a system of abuse and has been so since the beginnings of time. Most of society know, nor care, little about this. From the most loving relationships, right up to national and international relationships. If they could only learn the trick of cooperation, become fraternal, they'd have a real chance of survival. We are supposedly an intelligent species, but are still trying to figure out how to be fair and loving to one another.

The teacher known as Jesus, attempted to teach mankind how they should live loving, sincere, humble lives. He also taught them about how they should think of God. Within each of us there is something that tells us there is a God, some kind of higher power, some force governing the world, yet it is beyond our understanding as to what exactly this Being is. The simplest way to do this was to see him as a loving parent. A kind, generous father, who has given us life and will provide for us in the times ahead.

That was the first point that started me questioning the validity of the scriptures that had been agreed on. Where in this holy writing was the mention of the importance of a mother? Surely, God did not give us life? It was a union between a man and woman that created life. It is both parents that provide for us during our infant years. I understand the meaning behind Jesus' teaching, that we are all children of God. His own relationship with the "Father" was as unique as his Spirit was divine. In **John 10:30,** he is quoted as saying *"I and my father are one."* It was that statement that was a big stumbling block for me. Is he saying that he is actually God? That I cannot accept. He is a man, a holy man, but still a man. A man with a message for the world to hear. A world that was as corrupt then as it is now.

The darkness of the room is warmed only by the single candle that burns on the table. I turn to the next page in the thumb worn pages of my Bible. The ticking of the clock has a relaxing quality. As if it is a heartbeat at rest. The dark room is like a place out of time, a place to rest without consequence. It is my own personal sanctuary. A place where I can shut out the influences of the outside world and reflect on HIS teaching and the path set out for me.

The blackness engulfs my thoughts. The darkness overcomes any sense of purity, consumes all hope of cleanliness. It takes me back to that first time in prison. I prayed for the day to come, just as I did back then.

The shuffling sound in my cell echoes eerily from the past. I hear the door creak open and a shaft of light from the landing streams in. I can see the door from my bed but it seems miles away. The blackened shapes entering the cell, block out the light. It is only my second night in an adult facility and I have dreaded this moment.

Some people still see rape according to the old cliché, of vile men dragging innocent women into dark alleys and then brutalizing them. I quickly learned that the reality is more complicated than that. In here, male rape is common place, I just did not expect it to happen to me. The weight of someone holding me down as the bed sheets are pulled away is suffocating. A hand covers my mouth as my shorts are ripped from me. The sound is deafening; surely the guards must hear it and come to my aid. How naïve I am. Of course they would not come. How did my assailants gain access to my cell, if it was not in collusion with the guards? Money talks in this place.

My heart begins to accelerate as I fight to breathe through the pillow which my face is forced into. These were not lecherous, sexually oppressed old men. They were powerfully built, athletic young men who knew exactly what they wanted. One covers my sobbing mouth, while the other spreads apart my ass cheeks. Another holds down my arms so that I am unable to fight back. I try and scream as the one behind me slams his cock unceremoniously into my ass.

"Fuck, this fish is tight. You got this sexy. We gonna ride you all night!" His words are almost demonic and I feel the vomit rising from my stomach, as he thrusts himself balls-deep into me.

Inside I am crying and send my mind elsewhere, to think of happier times. Did I even have such times? Anything I have experienced is better that this nightmare. I wasn't handcuffed or tied up, but was in a version of dissociated shock. The invisible, immeasurable shackles of such a violation are immense.

The grunts from my rapist get ever louder and the ferocity of his lunges increase. I fear my ass cheeks will tear apart, such is the force of his hands on them. I feel a warm sensation as my first attacker shoots his load deep into my hole. My mouth is released just for a split second and I take a deep lungful of air. It is only for a short moment before another hand clasps tightly around my mouth. I relax as the brutes cock is pulled clear of me, but it is only replaced by an even bigger one, and I clench my eyes tightly shut and ride the pain.

One by one, they use my body as their personal cum bucket. When one is finished and his dick flaccid, my mouth is released and I am ordered to suck it hard again. All of the while my butt is being battered by another cock. I am covered in semen from head to toe. The warm, sticky fluid flows from my anus like a stream flowing to the sea. The tick-tock of the clock only makes me wish and pray for the dawn to come.

I was forever changed from that moment on. Over the next few months I was guilty of sodomizing men, as was done to me. An eye for an eye, the Bible says. I justify my actions by recalling the story of Johnathan and David and their homosexual relationship. If it's okay for the Scriptures, then it's good enough for me. That was how I lived my life during my first time in prison. Do unto them, before they do unto you. My own twisted version of the biblical teachings. To play the insanity card was my biggest stroke of genius. Just the mad-eyed stare was enough to keep the predators at bay. I quickly became a force to be reckoned with and someone that was to be avoided.

I close the Bible and lean back in my chair. I feel restless and have a compulsion to head into town. I have images of the girl Nancy in my head. Since Milton invited me to stay with him, we had enjoyed many parties with a lot of different girls. It was the age of free love and I grasped the opportunity with both hands. The ever present flow of narcotics only fuelled my sexual desire and being a friend of a famous singer, gave me access to all who followed him. Over time, I have asserted my own personality on his group and one by one they gravitated towards me. Some people are like that. They need someone to follow. Someone to lead them. I believe that is the reason I was put on this earth to carry on the message that Jesus conveyed almost two thousand years ago.

Out of all the women I have met over these past few months since moving to LA, Nancy has a certain quality about her I cannot put my finger on. Everyone is equal in the eyes of the Lord, but Jesus also had his favourites among his flock. I can see her bronzed skin laid out before me on the bed like a human altar, offering herself to be worshipped.

The twitch of my cock at the mere thought of it causes me to rise from the chair. I untie the belt of my robe and slip the garment off my shoulders. The warm air of the Californian night caressing my naked body. My hand wanders down my stomach until it reaches the base of my now erect penis. The sexual pictures that fill my brain cause my blood to rush to that area of my body. I have set myself rules just as the teacher did. I would abstain from self-masturbation as a penance for my impure random thoughts. It was all about control and self-discipline. How can I expect people to follow me, if I don't have rules and abide by them?

The cold metal of the cilice has been warmed by the heat from my body. Its barbs are imbedded deep in my flesh. I loosen the strap, securing it to my thigh and delight in the relief it gives. I insert my fingers under the links and pull the barbs free of my skin. Small rivulets of blood trickle down from each of the small puncture wounds and I observe, with interest, their path as they meander down my thigh. The cilice is worn by many members of monastic orders and some who are members of certain churches. It is to supress desires and atone for sins.

I position the cilice an inch higher so that it has new flesh to abuse. I take hold of the leather strap and pull it tight. The sound of the metal links running through the metal ring is so familiar. I have done this a thousand times but still get a thrill as the barbs penetrate my skin. I am reminded of the Christ's pain as he suffered for mankind. With the device firmly clasped around my leg, I tentatively walk over to the hook that is fixed to my bedroom wall. From it hangs a leather flogger that I have modified. At the tip of each fall, I have attached sturdy metal barbs to add additional pain to the instrument.

The practice of self-flagellation has been practiced by religious orders for centuries. In its religious context, it is a mortification of the flesh to mirror the pain of Christ prior to the crucifixion. I take down the leather flogger from its resting place and the handle creaks under my grip. I stride back to the centre of the room and give myself some free space. I take a deep inhalation of breath as I hold out the lash directly in front of me. I allow it to fall to the vertical, then in one swift action bring it up over my shoulder so that falls strike me on the lower back and upper buttocks. The searing pain from the metal tips, lift me off my feet. I stand on tiptoes for a second, as my body acclimatizes to the fire of its touch. I feel the skin break as I repeat the process. I count out loud as I deliver the next blow, then another. After each delivery, the pain increases until I reach fifteen and it all melds into one.

For this evening, twenty will be enough to curb my desires. The last five follow in quick succession and I drop the lash to the vertical in front of my body. My legs are quivering and breathing ragged. The sticky sensation as my life's blood trickles down my back, is electrifying. I wriggle as it enters the crack of my ass and runs down to my balls, before dripping onto the floor. I stand motionless and savour the after pain. Then, as always, I set about cleaning up the open wounds and blood from the floor. The hour is late and I must be about my father's business.

After applying some cream to my wounds, I dress in a pair of jeans and a t-shirt. There is no need for a jacket on this warm Californian night. I put my Bible back on the bedside table where it always sits, just at arm's length from the bed. I blow out the candle on the table and close the door behind me. As I descend the stairs, I hear the sound of snoring coming from the living room. On reaching the bottom, I look inside the living room. Drug paraphernalia is littered across the floor. A mass of naked bodies, both male and female, are contorted in twisted shapes. Legs and arms are wrapped around one another. The party was an epic one as always, but I slipped away early for my studies and to repent. I creep towards the front door and let myself silently out.

The night means downtown is lit by the neon lights of the clubs and bars, shining on the rain-kissed sidewalks. At night you can be anybody and no-one cares who you really are. I stare up at the sky and study the silver glow of the moon. It smiles down at me with a love so intense, it could warm the coldest of nights. But this is California and the night is warm and sultry. The darkness envelopes me like a warm duvet and my eyes take in the wondrous canopy of the heavens. It is the most beautiful canvas, alive with a raw energy. Surely, only a higher being could create such a magnificent masterpiece?

California nights in LA are filled with a buzz of excitement. The streets are filled with people, moving from bar to bar in search of pleasure. I move into the shadows to observe the street life. The hookers stalk the streets in their skimpy outfits and high-heel boots looking for work, their drug-addled bodies as thin as pins, and their cheekbones jutting out through pallid skin. I feel a deep sense of sorrow for these women, who are forced into this modern day slavery. Some might say it is their own fault for getting addicted to drugs. Their only option to feed their habit, to sell their bodies for money. I know that it is not as simple as that though.

I have felt that same old familiar sting, as the needle pierces the skin and the euphoria as the liquid enters my bloodstream. It is a sensation that is difficult to describe and nothing comes close to it. Well, maybe not everything. The swelling in my pants and the surge of blood that pumps at my temples, announces the arrival of my base desires. The barbs of the flogger were not enough to quell this insatiable appetite. Across the road stand two elegant-looking temptresses. They strut back and forth along their allotted space on the sidewalk. Although I cannot see anyone, I know a pimp or two will be watching their movements.

One of the girls has wavy black hair and is wearing a short, tight-fitting skirt and black top. She is a bit on the large side, tall and bulging out at the thighs, as well as the breasts. Her thighs and butt jiggles as she walks, exaggerating the sway in her hips. Her breasts are large, filling her top, and smashed down under the tight material. She walks slowly, blatantly, waving at the passing cars if they contained gentlemen.

The other girl was black and smaller than her. She was wearing a tight dress of black spandex and heels. Her breasts were large in proportion to her tiny stature, and her legs and arms were thin, especially in comparison to her companion. From her submissive attitude, and the fact that she was hanging back from her friend, I could tell that she was in training. She was not as confident as the larger girl and let her teacher do all the running.

I wonder to myself why she has entered into this lifestyle. Perhaps she has a child at home who needs to be provided for. Making money from your body might seem an easy option. If a guy was to take you out for a night, he might spend $20 dollars on you. These girls could fuck ten guys in that time, and make more than ten times that amount. That's as a beginner, and I am sure her friend would be charging something like $50. Enough of contemplation, these girls need redemption and to see the light that is the Lord.

I step out of the shadows and check the road. When there is a gap in the traffic, I walk casually in their direction. The teacher immediately spots my movements and her face lights up. I must say I am not a bad-looking guy. Not the skinny runt that I was as a boy. The hours spent in the gym have paid off when it comes to female company. That, and the fact that I seem to have some irresistible power over the female of the species. Not just females, but non-heterosexual males also. It is not my normal persuasion, but Jesus taught us that we are all brothers and sisters in God's eyes.

As I draw closer, the bigger girl pumps up her chest, adjusting her breasts so that I get a good view of what she can offer me. My breathing becomes ragged and heart rate increases. I lick my tongue over parched lips, savouring the sweet taste to come. Now only five or six paces away, the girl steps off the sidewalk.

"Are you looking for company, sugar?" Her accent is Hispanic, which explains her dark skin.

"It depends how much for that pleasure." I give her a cheeky grin and knowing wink.

"It will be $60 for full sex, $40 for a blow job and $20 for hand relief." At once, she goes into the price of her various services.

"How much for both of you, full sex?" She turns to look at her companion who is waiting nervously on the sidewalk.

"That will be $100 for the both of us and $5 for the room. I promise you that it will be worth it." A salacious smile crosses her lips.

"Done! Lead the way." I do not need any other rhetoric. These girls are in need of salvation and it is my path to lead them to it.

"So what should I call you, child?" I turn to the younger of the two, who is trailing us a few paces behind.

"I'm Summer and this is Gloria." She holds eye contact for a brief moment, before dropping her gaze to the floor.

"That's a beautiful name. I'm Curtis. Pleased to make your acquaintance." I offer my hand out and she timidly takes it, which causes Gloria to laugh out loud.

"It's a pleasure to meet you, Curtis." Gloria answers for the both of them.

We enter the rundown apartment building, just a stone's throw away from where they were plying their trade. It smells unpleasant and I instinctively breathe through my mouth to avoid the stench. I can't imagine that they live here on a permanent basis, and assume that this is just a base to work from. After paying a guy in a sweat-stained vest at reception, we walk down a narrow, dimly lit corridor. Gloria opens a door to the right and invites me inside.

A single bulb hangs from a flex with no shade to beautify it. It provides just enough illumination to make out the rather battered-looking bed. It has most definitely seen better days and the windows are thick with grime. I have never been the most house-proud sort of person, but this place makes my skin crawl. I can only imagine the multitude of bacteria and bugs that litter the stained mattress. On a bedside table, there is a wicker basket containing a multitude of different condoms. The wrappers are brightly coloured with various different logos on. Without a word, the two girls begin to strip off their clothing.

The desires in me are overpowering and I fear I cannot control them. I should stand firm on the rock that is Jesus Christ, but I am just a man. God is displeased with fornicators, that is why the book of Ecclesiastes, 11:9 says, *"You who are young, be happy while you are young, and let your heart give you joy in the days of your youth"*. We all take our own view on the Bible and interpret it to our own way. If I follow the way of my heart and what my eyes see, I know God will sit in judgement of me. We ought to keep our bodies holy. For the married, the Bible says "Be faithful and for the singles, keep yourself safe until you get married". Fuck that shit! I'm young and the boner in my pants requires attention.

The sight of the two ladies of the night, standing there naked before me, is too tempting to refuse. My mind is weak and the sight of bare flesh causes my temperature to rise, along with the increase of my breathing. Both Gloria and Summer are looking expectantly at me. For them, time is money and are eager to get on with things.

"You, caress and suck her tits!" My attitude has changed as quickly as the rise of my heartbeat. I point at the younger girl, giving her my instructions.

"So, you like a bit of girl-on-girl action do you?" Gloria grins at me. She will not be grinning when I finish.

"You bet! I would like to see you pleasure each other." I keep the tone of my voice low, hiding the excitement that is building.

Without another word, Summer begins to fondle and caress her teacher's breasts. She takes one nipple at a time, licking around the areola before sucking it in her mouth in a loud, slurping motion. My hand wanders down to the front of my pants and I rub the hardened flesh that is just waiting to burst free. The ache and throb is excruciating and I can feel a damp patch against my groin.

I fumble with my belt buckle and undo it with anticipation. I pull the leather through the loops and wrap the material around my right hand. I delight in the sensation it gives against my skin. With my other hand, I pop open the button of my jeans and unzip myself. I slide my fingers into the waistband and pull the jeans, complete with shorts, to the ground. The air that circulates around my balls and shaft is liberating and I run my fingers along its length, cupping my warm testicles. The sight of the two girls, now pleasuring each other, is enough for my resolve to break.

"Come here. I want you to take the serpent in your mouths, until he spits his fiery venom." My voice catches as I mouth the words and I step towards the pair, who immediately cease their mutual ministrations.

Their eyes open wide, feasting on the size of my manhood. God blessed me with this unusually large appendage and I thank him in my daily supplications. The pulsing of the blood, as it fills every cell of my cock, is mirrored in my temples as they pump in a rhythmic manner. I halt just before Gloria and Summer, who drop to their knees. Gloria takes the lead and takes me deep in her mouth, until the tip hits the back of her throat. I close my eyes as the shiver runs down the length of my body.

One by one, they use their mouths expertly on my weak flesh. As one mouth departs, it is replaced by another, all the time my cock is being stroked seductively. Sin starts from the mind, and the thoughts that are running through mine, are beyond sin.

"That's enough! I want you at the end of the bed and show me the glory which the Lord has bestowed on you." I pull my cock free of Gloria's mouth and she looks up at me, confused.

"So, you want to see our pussies, is that what you're saying?" She scrambles to her feet and is joined by Summer. They stand staring at me, awaiting my answer.

"Yes, go to the end of the bed and bend over, so I can see how much you have been defiled!" There is no hiding the venom in my reply, but it gets an immediate response.

"Now you're talking, honey." Gloria takes her friend by the hand and they wander across to the bed.

I pull the leather of the belt tighter around my hand. The pain only thrills me more. I notice the girl's discarded panties on the floor and stoop to pick them up. I inhale the sweet scent of each of the garments in turn. The blood pumps even faster around my already bursting cock. Both Gloria and Summer have taken up their positions, with their asses presented to me. I step towards them, panties still in my hand. On reaching the foot of the bed, I take each of the garments and place it in their mouths. They struggle a little at first, but then comply.

The ripe, well-rounded globes of their buttocks look so inviting. I run my hand over their surfaces and my touch produces the skin to raise in anticipation. They may get paid for having sex, but that is not to say there are times when it is not a little pleasant. With the right person, the body cannot lie when aroused. My fingers probe each pussy in turn, relishing the feeling of their wetness. Then, without warning, I unfurl the belt and strike each buttock with a resounding blow across its width. A muffled, surprised moan escapes from both Summer then Gloria, as the bite of the belt strikes home.

"God has sent me to drive out your sin. You are to receive his divine spirit and absolution by my hand!" I swing the belt so that it catches both girls, flush across the ass cheeks. They lurch forward under its ferocity.

My thoughts turn back to Upton Abbey and the numerous punishments I received by the monks. The sting of the paddle still burns bright in my memory. It is time for me to deliver God's deific wisdom. My hands swing back and forth, as I paint a picture on the voluptuous buttocks of the two prostitutes. Only pain and suffering can atone for their sins. The sins of the flesh require that special kind of deliverance. I am God's messenger on earth, a holy man. Like all holy men throughout history, celibacy is an inner demon that we must all face. I give myself over to lust and debasement. I will wash my sins clear after I have finished.

I throw down the belt and my fingers probe both asses and cunts in tandem. The sticky secretions soak me from their arousal. With a thumb in the ass and two in the pussy, I pleasure both of them at the same time. The lust in me has reached fever pitch and I withdraw my fingers. My attention is drawn towards the small wicker basket on the bedside table and I move towards it. The fluid still covering my fingers, I struggle to tear open the silver foil wrapper, and have to use my teeth in desperation. I finally retrieve the sheath from its vacuum-packed wrapper. I place it on the tip of my cock and using one hand, roll it down the length of my shaft.

I move quickly back to the girls, who are looking at me expectantly. The sight of my, now protected dick, causes Gloria to lick her lips. She cannot speak for the panties that are still stuffed in her mouth. I position myself firstly behind Summer, and without any reserve, drive my cock deep into her ass. She tries to spit out the material that is clogging her mouth, but to no avail. I grasp her hip and begin to pound into her like a beast.

"Feel the power of the Lord, be prepared to receive his holy spirit! You, my sister, must wait for your deliverance from sin!" I leer at the watching Gloria, as I pound that sweet anus into oblivion.

My Lord, I love doing your work!

CHAPTER SIX - CURTIS

That night was my personal epiphany, a moment of sudden and great revelation or realization. The two prostitutes were given a lesson in enlightenment and absolution of their sins. To say that they were spellbound and completely satisfied by my ministrations, was an understatement. It would seem ironic to the normal thinking person that forgiveness of sin is bestowed from such carnal acts. That is the true power of my message. I was brought into this world to preach my own form of the Lord's word. It gives me what I have been missing in my life. A purpose, recognition, attention, and dare I say it, adoration.

As I sit in the back room of the bar before our regular meeting, I muse and theorize how I plan to move forward with what has become a little movement. I chose the bar as it held regular poetry readings and talks on philosophical subjects. It was the perfect venue to get my message across and to seek out like-minded people. The kind of individuals I could mould into my own philosophy about life.

I have long contemplated ethical and religious theories. What is the best way to live one's life? I have come to the conclusion that the focus of right and wrong, is based on consequences that are derived from them. The actions we choose impact on us as individuals. It is time to move away from this and concentrate on an ideal where we focus on the interest of others. This was my way of interpreting the lessons that Jesus taught us during his lifetime. All I was doing was giving them a vehicle in today's society, making them more relevant. I was not being visionary, as scholars and philosophers have been thinking this way for decades.

Pain and pleasure have a fundamental role in all human life. You can approve or disapprove of someone's actions, dependant on the amount of pleasure or pain is a consequence of them. I have begun to read philosophy in conjunction with the Bible and have formed my own system of morality and lifestyle. If we are to measure both pleasure and pain, then we must quantify them against certain criteria. Things like intensity, duration, certainty or uncertainty are all factors. Pleasure is not necessarily followed by pain and vice versa. Yet these factors affect more than just one person and we must consider that when taking actions.

My hedonistic view is that, it is not the quantity of pleasure, but the quality of happiness, that is central to a utilitarian lifestyle. Most qualities cannot be quantified but there is a distinction between higher and lower pleasures. The overriding principle must be "the Greatest Happiness." I want to promote the capability of achieving happiness for the most amount of people. How we do that I am yet to fully decide. That will be my goal and with the right followers hopefully we will reach it. Not just for ourselves but for mankind as a whole.

Every day as I look around, on TV and on the radio, I see and hear nothing but misery. It's rather evident that something is not right in our world. In fact, something must be broken. The earthquakes, hurricanes, tsunamis. The hunger, pollution, threats of nuclear war, terrorism, mass shootings, greed and genocide. You can't be oblivious to the pressing reality that this is not a perfect world. We are far from the Utopia that I dream of. Some people ask where God is at horrible times like these, and how can they continue to believe in him.

I ask myself, do we look for God when times are going well? Honestly, in light of all the evil and tragedy, how can I not believe in God? I see devastation everywhere I look. Horrendous sights that shakes me to the very core. Beggars on the streets that bear little resemblance to human beings. I have wept while watching people who share horrible stories of abuse, rape, and betrayal. I sat in numbed silence, over tragedies, suffering and genocide on a global scale. It's all so overwhelming. Personal pain is sobering. Just as the pain Jesus suffered for mankind.

When God created this world and the people on it, he did so with all their imperfections. He could have built the world so that everything was perfect in every way. A world full of robots, who had no free will of their own. Mindless zombies incapable of emotion. With no ability to form relationships or love. In deciding on the former, he could not prevent them from using their choice for evil in the good universe he made. He created us with the freedom of choice to love him. On the other hand, he took away our freedom not to choose him, therefore he contradicts himself. God cannot contradict himself. He must be true to his character and nature.

The effect of the D-lysergic acid diethylamide pill I took about twenty minutes ago, begins to kick in. The use of narcotics has become a staple part of my life since my late teens. Now living and mixing in the show business world of LA, my habit has escalated. I feel disconnected from the room and my environment. The chemicals infuse my brain and temporarily disrupt the normal communication between it and my spinal cord. I feel as if I am trapped inside my own body, unable to move. I am in a waking nightmare. The sound of guns and explosions reverberate in my head. The deformed and brutalized bodies of women and children litter the floor around me.

It all seems so real, and I have to fight to convince myself it is only the effects of the drug. The images, sounds and sensations I am feeling do not exist, but my mind is telling me different. My perception of time and space, emotions, and consciousness, altered by the chemicals the pill contains. I feel the increase in my heartbeat and the veins in my arms are raised. I am in an induced state of detachment from reality. The use of these kind of natural hallucinogens have been used for thousands of years by indigenous cultures around the world. They precipitate visions or mystical insight and give me the ability to look at religious texts and the path I must take in another light.

The visions become less vivid and frightening. The beating of my heart in my chest slowly begins to subside to some kind of normality. I am gradually becoming adjusted to the chemicals that are firing the synapsis in my brain. They will help me think clearer and explain my theories to the small group of people that will be waiting in the bar. I shake my head and rise from my chair. The room spins a little and I wait until I have composed myself and everything comes into focus. Once I am happy, I step off to exit the room.

As I push down on the handle and pull the door towards me, my ears are filled with the sound of songs of peace and remonstrations, against the pointless war in Vietnam. There is no live show this evening, just a small number of people sitting around, chatting about putting the world to rights. I spot Nancy facing me, sat at a table with a few of the usual faces who have been regulars at these meetings over the past few weeks. The smile she gives me is warm and welcoming. It is something I have not experienced in my lifetime until now. There is a connection between us, but I cannot explain what it is. The lyrics of Dylan's "Times they are a-changin" greets my arrival. How very prophetic.

The room is a haze of smoke and I blink my eyes to peer through the gloom. The pungent, sweet smell of the weed, has a citrus scent to it. It has an essence of herbs too, rosemary and thyme drift up my nostrils. I never liked the smell in my younger days, but now I am drawn to it like a moth to flame. It is all part of the Bohemian culture that is LA in this part of town. I fight my way through the smoke until I reach the table where the others are already gathered. A couple of joints are being passed around and they all seem in a relaxed mood. My arrival causes a stir and they all turn to look at me through bloodshot eyes.

At the centre of the group sits Draven. Unlike the rest, his eyes are not as bloodshot. They are a clear, piercing blue and he seems quite lucid. He is a handsome fucker, I must admit. With his dark hair and swarthy complexion, he looks almost Latino. Either side of him sits Gloria and Summer. He seems to hold them captive with his hypnotic gaze. Many women are attracted to men who come off as "mysterious", and his aloofness or withdrawn characteristics tend to pull them in.

Draven is intriguing with hidden depths. It is as if he knows some secret about life that we don't. Or is he just weird? I have yet to peel away the surface of his character and get to know the real Draven. He could be just shy and uncomfortable in the company of others, but I do not think that is the case. He is a watcher, observing everything that is going on around him, before passing judgement on it. That is a good trait to have and one that I have cultivated myself. He listens more than he engages in conversation. Maybe he doesn't want to say something he doesn't mean, or it takes him extra time to get the right words to express himself. Whatever the reason, it lends to his mystique.

It takes a few moments for him to acknowledge my presence, so I observe him a little more. He has an aura of confidence about him. Not arrogant. He doesn't need to dance on the tables to get the attention he desires. The air of confidence does fall just short of cockiness, though. I have yet to make up my mind if he is an adversary or friend. What I have deduced, is that he seems genuinely interested in my theories.

"Good evening, brothers and sisters." I address the whole group which numbers three guys and six girls.

"Good evening." They all answer in unison except for Draven who sits stoically in his seat.

I take a seat and everyone immediately, including Draven, focuses their attention on me. I leave enough time for the tension to build before speaking. For the first time in my life, I am given the devotion perhaps I craved as a child. Whatever the reason, I drink it in and enjoy the adoration.

"To be worthy of worship, God must be good and all-powerful. There are some of you sat around this table, who think that evil and suffering are signs that God is not powerful enough to stop evil, or not loving enough to do so. Am I right in that assumption?" I look at each person in turn, my eyes boring into theirs to search into their souls. The eyes are a window to the soul, they say, and it is true.

"There is so much suffering in the world. If God is so powerful, then how does he let it persist?" It is Summer who breaks the silence, her innocent face imploring me for an answer.

"I disagree. I think that God is all powerful and more loving than we can understand. Let me try and explain." I have them hooked and they shuffle forward in their seats, as if what I am about to impart is a closely guarded secret.

"We were all entrusted with the care of this great garden we call Earth. We are in a cooperative alliance, to see that we nurture this place as God intended." I let my initial sentence sink in before continuing with my rhetoric.

Draven holds out a joint for me, which I take gratefully. I draw a deep lungful of the sweet smelling smoke into my lungs. I gradually exhale the smoke through my nostrils and delight in the tingle it gives my cheeks. The group, already half-stoned, still give me their undivided attention.

"Mankind has, somewhere along the way, separated ourselves from God, making choice after choice to disregard God, doubt his character, mistrust him, and hide from him. We have ignored the guidelines that he set out for living in the world that he created by his own hand." There is an edge now to my voice, a little hint of malice. Just enough to make the group drop their eyes in shame. It is true and they know it.

"Then teach us the way. What do we need to do to seek the truth?" In that one moment, and with those words, something strikes my very heart.

"Nancy, that is just what we need. To find the one true path that leads the way to that which we all seek." Each of my new acolytes nod their heads in agreement and a murmur builds up to an excited whisper.

"Tell us more, teacher." It is the rather petite Jasmine who speaks now. Her voice is so timid, but she is barely out of high school and is a very shy girl.

"What God originally intended, was that his creation should be an alliance between man and woman. This has now disintegrated into all levels of abuse. We use each other for our own purposes, to fulfil selfish desires rather than living in a trusting compatibility with each other. We have become selfish and mistrusting. We are interested in our own self-protection. We are envious of what each other has, and grab and claw at it for ourselves. We have become greedy and unwilling to share. That is what I believe to be the crux of the problem." My words hang as heavy in the air as the smoke from the pot.

"Then what is the answer to this problem, teacher?" It is Nancy again, who leads the conversation on.

"We must reintroduce this blessed alliance, between man and woman that God originally intended. It is time to put away personal jealousy of what one man or woman has over another. We are all God's children and should share everything that he has provided for us." I smirk inside when I deliver this part of my lesson.

"What does that mean, teacher?" It is Steve, one of the other guys that speaks up.

Since he found the group, when he attended a poetry reading a couple of weeks ago, he has always been full of questions. That is not a bad thing, but I should have known that he would need clarification on the meaning behind my statement. He was an awkward-looking guy and did not seem to be confident in the presence of females. That was the polar opposite to his friend Jack, who he invited along a week later. Jack was full of himself and was always flirting with the girls in the group. They did not seem to mind, as he was a pleasant enough guy and was quite humorous.

"Jesus, in his short life, lived it to the full and we should copy his example. There will be no jealousy between us and we will love each other without barriers. If you wish to make love to Summer or Gloria or both at the same time, that should be something to celebrate. The sharing of ourselves, without restrictions to today's conformities, is how we will build our house. A temple, glorifying the Lord and the gifts that he has endowed us with."

"Is that not just free love? I can get that anywhere here in LA." Jack immediately interjects on my explanation. He grins at the girls in a lecherous manner, which makes my blood boil.

"You misunderstand me, brother. What we will build together, will be nothing like the false idolatrous actions carried out by those who merely lust for carnal knowledge. Ours will be a journey of spiritual enlightenment." I can tell by the glazed look behind his eyes that Jack is still not convinced of my explanation. In time, he will know what I mean.

"Cool man. I can live under those kind of rules." There is a murmur of excitement now, between everyone, as they discuss the enormity of what I have revealed.

I sit back and contemplate what I will say next. It was Nancy who had given me the idea with her earlier question, about seeking the truth and finding the way. I have been thinking about the direction of this fledgling group. We will be known as the "Seekers of The Way" and like Jesus, these are the first of my disciples. As I regard each of them in turn, names are conjured up in my head from readings of the New Testament. If we are to have a new identity, it is time to throw off the shackles of our old lives and identities. I will rename them all, and baptize them with their new Christian names.

"To begin our new journey, I will now give you the names that you will go by." Every head turns in my direction.

"We will be known as "The Seekers of The Way" and I would like to thank Nancy, or should I say, Magdalene for that inspiration." My remark causes Nancy to blush.

"Thank you, teacher." She seems happy with her new name as she grins back at me.

"Steve and Jack, you will now be called Thomas and Luke." I smile inwardly at the irony of giving Steve that name, after doubting Thomas from the scriptures.

"Gloria and Summer, your Seeker names will be Lydia and Bethany." Their faces light up, confirming they are happy with my choices.

"Thank you, teacher".

"Jasmine, Sky and Moonbeam, your new names are Martha, Priscilla and Tabitha." They nod their heads in agreement and I sit back as if I have completed my naming ritual.

There is an eerie silence in the room. The jukebox has finished playing its selection and there is only a murmur of whispered voices from nearby tables. All of the group have turned their attention to Draven, who is sitting there with his hands in front of him. His fingertips are joined together, as if he is in silent prayer. He lowers his hands and looks directly at me.

"What am I to be called? You seem to have missed me off your list." His question sounds a little sarcastic and I have to fight to control the anger that begins to rise.

"I have saved you a special place, my friend. It took me a while, but I will call you Peter. Just as the same Peter that carried Jesus' message after the crucifixion." The scowl that covered his face moments ago, breaks and his lips turn upward showing a perfect set of white teeth.

"You honour me, teacher." Now there is a genuine ring to his voice, its timbre a little shaky from the emotion it contained. It is also the first time he has called me by the same title as the others. The journey has begun.

CHAPTER SEVEN - BAPTISM

Up until this point, my life has been one big struggle. The thing about life is, it pushes you until you break, just to see if you can put yourself back together. That might seem a little melodramatic, but they do say that I was always that way. No, I fucking wasn't. I just wanted the love and attention every child wishes for. Yesterday is history, tomorrow is a mystery and today? Today is the present! It is the beginning of a new life for me. The bible taught me that things I have done in the past, God has forgiven. Not because of anything that I have done, but that Jesus paid for all our faults. He gave up his life so that mankind might start again. I am going to grasp that opportunity with both hands and deliver my own brand of twisted religion.

Here I am anticipating life's thrilling adventures, waiting to impart its deepest mysteries on my new flock. I choose to live it to the fullest and celebrate every aspect of it! To me, life is sacred. I have lived it as a secret and told it as a lie. Of course I have shared parts of my daily life in the past, but not all of it. This being a simple act of human nature. We guard moments that we don't want people to know about. The times when I was left abandoned to amuse myself, while my mother lived her life how she wanted. Now it is my turn. I am the main focus of people's adoration and I will use every part of me to see that is how it stays.

It is prophesized that Jesus would return one day to make things right. Our hero and rescuer will restore what was lost and damaged by our betrayal. All people will be judged with perfect justice. The guilty will be sentenced and their lives of separation from God will culminate in endless anguish, as they continue on their path of self-absorption and self-centeredness, on and on forever. I have assumed that mantle and I am ready to do the Lord's work. People are like sheep and will follow, if you give them the right incentives.

My disciples, and those that follow, will enjoy life as God designed it; without selfishness, greed, hatred, pain, sorrow, abuse, and suffering. He will satisfy their deepest longings and desires and I will show them the way. All of the years of neglect and abuse, by the monks at Upton Abbey, will have been worth it. It is my time to shine and grasp the opportunity that has been given.

The room is a kaleidoscope of colours as it moves in and out of focus. The cocktail of drugs I have taken throughout the day have rendered me immobile. They give me clarity to see things in my own peculiar, but visionary way. The problem with narcotics is the more addicted a person is, the more love they need, the more support they are crying out for. In my former years when I began taking drugs, I was not fortunate to have a stable family to give me that support. It was inevitable I would spiral out of control.

I was not the only one who found themselves in this kind of dilemma. After leaving Upton Abbey, I fell into the wrong company. That is when my story with substance abuse began. One of the guys I became friendly with, was much older than me and was already way down the path to self-destruction. He was called Chester and he told me how addiction not only affected him, but those close to him.

He had been using crack for eight years. He lived with his mom who did his laundry, made him breakfast and gave him money. High one night, he sold his truck for $300 which he spent on crack and a hotel room. He made one bad choice after another. He didn't think about the consequences to himself or to others. His sister talked about her outrage at watching Chester self-destruct. She suffered as she watched him refuse help, live life on his own terms and continue to make bad choices. Chester's sister's anger is evidence of her love for him. She knows, just as God does, that life can be better. Anger isn't the opposite of love, hate is, and taken to its end, hate becomes indifference. Even after these wise words, here I sit with the poison running through my system.

I just need to take matters into my own hands and enact vigilante justice. I am not the final judge or authority. I can live freely loving and freely forgiving. *The day will come when evil will be avenged, when brokenness will be healed, and justice will reign. He will wipe every tear from their eyes, and there will be no more death or sorrow or crying or pain. All these things are gone forever. –* **Revelation 21:4**

The anxiety in me begins to build, which makes my heart race and hands tremble. My palms are sweaty, as is the rest of my skin while I mumble incoherently to myself. I am in a state of inner distress but need to get my act together before the group arrives. A feeling of self-loathing, accusation and pain swirl into an inner storm unlike any I've known. The thoughts invade my brain and I fight to gain control over them. I think that I have overdone my dose of habituates for the day and I rise from my chair and walk to the rest room.

I am ungainly on my feet and reach out to a chair by the bed to steady myself. The room moves in and out of focus and I pause for a moment, until I am confident I am stable. I take the four or five paces to the rest room and use the handle as a support before opening the door. I run my hand up the inside of the wall and finally find the light switch. I flick it down. I am met with the kind of brightness that sears into your retinas, making you close them for fear of going blind. It is a brightness that would make fresh snow look grey and dull. It is a brightness to rival the sun itself. I blink my eyes a few times to allow them to become accustomed to the glare.

I stumble to the basin and fill it with cold water. The water moves softly around my outstretched fingers, caressing coolly, eddying in their wake. I pull my hand out and watch the drips, both transparent and opaque at the same time. They fall, snatched by gravity to the basin below. Each one swiftly haloed by ever-growing rings. They have me hypnotized for a moment. I cup my hands and scoop up some of the refreshing liquid. The coolness permeates my skin and I splash the water on my face. The effect is immediate, taking my breath away at first. It is the jolt I need to bring me around to some sort of lucid state. I repeat the process until my flesh is tingling from its cooling properties.

My voluntary state of euphoria, confusion and difficulty in speaking, is gradually subsiding. I lift my arm and glance at my wristwatch. It is already early evening and my flock will be arriving in an hour. Through my confused state, I try and recall if I even mentioned it to Milton. He has been a bit of an asshole lately. Perhaps I might have overstayed my welcome. I will give some thought about that later, but I better have the courtesy to tell him of my plans for the evening. I wipe the water from my face and head off downstairs.

The melodic strumming of a guitar gets louder, as I descend into the open space which is the main living and entertainment area. The familiar sound of Milton's voice drifts up towards me. I must admit, you have to give credit where it is due. He is a phenomenal singer, song-writer and poet. The fact that he saw some promise in me was what drew me into his company. As always, it was good to be appreciated and given the attention I craved. I know though in my heart of hearts, I will never succeed in this cut-throat music industry. I need to put some plans in motion about finding a place of my own.

"Hey man, come join the party!" Milton calls to me as I reach the foot of the stairs. From the sound of his voice, he is already wasted.

"I'll take a drink with you, buddy, but I've got some guests arriving shortly." My response doesn't go down too well. There has been a tension building between us lately.

"I wish you would stop treating this place like your own private hotel, man." Just as I suspected, he immediately berates me for inviting people over without his permission. In the beginning it wasn't like that, but things have changed.

"Okay, dude, cool it." I try to appease him, but I can see from the look in his bloodshot eyes that he is pissed at me.

The doorbell sounds just as I'm about to try and calm him down. I ignore his accusing looks and go to the door. When I open it, I'm pleased to see that the group have arrived as one. At least that will prevent Milton being disturbed every five minutes with the doorbell constantly ringing. Magdalene is at the front of the group. She is wearing a flowery dress which is almost translucent. I can see every curve of her shapely body and am immediately aroused knowing that my hands will be wandering over her skin very shortly. The remainder of the group are huddled together behind her, with Peter bringing up the rear.

"Come in brothers and sisters. Milton has some guests over, so we'll go straight out back to the pool." There is an excited, anticipated buzz to my flock as they shuffle past me.

We transit through the main living room and they greet Milton, walking past him and his guest. He gives them a derisory look and goes back to strumming his guitar. I hurry them along not wanting to piss Milton off more than he already is. We exit the house via the rear of the living room. Magdalene glances at the sofa where I explored her body that first time. She looks back over her shoulder and gives me a cheeky wink. I can't help but chuckle thinking of her licking up my semen from the floor.

As Magdalene brushes past me, she is close enough for me to breathe in her scent. I reach out and our skin touches. She turns to face me and her face lights up. The mere thought of pulling her close and having her there, out in the open, is stronger than any drug. There is an invisible quality that she possesses that has the ability to bewitch me. I must attempt to stay true to my teaching and not favour one woman over another. It is going to be a difficult task, but one I must achieve.

"We all know why we are here, brothers and sisters. Take off your clothes and make a line by the pool. When I call your Seeker name, come and join me in the pool." As I deliver my short instructions, I myself begin to undress. The rest of the group, without question, do the same.

I watch each one in turn as they discard their clothing at the side of the pool. I am not drawn towards the male form, but the other three guys are not lacking in the attributes that most women yearn for. Flat stomachs and chiselled torsos that only a healthy lifestyle can manufacture. Who am I trying to kid? These guys are far from healthy. With the amount of pot and barbiturates they consume, their bodies are inwardly defiled. From the outside they are sculptured Gods. The ladies are of varying shapes and sizes, but all of them are pleasing to the eye in one way or another.

Out of all of them, there is nothing more tantalising than Magdalene's naked form. Everything about her is natural and I love it. Perhaps that is the wrong word to use. All I want is to taste those sweet orbs, suckle and tease those taut nipples. The rush of blood from my now pounding heart has quickly entered my dick and it begins to rise to an elevated angle. Magdalene is the first to notice and she gives me a rather coy look. That sweet mouth and ruby lips will be tasting me before very long. I shake my head to dispel the lust that is building inside and step down into the pool.

"The first one to join me is Tabitha." As I reach the centre of the pool, I call out the first disciple's name. It is not arranged, merely that she is standing closest to me in the line.

She lowers herself down so that her feet are dangling into the water. Then, with a push, she submerges herself in the warm liquid. Step by tentative step she draws closer to me until she is only a few feet away. I reach out and take her hand, pulling her to me. I kiss her softly on the lips before turning to the assembled group.

"I would like to explain why I wish to baptise you. The purpose of Jesus' baptism by John, was first of all to provide an occasion for Jewish people to confess their sins and repent and get right with God." They all nod their heads to confirm that they have understood the solemnity of the occasion. I continue.

"Second, John was making it clear that his baptism of repentance was bringing into being a people of God for the coming Messiah. It was a way of giving them an identity, just as I want to give us an identity. As Jesus said to John *"Let it be so now, for thus it is fitting for us to fulfil all righteousness"*. With those words, I place my hand on the top of Tabitha's head and push her down until her head is submerged below the surface.

"I baptize you, Tabitha, in the name of the Father, and of the Son, and of the Holy Spirit." I release the pressure on her head and she emerges from the water. I kiss her once more fully on the lips.

"Welcome to the way. Now go join your brothers and sisters. Thomas, will you join me please?" Thomas looks up and hesitates before entering the pool.

The anxiety sits below his smile as he nervously edges to the centre of the pool. It is as though the water is charged with electricity, not enough voltage to kill, but sufficient to keep things uncomfortable. As ever he is doubting my methods, but he continues until he reaches me. I lean forward and kiss him on the cheek. He flinches initially then a broad grin spreads across his face. The nervousness seems to drain from his body, as I place my hand on top of his head. As before, I go through the same procedure as with Tabitha. As I push him under the water, I give him his new Seeker name. He explodes out of the water coughing and spluttering and I take him in a warm embrace.

"Go join your brothers and sisters." I gently push him away coaxing him back to the waiting line of my flock.

One by one, I call them forward and baptize them in the holy trinity's name. I baptize Draven, or Pete, to give him his new name second to last. There is most definitely some kind of chemistry between us both, not a sexual one. Something that beasts of a similar nature share. He is not pushy but is definitely the Alpha male type. As long as he knows his place, that is all I ask.

Finally, it comes to Magdalene and I motion her to join me. Like a woodland nymph, she strides around the edge until she reaches the steps. This allows her to maximise the gracefulness of her entry. With her eyes fixated on me, she slowly descends until the water is just below her breasts. As she moves, they jiggle ever so slightly. They are round and pert at the same time. Nature has yet to ruin them by the suckling of infants. I tear my gaze away from them and look deep into her eyes as she approaches me. It is if she is in some hypnotic trance. I wonder how much weed she has taken prior to her arrival. There is a dream-like state about her and I hear an audible sigh as I reach out and touch her. I cup her jaw with my palm and plant a sensual kiss on her lips. I linger a little longer than with the others, hopefully that will go unnoticed. Also, the throbbing of my now fully erect cock is hidden from view of the onlookers, by Magdalene's body.

I perform the baptism ritual and as she emerges from the water, as before, I seal the deal with a kiss. This time, I feel fingers running across my buttocks as her hand squeezes them in turn. Memories from our first assignation, here just weeks ago, obviously rekindled in her mind. I have to break the embrace for fear that the flock will observe her actions. Not that it really matters, as I will be balls deep in her before very long.

"Brothers and sisters. We must now consummate the proceedings by sharing each other. Please feel free to enjoy the first night of many more to come." I throw my arms open like a circus ringmaster.

The mood of the group becomes suddenly energised. The ritual was sombre and meaningful. You can use all the rhetoric and paraphrasing from the bible you want. Nothing is more stimulating than to confirm it all by good old-fashioned sex. I wade back from the centre of the pool and as I climb the steps I am met by both Tabitha and Magdalene. If I was to make a choice, they would have been the first on my list. I drape my arms over their shoulders and guide them to the rear of the garden, which is shrouded in darkness from the lights around the pool.

There is a cluster of trees to the rear of the property. I'm not a prude by any stretch of the imagination, but it is nice to have a little privacy from time to time. The path beneath my feet turns into a deepest brown and the moonlight bleaches the stones that are strewn across it. The canopy above and the foliage below cool the air a little and I breathe a little rapidly through my excitement. My eyes dart this way and that, searching for that perfect spot. Then I see it. Two sturdy trees standing only feet apart. I lead my two disciples towards them.

"I want you both to lean against those trees, so I can get a good look at your asses and pussies." I am straight to the point and eager to thrust myself into these pair of woodland nymphs.

"Yes, teacher." They answer together and make directly for the two trees.

They halt just before the trees and turn around to look back at me. I hold my erection expertly in one hand, running the fingers along the shaft. Their eyes are drawn to it and both of them grin as if pleased at my arousal. They seem to hang on my every movement, transfixed on the motion of my hand. They are polar opposites of each other, Magdalene blonde and Tabitha dark-haired. Both of their bodies glisten in the moonlight, highlighting every bump and curve. Their nipples and areolae are bright pink and provide a striking contrast to the surrounding pale, white skin of both of their bare breasts. The nipples, already engorged with blood, protrude indignantly, while their large areolae look raw and sumptuous. I want to stride towards them and take each one of them in my mouth, but restrain myself.

"You want to touch it, don't you?" I indicate my cock that they are both locked onto.

"Yes, teacher. We would like that very much." Magdalene answers for the more introvert Tabitha, who simply nods her approval.

The pair of them look on in anticipation as I step forward. I stop just before them and hold out my penis for their inspection. Magdalene places one hand on my waist and the other on my bare buttocks. I clench them instinctively. She takes a hold of my jutting member, holding it in place as she studies its full magnificence. She kneels in front of me and beckons Tabitha to do the same. My twitching dick is only inches from her face. I offer no resistance as she lifts up the shaft to get a look at my balls.

"It's beautiful, isn't it?" She whispers to Tabitha who shuffles a little closer.

"Fuck, yeah!" The once shy Tabitha has become a she-devil as she licks her lips at the sight of my cum-filled swollen plums.

Magdalene tosses her hair over her shoulder and places a firm, yet gentle kiss on my bulbous scrotum. Using her tongue, she traces a line straight up the underside of my shaft, until she arrived at the glands. With a flick of her tongue she teases the mushroom-shaped head of my circumcised member. I feel butterflies in my stomach over the sensation. Her tongue is joined by Tabitha's lips as she sucks on my testicles. I think I will explode right here, right now and close my eyes to distract myself.

Magdalene is now slurping on my cock as if she was licking the top of an ice-cream cone. Then she takes me fully in her mouth and my stomach and thigh muscles twitch. Bobbing her head, the beautiful creature lets my cock slide back into her throat, ensuring the length is covered in saliva. She removes her mouth and uses her hand to smear it up and down its length, gently jerking me off. They take it in turns to sample every inch of my tasty, virile genitals. I cannot take it any longer.

"Get against those trees and show me those asses!" I withdraw my cock from Tabitha's mouth, who has taken over from her sister.

"Yes, teacher." They both rise from their kneeling positions and using both hands lean against the two trees.

With their asses thrust out towards me the wanton women arch their backs and glance over their shoulders. I take a further two paces forward so that my hip makes contact with Magdalene's ripe, rounded ass cheeks. The end of my cock is still sticky from both of their combined saliva and it nestles between her cheeks. I lean forward and grasp her by the jaw, pressing my lips hard against hers. At the same time grasping her right breast, and squeeze her rigid nipple. Stretching and tugging at her lovely, ripe protrusion until she winces with pain.

"You like a little pain. That is good." Her murmurs have excited me even more. There is an inner demon within us all and mine is rising from the gates of hell.

Tabitha is only a few feet away and I end my passionate kiss with Magdalene and position myself between the two trees. They could not have been placed any better if I designed it myself. I am at a perfect arm's length from both of their lush buttocks. I pull back both of my hands and Tabitha's eyes open wide as she awaits the short, sharp sting as my palm explodes against her delicate milky white flesh.

"God, yes!" I swivel my head to catch the clenched eyes and satisfied smile on the lips of Magdalene. I knew she was my chosen one. Someone who enjoys pain as a means of repentance of sin.

For the next five minutes, I alternate the speed and intensity of my smacks against their now quivering asses. The glow from my palm transferred tenfold to their flesh. Now that they were both warmed up sufficiently, the ache in my cock needs to be satisfied. I step across to Magdalene and slap the throbbing appendage against her upper thigh.

"You want this inside of you, don't you?" I put my face next to hers and hiss the words but loud enough that Tabitha can hear.

"Yes, teacher! I want it so bad!" She almost wails her reply and it makes me smile.

I move so that I am in a position directly behind her. She removes one of her hands that is steadying her against the tree and reaches back. Her fingers first touch the end of my pre-cum coated dick. I shiver as the electricity surges through my body. Looking down, I admire her flagrantly displayed creamy-white buttocks and watch as her fingers rub the reddened area where my handprint is clearly visible. Then, she revealed the plump pillows of her pink vulva, peeking back between those shapely legs. Using two fingers, she prises her lips apart, so I can see exactly where to stick my cock. I take hold of her hips and direct the tip to the edge of her opening. It slips smoothly between her soaking wet lips. A surge of creamy moisture greets my swollen, pink head, which dipped effortlessly inside Magdalene's crimson cavern.

Tabitha watches on with approval and a little sadness as she observes me, as I thrust my hips forward so I am fully seated inside of her sister. Magdalene lets out an exclamation of joy, as I wriggle slightly, adjusting myself to the optimum position.

"That is where she wants to be. Held captive, with your erection deep inside of her." Tabitha screams out in encouragement and I give her a cheeky wink. She is going to fit in quite nicely, I think.

I am completely engulfed by Magdalene's saturated opening. I begin to thrust in and out of her. The flesh of her buttocks quivers and cushions each gyration of my hips. She feels so warm and lush as I pound into her faster and faster. At the same time, I release one hip and grasp hold of her throat. I squeeze it with a firm, but not aggressive, pressure. I can feel the pulse in her carotid artery and the movement of her body tells me she is close to the edge. I do not want to cum just yet. I have another young disciple to pleasure yet. I slam in and out of her and her legs begin to shake as I ride her into a full-blown orgasm.

"Fuck, yessss!!" Her legs clench together and the pressure around my cock tightens as she discharges her juices all over me.

I look across at Tabitha whose eyes are as wide as saucers. From the heaving of her shoulders, I would say that she was close to her own climax just watching me fuck Magdalene. The cum in my testicles has reached simmering point and I need to expel it.

"Give me some of that cock, teacher. Make me cum like you did my sister." Tabitha is begging for it and I am eager to oblige her.

"Then get yourself ready, my child." I pull myself clear of the now quivering Magdalene.

"Thank you." She whispers her gratitude, head falling for a moment and she gathers herself.

I make my way the two or three paces to the right where Tabitha waits in excited anticipation. Stepping in behind Tabitha, I line myself up with her glistening skin and tease my bulbous head against the knotted flesh of her inner labia. Reaching back, she ensures her lips are sufficiently spread for my insertion. She frowns, then lets out a soft moan of approval as I force myself inside of her. I grind my pubic mound firmly against her soft buttocks.

Grasping her pale fleshy mounds, I spread her cheeks in a bid to drive my cock even deeper into her. I can see her tight, pink anus sitting utterly exposed as I hold her cheeks agape in front of me. Pulling back a little, I drive my dick in as hard as I can and hold it there for a second. Then with no finesse and the threatening orgasm only moments away I pound into her like a wild beast. Her breasts bounce in rhythm to my rather aggressive thrusts. The sound of my stomach slapping against her ass cheeks reverberates around the small group of trees. This only adds to my arousal and I pump even faster, the tingling in my testicles announcing the imminent arrival of the sticky white love express.

Tabitha drops her head and pushes back, sensing my pending ejaculation. Her heartbeat pumps against my palm as I grip her breast tightly. I can feel her body begin to shake and her legs tremble as she nears her own orgasm. I move my hand from her hip and my finger finds her swollen clit, which I rub vigorously. She moans out loud and I feel a hand now on my buttocks. I look back over my shoulder to see Magdalene forcing me deeper into her. There is a playful smile on her lips as I submit to her coaxing. I pound even harder in and out of Tabitha's now saturated opening. Not able any longer to hold it back, I delight in the electrifying sensation as the cum travels up through my cock. She convulses beneath me and I pull myself clear, still rubbing her clit for all I am worth, bringing her off to a sweet release. I jam my cock into her gorgeous, pink tight ass just a few pumps.

I glance down, and my swollen dick is glistening with the juices from her cunt. I slip it out of her ass and it slides beautifully between her buttocks and I shoot a hot trail of sticky, warm cum up her back. Her ass cheeks clench around the shaft, milking me for every last drop. In a few moments I am totally spent and drop against her. My body weight causes her to sag a little, bearing the whole of my weight. We remain stuck together for a few moments until we have gathered ourselves. After a short while, I stand erect, the blood in my cock now retreating to other parts of my body and it becomes a little softer. Magdalene embraces me along with Tabitha, smothering my mouth and neck with kisses. I drink it all in, bathing in the admiration. Voices not far off, draw our attention and we break our little party.

"It sounds like someone is having fun." I wink at my two disciples as the sound of joy rings through the small dark woodland.

"Let's go investigate." Tabitha grabs me by the hand and pulls me in the direction of the sounds.

It is only a short distance before we find the source. Lydia and Bethany have been trussed up in two child's play swings. They have their legs inserted around the ropes so that they are suspended with their legs open. Their asses rest on the seats, and being at waist height, both Peter and Luke are driving mercilessly into their pussies. The air is filled with sounds of ecstasy as the group carry out my earlier instructions. Thomas is standing with his hands on the heads of Martha and Pricilla. They are both kneeling before him, worshiping his cock. They feast hungrily on him, taking it in turns to suck his balls and tease his shaft. The look on his face is that of an angel, a fallen angel who is revelling in Satan's delights.

As I take in the whole scene, one thought enters my mind. We have such an exciting journey ahead of us and I, for one, am going to enjoy every last second of it. Who knows where it will lead, but the possibilities and pleasure are limitless.

CHAPTER EIGHT - PETER

I stare at the photograph on the table by my bedside. The two figures in it have almost become silhouettes. It is as if I have walked away from them, only leaving blackness behind. There is an ache that comes and goes, always returning in quiet moments. I want so much to keep her close, to talk and laugh like we did, before I entered the program only nineteen weeks ago. Time is subjective and cannot be measured when it comes to matters of the heart. All I know in mine, is that I am doing this for the right reasons. To build a better and more secure life for my family. To defend the Constitution of the United States against all enemies, foreign and domestic. I will bear true faith and allegiance to the same. That was the obligation I had taken, and the words resonate with me now as I think about my family.

I see them both everywhere I go, and in everything I do. In the things we both love; in nature, music, and in those silly things. Even though they are gone, their aura remains, beautiful and strong, making the pain all the worse, keeping the feelings so raw. I keep myself focused on the end goal and promise myself that it will be all worth it in the end. To leave a wife and young child alone to fend for themselves, is not an easy thing to do for a man. He is a protector, a provider, a safe haven for those he loves and cherishes.

The high-pitched continuous beep of my alarm clock breaks my train of thought. I wipe away the water that has welled up at the corner of my eye and focus on the day ahead. The end is so close, but I must concentrate my efforts to make sure I make it to the end. We were told in the beginning that we can be dismissed from the course at any given point and I'm not about to let that happen. I throw back the covers and swing my legs out of bed. The coldness of the hard, linoleum floor seeps through the base of my feet and I shiver in the twenty-man dormitory. Some of my classmates are already stirring, others pull the covers over their heads not wanting to face the emerging dawn. I pull on my shorts and a vest, tie the laces of my running shoes and creep out silently.

The FBI Academy at Quantico, Virginia, is situated within the immense Marine Corps Base. With its 547 acres of real estate, it is the perfect location for an agent's training and development. The FBI Academy is just one of many facets of the

Training Division, whose work reaches far beyond the confines of the campus grounds. We are only thirty-six miles from Washington DC, but it's almost like another world. Cut off from the outside by a perimeter that is permanently guarded and patrolled, we live our lives without disturbances. I have undertaken firearms training in various weapons issued and used by the Bureau. My adeptness and skill in their use marked me out from the beginning, as one of my courses shining lights. It was not surprising to me, having been brought up in the town of Appleton, Wisconsin. It was, and still is, a hunter's paradise. Over 150 years ago trappers and fur traders chased the promise of lucrative beaver pelts up the Fox River and settled in the town of Appleton. My father raised me in the ways of hunting and to study and love nature. These skills served me well in that part of my training.

As a New Agent in Training (NAT), I have undertaken a variety of subjects. These included legal training, informant development, investigative techniques, ethics, surveillance, interviewing, interrogation, intelligence, physical fitness, defensive tactics and practical application exercises. A lot of these subjects were carried out at Hogan's Alley. This was the Academy's training facility that looks like a town square. It has its own bank, shops, hotel, restaurants etc, so NATs can practice real life scenarios. With the use of role players and SIMs, which are basically paint guns, they provide an excellent training environment.

It is not all physical but mental as well. I have taken a number of academic, psychological and legal exams during my time here. This morning will be my final legal one and my mind needs to be sharp and focused as it is this area I find most difficult. Failure of any of the tests would mean an instant removal from the programme. I have always found that exercise gets my brain firing at the start of the day. Along with my daily rigorous physical training, I run every morning.

I raise my left leg and grab hold of the toes, stretching the muscles in my thigh. I hold the pose for about ten seconds before repeating it with the other leg. After making sure my legs are warmed up, I stretch my arms and upper torso ensuring that I am fully loosened before I begin my work out. I take in lungsful of air to oxygenate my blood before setting off at a steady jog.

Only a few short months before I decided to apply for a position as a member of the FBI, I had a loathing for exercise. It *was difficult at first to train myself into getting up early in the morning and running before work. Now, I relish the prospect and wonder why on earth I had not done it sooner in my life. The chemicals the brain releases during exercise is almost like a drug. I have become addicted to it and get agitated if I miss my morning fitness. I flew through the physical entrance exam with flying colours. In fact, I was in the top 5% of the applicants on my course.*

My body was built for speed, although my feet pound the tarmac with all the grace of a sack of wet concrete. It is not long before I am in my rhythm, breathing regular and my pace becomes more graceful. There is now a spring in my step and as I enter the woods, I pick up the pace just a little. The ground is soft from the dew and overnight showers and absorbs my weight, making it a little more challenging to keep my balance. My head bobs loosely from side to side as I navigate the trail through the sweet-smelling pine trees.

The slapping noise of my running shoes resonate around the closely packed trees. I cover the ground in a great lolloping gait, as if my ankles were made of tightly coiled springs rather than just sinew and bone. I have not even broken out in a sweat or needed to get my second wind before I emerge out of the forest and hit the perimeter fence. I follow it for about two miles before turning left and heading back towards the base. It is only when I am about a mile away, that I feel the perspiration building beneath my vest and my breathing now coming in pants. I ignore it and double my efforts, gaining even more speed as I eat up the ground. Every few paces I check my wristwatch to ensure I am on time to beat my record. With the gates in sight, I smile to myself knowing that once more I have improved.

As I approach the gates, the marine on duty raises the barrier for me. I dutifully hold up the pass that is hanging from the lanyard around my neck. It is not necessary as he has seen me run the wire almost every day since I started the course.

"Push it, man! You're looking good!" He waves me through like a traffic cop on a New York intersection. I glance at my watch. He is right, I have smashed my previous time by almost thirty seconds.

I warm down a little outside the dormitory, performing a few stretches and allowing my body to relax a bit. The perspiration is flowing freely now, and the colour of my vest has turned from a light to dark blue. On entering the room, it is a hive of activity. Most of the course are already dressed, laid on their bunks reading in preparation for the exam. Others are returning from the washrooms with towels around their waists, while others stroll through the accommodation with dicks swinging freely. Fucking extroverts, I think to myself. Okay, my own cock is bigger than average, but I don't see any reason to flaunt it in front of everyone. I grab my towel from the locker and head off for my shower.

The sweat has ceased as we line up outside of the classroom where the exam will take place. Some of the guys have their heads buried in notebooks, hastily trying to cram as much knowledge in before we begin. It is too late now; if I don't know it now, I never will. The run had cleared my mind over any worries I might have had, but as the door is opened and we are invited inside, the fear returns once more. In the past I have had the ability to recall information, but for some reason I have a bad feeling about this one.

As we shuffle inside, I find the desk with my name card displayed on the table. There are four rows of ten and I am in the first one. No chance, even if I wanted to, of cheating. The Proctors would be constantly monitoring the class prowling up and down the rows as in previous exams.

"Okay, gentleman, take your seats and settle down. This is your final exam. If you have any questions, simply raise your hand and someone will come to you. You have three hours for the exam and I will tell you when to begin. Are there any questions?" The head Proctor looks around the room, but is met with a silence that is deafening.

"The time is now 9am. You may turn over your papers!" I haven't had time to gather my thoughts, which is probably a good thing really.

I arrange my writing implements on the desk and turn over the paper. All my senses are tingling. My body is reacting like there's a gorilla about to beat the crap out of me instead of being faced with a sheet of legal scenarios and questions. My body is preparing for a marathon instead of sitting still for a couple of hours. I can ace this stuff, I know I can. I fill in my name, date and course number. One task complete. Then I begin to read the first scenario and the words seem to dissolve into the paper. The increase of my heart rate causes my temples to throb, as I fight to concentrate. It is only initial nerves and it doesn't take long for me to settle down. I read the scenario over *and over and finally it becomes clear. The nerves are quickly banished and I pick up my pen and begin to write.*

"You have fifteen minutes remaining!" The voice of the Proctor startles me. I look down at my paper and am relieved to see that I have almost finished the last question. The time has flown and my fingers ache.

The last few minutes fly by. I look up at the clock as I put down my pen. I have finished with five minutes to spare. I exhale loudly and receive a vicious look from the person to my right. He obviously has not made as much progress as myself and I can tell how frustrated he is. I mouth a silent apology but can't help leaning back in my chair with a self-satisfied smug look on my face. For the remaining couple of minutes, I run my eyes over the paper making sure I have answered every question.

"That's it. Put your pens down!" The Proctor's voice rings out across the room and is met by a series of groans and pens being slammed down on the desks.

I give an inward sigh of relief, happy in the knowledge that I have answered everything to the best of my ability. This was the last stepping stone to me graduating a fully-fledged FBI field agent. There is only a few more days of driving skills and firearms proficiency before the course ends. The Proctor sweeps through the room collecting each person's paper before dismissing them.

I leave the exam room with a certain sense of relief and anticipation to the last visit to Tactical and Emergency Vehicle Operations Centre (TEVOC). The unit teaches safe, efficient driving techniques to FBI, DEA and other government and military personnel. Apart from the firearms training, this is one of the most enjoyable parts of the course.

Six of us will be running through some of the training scenarios before being relieved by the next group. I am paired with Shaun O'Hagan, a thick set Irishman from Boston. His family came from County Cork in Ireland and arrived on these shores back in the time of the potato famine in the "Old Country". As I was of Irish descent, we got along great together. He was a no-nonsense kind of guy and spoke his mind. Everyone I met during my time at Quantico would become friends for life, but some you held in a closer tie than others. Shaun was one of these. We drew our firearms from the armoury. A Remington shotgun and semi-automatic pistol. We moved to the loading bay and prepared our weapons.

From the armoury, we make our way to the motor pool. Here, there were an assortment of high-powered vehicles that were used by the NAT's. This morning we were assigned a black, armoured sedan. The scenario was that we were escorting a high-profile prisoner to a court hearing. The prisoner was played by one of the Quantico instructors. He was placed in the middle vehicle with an armed escort. Shaun and I were in the lead vehicle and waited patiently for the order to move.

"Move out!" The silence is broken and Shaun, who is driving, pulls away smoothly.

We roll down the main street of Hogan's Alley and as we come to an intersection, the lights change. I am constantly scanning left and right at the buildings and on the sidewalks. Threats can come from any angle. What may look innocent to the normal person, is something to be suspicious of for an agent. Danger lurks behind every pair of eyes that observes us, as we escort our package towards the court building. The lights turn to green and Shaun places his foot on the gas. From my peripheral vision, some second sense causes me to look to my right. The looming shape of the dark vehicle is only ten yards away.

"Contact, right!" I just have enough time to scream out a warning, but Shaun has already reacted.

He coolly turns the wheel so that he can lessen the blow which we know is going to be unavoidable. I cock my pistol, chambering a round, and brace myself for the impact, which comes with a violent thud. I am immediately thrown to my left from the inertia. The seat belt does its job and digs into my shoulder. It is only a matter of seconds for me to gain my composure. With my heart racing, I look to my left and see that Shaun has already discarded his belt and is out of the car. With his shotgun resting on the roof, he is firing into the side of the target vehicle.

I slide across the seat and exit through his open door, keeping low, using the vehicle as protection. It was text book stuff and if it wasn't so fucking real, I would have a hard on. I take up a stance to the rear of the vehicle and open fire. The dark vehicle is covered with the paint from the SIM's. I glance over my shoulder and see that the vehicle carrying the prisoner has taken an alternative route just as we would do for real. It was our duty to protect it and that we did.

"Okay, cease fire. Cease fire!" an instructor wearing a baseball cap steps out of a nearby building with a megaphone in

his hand. I immediately lower my firearm and apply the safety catch, as does Shaun.

"Good job, guys. Get your weapons cleaned and hand them back to the armoury." The scenario had only lasted a maximum of ten minutes, but the instructor seemed pleased with our reactions and the drills of the other two vehicles.

"Devlin. The director wants to see you in his office." For a moment my heart sinks. Surely, I'm not being dismissed from the course this close to the end?

"Yes, Sir!" I return my pistol to my shoulder holster and we get back into the Sedan and drive back to the motor pool.

I unload and hand the weapon back to the armourer and sign the sheet of paper to say I have done so. My heart is still racing, and a sickening feeling rises from my stomach. The central administration building is just a short walk from the armoury, but it is the longest walk I have ever taken. Has the last nineteen weeks been for nothing? I'm about to find out. I find the Director's office and wait patiently outside. The perspiration has built up on my lip and I run my tongue across it and taste the salty liquid. I don't have long to wait until the door is opened.

"The Director will see you now." A pretty young girl with heavily applied makeup steps out of the room and holds the door open for me.

"Thank you." I can't hide the tremble in my voice as I step past her.

The room is spacious with a single large desk at the far end. A window runs almost the full width of the room and I have to shield my eyes against the afternoon sun which streams through. The Director of the Quantico Academy is sat behind the large desk, but rises as I enter. He is dressed, as always, in a suit of the highest quality and cut. His hair is high and tight, reflecting his military background.

"Patrick, come in my boy. Take a seat." He extends a hand and a warm smile. I take it and feel the strength in his fingers.

His greeting is welcoming, and the tone puts me immediately at ease. If I was to be dismissed, his attitude, bearing and voice would be different I am sure. So why have I been summoned into the Holy of Holies? It is only then that I notice another guy in the room: he sits silently, not moving. He is dressed in jeans and a checked shirt. On his right arm, surrounding what I can observe is a massive bicep, is a white armband. His eyes wander over me from tip to toe. It is as if he is assessing me. I take the seat the Director has offered.

"I've been hearing good things about you. Your instructors tell me you are in the top 5% of your class." As if to confirm this, he shuffles through a folder, which I assume has all of my information contained within its buff exterior.

"That's pleasing to hear, Sir." I can't help allowing myself a silent pat on the back. It feels good to be praised, but especially so from someone as revered in the service as Kurt Steinbeck. The stranger remains silent.

"I've been through some of your results and your firearm and psychological evaluation scores are some of the highest I have seen in my time here. How have you found the course?" I don't know why, but this seems like a loaded question. A way for me to make a mistake. I ponder my reply, thinking what does he actually wants to hear? I decide to be honest.

"It is something I never thought I would get to experience. Of course, I found some aspects more challenging than others. The legal side is one of those, but I think I have finally got my head around it." There it is, I have left myself open to scrutiny as he sifts through the pile of papers.

"Your first legal exam was about average, but we will see what your final is like. How did you think it went this morning?" He sits back from the desk, but still holds onto the folder containing my life at the Academy.

"I'm quite optimistic to be honest, Director. I feel I answered all the questions fully and gave validated evidence to back up my conclusions." He seems happy with my reply, but his cool grey eyes never leave mine. He watches every bit of body language and I feel like I am in some form of interview.

"I see you have a young family." Once more he opens the folder and takes out a sheet of paper, which must contain my family history. He scans down the page.

"Yes, I have a wife, Siobhan, and a young son, Liam. He is three next birthday."

"The course must have been difficult being parted from them for so long." Again, he probes me, looking for any sign of weakness.

"It was at first, but I think I have managed it well." My reply seems a little too defensive and he examines my reaction carefully. Then he gives the guy in the corner of the room a wistful stare.

"Can you tell me why you applied to be a member of the FBI, Patrick?" This question came way out of left field and I wasn't expecting it.

"To serve my country against all enemies, foreign and domestic." I give the stock answer that all candidates give. From his knowing smirk, I can see he is not convinced.

"I see you were raised a Roman Catholic. Are you a good Christian? Attend church regularly?" Once more he examines the folder he is still grasping, turning over another page of my history and background.

"I like to think so, Sir. I was raised to believe in God and the Virgin Mary." Religion has never cropped up in my time at the Academy, but I think there is a reason behind his line of questioning.

"There are many threats to our country. Some of them are external while others are home grown. There is a new emerging threat that we have been watching recently. I would like to show you a quick videotape before I continue." He rises from his chair and wanders over to a TV and video recorder. He presses the button on the device and returns to his seat.

At once the TV springs into life. The images are a little grainy in places, but the subjects are the same. Groups of people listening intently as enigmatic characters speak to the assembled masses. Some are only small in number, where others are a vast sea of adoring faces. They hang on every word they are being fed. The tape continues for the next ten minutes and I fidget in my seat as I attempt to comprehend what on earth this has to do with me. The video footage comes to an end, but the Director remains seated.

"Do you think you could live a life under another identity? Have no contact with your family for an unspecified duration?" He waits until his question has permeated into my, now confused brain, glancing surreptitiously across at the silent guy who has now got up from his chair.

"Having never experienced that kind of life, I cannot really give a truthful answer on that, Sir." I feel that there is something coming that I never expected when I entered the room only twenty short minutes ago.

I hear the door open behind me but keep my attention on the Director. He leans forward and closes the folder, placing it on top of the desk. From my peripheral vision, I can see the stranger move towards me.

"Look at me." The voice comes from my right. The accent is foreign, but I have heard it before when watching old movies about the Second World War. I turn my head to look at the stranger who is now stood directly next to me.

"I am the Umpire. Look at my face. The next time you see my face and hear my voice, it will be over. Do you understand?" My mind now is swirling in the deep depths of confusion. What the fuck is some British guy doing in the Director of the FBI Academy's office?

Strong, rough hands are placed on my shoulders from behind. I never heard the person approach. I am forced down into my seat and I try and struggle but am kept firmly in the chair. A rustling sound comes from over my shoulder and I feel something coarse against the back of my neck. I stare into the unsympathetic eyes of the stranger and then everything turns black.

CHAPTER NINE - MAGDALENE

The first time I heard the husky lilt of his voice, I was hooked. He has an aura surrounding him that is almost something you can touch. If I were a young girl once more, I would say it was a crush. Yet that is such an infantile word and nothing like I am feeling. It is a word invented by the older generation to belittle young love. What I feel inside is a passion hotter than a thousand suns. When I heard him sing, it was like liquid adrenaline being injected right into my blood stream. Not so strong that it would freak me out, but just enough to make my body tingle with desire.

My skin prickled where he touched me and my heart beat erratically in my chest so hard that I thought it might fly out. I felt like a teenager again, only the butterflies in my stomach were exaggerated tenfold. I liked him. A lot! When he approached me in the club, time stood still. My stomach turned unhelpfully and I felt my skin turn clammy. I am the moon to his sun. As the sun and the moon perform their duty regularly and harmoniously according to the unfaltering laws of nature, so a couple are reminded that their lives should also reflect this. I hope to spend the rest of my life, waxing and waning as he rises each morning to banish the darkness.

The mere thought of thinking about him makes me begin to perspire. My hands are sweating and I rub them against my skin. The release of the chemical dopamine and the increase in the amount of testosterone surging through my body has caused this reaction. It is natural in all men and women when they feel a certain way about a person. It is involuntarily and cannot be controlled. Why would anyone want to control it? The sensation and feelings it produces is more addictive than any drug I have taken up until this point in my life.

A woman also produces norepinephrine and phenylethylamine. It is these chemicals that are increasing my sense of euphoria as I think about Curtis. I am totally focused on him to the exclusion of other things. I am feeling extra alert and alive, but am having trouble getting to sleep. I remember that time at Milton's place when he shot his load on the floor. The Oxytocin which is released in these moments of passion and intimacy breaks down emotional barriers, making people feel comfortable and getting them to "drop their guard". My guard was definitely down as I got down on all fours and lapped it up like a kitten. It is this particular chemical that is the most addictive. When the person you are falling for is not around, you do not produce as much of it so that's where the craving for more comes from.

Although these chemical imbalances are a factor of why I like certain types of men; there is also personal preference be that physical or psychological. I have always gravitated towards the dark and brooding type of person. I don't care about the size of a guy's cock, although I would never say no to a large portion of meat. He must have a brain and be able to engage me in meaningful conversation. Someone who pays attention on my habits, behaviours, and preferences. That is to say without criticising them. I am a secure kind of person and am comfortable being on my own until the right one comes along. I'm not the type that would hang around outside someone's apartment, just to get a couple seconds of their time. I might want to spend more time with a person, but would never resort to inappropriate or manipulative ways of getting their attention.

Curtis has physical attributes that draw me to him. We are all different in what we see in the opposite sex, but I am sure his characteristics give him that special attraction. Just his expansive body movements. Like everyone is in reach and he is reaching for everyone. His free, loud, contagious laughter. He's not afraid to show his teeth and laugh the more sincere laughter he can offer. He has a verbal wit. Very quick at jokes and snaps comebacks just to stir the social environment.

He has a way of relating stories from the scriptures that gives it a relevance in today's society. I was never very religious but he makes things all so much clearer. His vision of a new lifestyle is something that I believe will grow. He is not self-obsessed hearing his own voice. Every silence is filled by a story that entices other people's ideas and start a general conversation. And still keeps people interested in the meaning behind the original story.

I loved his idea that our culture is one where people make their better natures subordinate to wealth accumulation because not to do so means they can't survive. It is a culture where the purest souls are viewed with suspicion; of course, they must have an ulterior motive. It is in itself toxic in nature and something that we should try and avoid. That is his vision in a nutshell. To love each other unconditionally, without jealous thoughts of what one person has over another. I get that, I really do. The only thing I question is how I will handle the jealousy thing. Like I said, I am of a secure nature, but my feelings for Curtis are something that I have never experienced. Will I be able to keep those in check? To share him with the others?

The night of our baptism was the first test. As he guided us through the small group of trees to the rear of the garden, I was a little nervous. Although his arm was draped over my shoulder, I knew that his other was touching Tabitha. For the initial first five minutes I must admit I felt the green eyed monster emerge. We were both naked with the man I am quickly becoming attached to. For the first time in my life, I was comparing myself to another woman. Did he find her body more attractive than mine? Did he desire her more than me?

When he held out his cock for us to sample, I wanted to be first to taste him. I hastily grabbed it, taking control over the situation. Not to anger him and to show that I was good with his philosophy of sharing each other, I gladly shared him with my new sister. The fact that he chose me first to fuck made me feel special. It was only when he withdrew and decided to spill his seed in and over Tabitha that I felt a pang of jealousy. I must say, though, the sight of him fucking her like a wild beast was so erotic. The thought of it makes me bite down on my lip.

As I lay in my bed, I slowly run my fingers over my breasts. Before I realized it I was squeezing them with need. All of the time I am thinking of Curtis, lurking in the shadows at the foot of the bed watching me. I begin to flick and pinch the nipples, squirming in the delight of the sensation. I think of his mouth surrounding my breasts, his tongue teasing them to taut peaks. I gradually remove one hand from my tits and gradually run it down my stomach. The tiny hairs on my skin react immediately sending a shiver through my body.

It does not take long before the finger tips touch the top of my sex. It is already wet from my imaginings. I spread my legs wide and I slowly take one finger and trace around the lips of my pussy. Already soaking wet, I whisper to myself and to the shadow of Curtis observing me. Slowly, I slide one finger two knuckles deep, slowly sliding in and out of my pussy. I only wish it was Curtis' thick, strong fingers pleasuring that hole. Even if he was there, I was far too gone to care, or to stop.

My hips convulse as I slide my fingers in and out, first one then two. I am so close to falling over the edge of an orgasm. In my mind's eye I can see him rubbing the front of his pants. His swollen dick forcing itself against his tight fitting jeans. It only spurs me on and my fingers work even faster. It turns me on thinking about how excited he is watching me masturbate. From his vantage point he would have the perfect view of my now soaking pussy. The juices from it coating my fingers and dribbling down my lips into the crack of my ass. I slow down a little to tease my imaginary voyeur.

His cock is now free from his pants and he seductively runs his hands along the shaft. The veins on the surface are standing bold, and proud as the blood swells them. I continue to use my two fingers to slide and explore my now flowing cunt. The strokes of his hand become more vigorous, in time with my own ministrations. I so wish that cock was driving in and out of me. Stretching my skin, my hips moving to meet his thrusts. His hands grasping both of my ass cheeks pulling them apart as he pounds the fuck out of me. His balls slapping against me with that delicious sound. Before I know it I scream.

"Oh god I'm….." I hear a hitch in his breathing and realise he is also close. His fingers are a blur as he prepares to discharge his sticky, sweet juice over my body. Showering me with his generosity.

I am sure I feel the bed move under his weight. It is all in my mind, but it feels so real. A whispered voice in my ear.

"I have to put my cock in that wet pussy before I lose my mind" His gravelly, deep voice is full of lust and desire. I open my legs to allow him access.

My fingers rub my clit as I feel his cock slam into me. The lubrication from my masturbation making the entry effortless. He begins to pound in and out of me his mouth biting down on my shoulder as he brings himself off inside of me.

"Fuck, yesssss!" I wail out to an empty room as my phantom tips me over the edge. My whole body twitches with ecstasy as my cum flows like a stream down onto the bed sheets.

It is not over then. He pulls his still hard shaft from me and pinches both of my nipples in unison. I quell the pain by once more biting down hard on my lower lip with my teeth. It is more of a pleasant pain than excruciating.

"Get over on your knees!" He does not wait for me to comply.

He can't get me on all four fast enough, his rough hands throwing me over so that my ass is in the air, face down into the bed. It is amazing how the mind can conjure up the things that we desire so much. On the exterior he is a gentleman, but within, he is a hungry wolf eager to sate his hunger. My fingers move once more to my clit, which is still super sensitive from my orgasm.

"Grab the headboard," He growls. I do as I am instructed without reservation.

The sensation of the tip of his cock against my anus makes me wriggle. I push back a little and wince as the head stretches my sphincter muscle. As he pushes himself forward, I swear I can feel that massive tool in my stomach. He begins to slam into me really hard and I rub my clit in timing with him. Although I have just cum, it is a different feeling having my ass pounded like this. I frantically await that warm sticky feeling as his sweet juice spurts deep in me. I don't have long to wait and his grip tightens on both my hips. His fingers bite down hard and I look back as he throws his head back.

I am breathless, but so need another orgasm. His whole body tenses, the muscles in his stomach tighten and his thighs lock. His lower stomach bangs against me as he fills my ass with his seed. Pumping every last drop into me. I flinch as droplets of sweat drop from his head onto my naked back. He slumps forward on me, his weight breaking my hold on the headboard. We lay there gathering ourselves for a moment, still joined together. I sigh, dreamingly as the vision slowly dissipates back into the shadows. All that remains of his incursion is a wet stain on the bed sheets and the silver trickle of my juices running down my inner thighs. I cannot remember a better wank in all of my life and I fall asleep with the biggest smile on my face.

The drapes add an orange glow to the morning light. Every morning here in California is a perfect sunrise. The smell of the ocean drifts through my open apartment window. For a moment my mind conjures the rhythmic waves, soft on the sandy shore and my heart beats to the same slow pace. I am beautifully rested and feel alive. Ready for the day ahead and excited at the party and meeting at Milton's place later that day. Curtis seemed pretty stoked about the meeting and said that he had a proposal for us later. He is a mysterious guy at times. I think that is what adds to his allure.

I take in a deep breath. A new day has begun and I throw back the duvet and swing my legs out of bed. Collecting my thoughts, I wander over towards the window. I reach out to the fabric, noticing how up close the light pours through every open space between the fibres. The material is warm beneath my fingers, and pulling them to the side, the sun floods the room. It paints the colours anew. I feel a little of those golden rays soak into the skin. A chorus of birds breaks the drone of the city traffic. I know it's too early to be up, but I'm excited about meeting Curtis again. I know there will be others at the party seeking his attention, but it is enough for me to admire him from afar.

After my shower, I cook myself a breakfast of ham and eggs. The kitchen's air is thick with the scent of coffee. I need at least two to get me going in the morning. I hum softly to myself as I turn over the ham and eggs in the small pan. The smell is driving me crazy and I begin to salivate. This will set me up nicely for a stroll along the beach. I just need to be doing something so that the day passes quickly. I take my time over consuming the gorgeous offering, savouring every last mouthful. I place the plate and knife and fork in the basin. Fill it with warm soapy water and drain the last bit of coffee from my mug. I will wash up later and decide to take my walk.

It is only a ten minute walk for me until I reach the beach, which is now beginning to fill with people. The shore is a graceful arc of sand, glittering under the summer sun, a place for the placid Pacific Ocean to lap. The waves roll in with a soothing sound, the salty water a brief flurry of sand. Every few feet or so lay a shell, a treasure of the aquatic world just out of reach, and the footprints I leave behind will soon be erased by the incoming tide. As I stroll along the sand, I think about Curtis. I can't wait for the hours to fly by so that I can see him again. The calling of the sea-birds above me distract me a little, but my thoughts always return to him.

The temperature has dropped, if only by a few degrees by the time I arrive at Milton's luxury home. It is still very oppressive and we could do with some rain to clear the humid air. The front parking area is already full of expensive high end motor vehicles. It was obviously a party for the rich and famous. I guess we only got an invite because of Curtis influence. When we arrived for the Baptism, I felt a tension between Milton and Curtis. He seemed agitated and not his normal calm self. I have never seen him lose his temper or raise his voice. Yet, there is something hidden behind those eyes that hints at another side to his character. Maybe in time he will let me in and see that other facet to him. I must make a concerted effort to try and distance myself from him in the company of the others. I don't want my emerging feelings for him bubbling to the surface for all to see.

The door is wide-open and I saunter inside. The coolness of the room is welcoming from the sticky air of outdoors. The party is already in full swing and the music from the sound system reverberates off the walls. The sweet pungent smell of pot hangs heavy in the air. I squint my eyes, which have begun to water under the effects of the smoke.

There are groups of people spaced around the room. Some are deep in conversation, while others are dancing their asses off to the music. All of them seem to be high on either alcohol or drugs. I haven't taken anything today and feel better for it. I know that I will not last the night without a little something to help me party until the early morning.

I sweep the room until I find Curtis. Both he and Milton are laughing and drinking in the corner of the room. They seem to have made up any differences that I noticed on our last time here. Two girls cling onto them, obviously a little worse for wear. I glance at the clock on the wall. It is only 7pm and the party has only just begun! I doubt it very much if these two will see it to the end of the night.

Curtis turns towards me and our eyes meet. The upturn of his lips at the corner of his mouth indicates he is pleased to see me. Milton follows the direction of his gaze, he smirks as he notices the sign of affection from his friend. The blonde girl that is draped over Curtis shoulder loses her footing and he has to catch her. The spell is broken and both Milton and Curtis return to their conversation.

"Hey, babe! Over here!" Tabitha calls out to me from a corner of the room. All of the group have arrived and taken up residence on a series of sofas and armchairs.

The music is so loud that it makes my skin tingle and my lungs feel like mush. The bass thumps in time with my heart beat as though they were one, filling me from head to toe with the sound. I am surprised I even heard Tabitha's call over the cacophony of sound. Over the roar of music, a distant, hazy chatter can be heard. I can't make out any words, but laughter rings in my ears. As I make my way through the people dancing,

I feel compelled to join in. I need a drink and maybe a hit of something to relax me first.

The group makes room for me on one of the sofas. Tabitha greets me with a warm kiss. As our bodies touch, I feel her hardened nipples press against me. I have never been interested in women in a sexual way, but since our Baptism I sense a connection between us. Not just a spiritual one, but a physical one too. The sight of Curtis pounding her pussy and watching his semen spurt all over her ass and back was so erotic. I clench my thighs together over the thought of it. I have to catch my breath as the throbbing increases down there.

Luke seems already to be intoxicated, slurring his words. His hands wander over Bethany and Lydia, who are sitting either side of him. They reciprocate by running their hands up the inside of his thighs, massaging his balls and cock. It looks like the party is going to turn out to be a fuck fest. Thomas is in hushed conversation with Priscilla. Peter sips quietly on a whiskey while smoking a joint. He seems lost in his own thoughts as Martha tries to get his attention.

"Good evening, brothers and sisters." I raise my voice so it can be heard over the sound of the music.

"Good evening, Magdalene." Both Bethany and Lydia break from their rubbing of Luke's cock long enough to greet me. It is quickly followed by the rest of the group. I take a seat next to Tabitha and she passes me a joint.

I settle down and inhale deeply, letting the smoke enter my lungs. My face begins to tingle after a few minutes, but I start to relax from its effects. Tabitha runs her fingers through my hair as if she was grooming a pet. I sigh at her touch and move my body along the sofa so we are a little closer. Just as I feel at home, she suddenly jumps up.

"Come on, let's dance!" She is like an excited teenager and drags me to my feet. She giggles as she leads me into the area where the guests are gyrating their bodies to the psychedelic music.

Before we have a chance to begin dancing, Curtis approaches. He has a serious look on his face and strides across the room. He moves directly to the group and whispers something to each of them in turn. They nod their heads and he turns towards us. His demeanour seems to have changed from only moments ago. Gone are the laughter lines to be replaced with a look of earnest resolve. He cuts through the other guests until he reaches us.

"Try and not get too wasted. I've something I need to speak to you all about a little later." He delivers his rather mysterious message before returning to Milton and the two young girls.

"What do you think that is all about?" Tabitha shouts into my ear, but I am as confused as she is.

"I have no idea, but he seems pretty serious about something." I try and dismiss the feelings of foreboding that have been created by his cryptic message.

Tabitha begins to sway to the music. She flows in dance as if it were the only way her body truly knew how to speak. Verbally she was usually quite guarded, physically she would shrink and fade into the background. Since we shared Curtis, she seems to have come out of her shell and her sensuality bursts through into the most vibrant picture of a beautiful soul. I can see why Curtis chose her to consummate the baptism ritual. She was so innocent, but is gradually emerging like a butterfly from a chrysalis.

We dance for the next twenty minutes or so. From time to time I glance across the room at Curtis. The young girl is still all over him as if he is a lifeline preventing her from sinking. Milton has become bored with her friend and is standing alone, his eyes searching the room for a suitable piece of ass. As his attention is diverted, I notice Curtis slip something into his drink. I have to blink to make sure I have seen correctly. His eyes meet mine and he raises a finger to his lips as if to tell me to be quiet. The girl does not notice as her head is buried on his shoulder.

"I need a drink!" I lean across and call into Tabitha's ear.

"Yeah, me too!" She replies smiling that innocent smile.

We look for the nearest place to get a drink. Milton has a number of bars set up around the room. I take Tabitha by the hand and we fight our way through the dancing crowd to one where a young guy is cleaning glasses.

"What do you want?" I turn to Tabitha, who has taken up a position to my right.

"I'll have a Manhattan, please." She glances shyly at the young man who grins back at her. She oozes sex appeal, that vulnerable innocent look does it every time.

"That'll be two Manhattans then, please" I give my order and just as I do I feel something hard pressing against my butt cheeks.

The distinctive smell of expensive cologne and even more expensive weed drifts up my nostrils. Hot breathe is blown over the surface of my neck. A hand rests against my right ass cheek before squeezing it roughly. I swivel my head and come face to face with Milton. He has a lecherous smirk on his face. The same look he had given when he noticed Curtis looking at me.

"I hope you are enjoying yourself, babe." His words are slurred and he appears to be as high as I've ever seen him.

"Yeah, it's a great party. Thanks for having us over." I pull my arse cheeks away from his stiffening cock. It is then when his attitude changes.

"What say you and me have a little party of our own?" He pulls me to him once more, pushing his dick hard against me.

I look to Tabitha for support, but she is already flirting with the young guy fixing our drinks. Next, I sweep the room for Curtis. At last I find him and the young blonde is all over him like a rash. Her hands are running through his hair as she pulls his face against hers. They are locked in a deep embrace and his hands are wandering all over her ass. My heart sinks and I feel lost at sea. Fuck it!

"That sounds just perfect." I turn to look at Milton who is trying to focus on me.

"Cool, baby. Let's go!" He grabs my hand and pulls me after him, like I am some kind of possession.

The guests in the room part as he drags me away to a far corner. The location he has chosen is not random. We are in direct line of sight of Curtis. He lifts his head from the amorous young female and his attention is focused on our movement through the room. Milton leads me to a sofa in the corner of the room. He pulls me to him so that my back is to Curtis. I begin to feel a little awkward and apprehensive. His head leans forward and as his lips press against mine, and his hands move around to my ass cheeks. He pulls up my dress so that my buttocks are exposed. I open my eyes to see him glancing in the direction of Curtis. It is then that the penny drops. This is all for his benefit. He obviously noticed the look on Curtis face when I entered the room. Why do people who have money have to covet that which is not theirs?

Once he is sure that he has Curtis' undivided attention, he breaks the kiss. He grips me by the jawline, his fingers squeezing against the bone. As I look into his bloodshot eyes, I notice a glazed look. His eyelids blink once or twice and he tries to focus on me. This is not just the drugs that he has consumed, it is something else. Then I recall Curtis slipping something in his drink. I do not have time to ponder it. Milton roughly turns me around so that the tops of my thighs are against the back of the sofa. Again, he lifts up my dress and I feel the cool air flow over my ass.

Without warning a sharp stinging sensation followed quickly by a slapping sound causes a few people nearby to look around. I must admit, I can't resist smiling in the pleasure it produces. All I can think of is the words Curtis used when he talked about sharing. No one belongs to anyone, we should give ourselves freely in the service of the Lord. It is a way to glorify his name. I relax as he pulls my hips away from the sofa, using his feet to spread my legs a little. Then, with one hand, my panties are pulled down and his fingers go to work on my pussy. It surprises me how wet I have become and I give myself over to the sensation. His action is slow and sensual, not aggressive. I push back against him, letting him know that I am enjoying the feeling.

He withdraws his fingers and I look back over my shoulder as he unbuckles his belt. He may be under the influence of drugs and alcohol, but that does not stop him gaining an erection. The bulbous head of his cock is glistening with pre-cum and his hand grasps the girth of his shaft. It is only then that he has difficulty aligning it with the opening to my pussy. He wavers a little, but finally I feel the tip rub against my outer lips. In one fluid movement, he pushes forward and enters me. I exhale deeply as I am forced to stand on tip toes, before lowering myself once more to the floor. With one hand on my hips the other on my shoulder he pounds into me.

The room is now full of cheers over the sound of the music. This kind of thing was common place at Milton's parties and we aren't the only ones engaged in sexual activity. Couples and threesomes cavort in various degrees of undress throughout the room. Milton, being the host, is the star attraction and now so am I. Lifting up my head, I can see that the blonde girls is now on her knees sucking hungrily on Curtis' cock. I feel a pang of jealousy. That is until I see the look of venom and despise in his eyes as he watches Milton defile my pussy. Before I know it, and without Milton reaching climax, I feel him slump against me. Whatever Curtis slipped him earlier has done the trick, and I watch as a wry grin crosses his lips.

I shuffle forward so that I am free of Milton's now ever shrinking shaft. His weight against me causes me to dip slightly. Some of the guests rush across the room and help him off me and down onto the sofa. After checking that he doesn't require any medical attention, they go back to the party. He is mumbling something as if in a drunken stupor. The waistband of his trousers are still open, but someone has kindly tucked away his dick in his shorts. I pull up my panties and straighten my dress. As I look across the room, Curtis gives me a satisfied nod and the anger from his face has vanished. I feel an overwhelming sense of relief as I leave the corner of the room and return to the rest of the group.

CHAPTER TEN - PETER

The blackness engulfs my thoughts. It stretches out into the distance, a map of my fears, testing my courage. The darkness overcomes me, and I fight to breathe. The cloth sack on my head is sucked into my mouth with every inhalation of breath. The coarse prickly material scratching my lips. Being sightless gives free reign to the imagination in a way that daylight renders impossible. This can be a positive thing, but in this situation it can also be negative. My mind runs riot, trying to figure out what is happening. One moment ago, I was engaged in pleasant conversation with the Academy Director. Now, something is wrapped around my neck squeezing against my windpipe. I fear I might pass out at any minute. The blackness is replaced by bright stars dancing before my eyes.

Fear is caused by many variables. Some are known, others are unknown. Or you just don't know when they will happen. Fear of the unknown is probably one of the worst things imaginable. The things that happen randomly and out of the blue are a form of torture on the mind. It elevates primal fear, decreasing logic and self-control. My breath is now ragged and harsh. As the fear of uncertainty takes hold, my brain speeds up. Although I am thinking faster, it becomes more difficult to rationalize things. Especially as the air is being restricted to my brain from the pressure on my airway.

I am being pulled from the leash around my neck and pushed by the gnarly, strong fingers on my back and shoulders. The smell of a manly odour pervades my nostrils, as I am manhandled to, I don't know where. I am disoriented but can tell from the motion of the pushes and pulls I am changing direction. I try and visualise a map in my head to attempt to ascertain where the hell I am in the building. We have not descended any stairs, so I know we are still on the same level. All of a sudden, my movement is halted by the hand on my shoulder.

The creaking of a door's hinges in desperate need of lubrication. Then I am pushed from behind and pulled from the front so the leash around my neck tightens once more. I stumble into a wall of sound. I have heard it before during training and recognize it as "White Noise". The term White is used to describe this type of noise because of the way white light works. White light is light that is made up of all of the different colours or frequencies of light combined together. Just as a rainbow acts as a prism separating white light back into its component colours. In the same way, white noise is a combination of all of the different frequencies of sound. It is as if thousands of sounds have been mashed together but delivered at the same time. The effect is that it drowns out any other sound around. If I wasn't confused and disoriented before, I certainly am now!

There is a marked difference in the ambient temperature of the room and I shiver. Up until now, I have heard no voices. I have worked out that there are at least two people in the room, as I was being pulled and pushed from both directions. The restriction on my throat lessens but is replaced by two firm hands grabbing me by the collar and pulling me forward. It takes me off-balance for a minute, then I am forced back into something. It is my shoulder blades, followed by my head that strike the surface of the object. It seems to be flexible and not rigid. It makes a hollow sound as my body makes contact, loud enough to be heard over the white noise. I rebound off the flexible surface, but the grip on my collar forces me back against it. The grip is released, and I sway from side to side.

Just as I am getting accustomed to my new surroundings, I am pulled away and turned around several times. I have no idea in which direction I am facing. The perspiration that has built up inside the cloth hood, begins to run down my forehead and into the corner of my eyes. I lift one hand to reach up and rub the hood to absorb the sweat. I feel a sharp pain as my hand is slapped down to my side. Still nobody speaks.

As I try and make sense of it all, hands begin to pull away at my clothing. My jacket is removed along with my shirt and tie. I shiver even more as my naked flesh is exposed to the cold of the room. Then I feel my belt being unbuckled, and at the same time, my shoes and socks are removed. There must be at least two people in the room to perform this, I think to myself. I curl up my toes as they make contact with the hard, cold, wet floor. We are indoors so why the fuck is the floor wet? Once my trousers are removed and I stand there completely naked, the hands leave my body and I am left alone for a minute or two.

It is just enough time to cause psychological discomfort, as of course, this technique is designed to do. The insecurity of being laid bare in front of an unknown number of people, is frightening in itself, bearing in mind I don't know the gender of the people in the room. I imagine it would be worse if they were female and during my time at the academy, we were told that this ploy is often used. If there are any sniggers or remarks of ridicule about my physiology, I cannot hear them for the incessant white noise.

I gradually become used to the ambient temperature of the room, but my whole body is shaking in an attempt to warm itself. Two hands are laid on my shoulders and I am pushed forward. I count the paces, one, two, three, four, then the hands restrain me from taking another pace. My hands are lifted by the wrists and stretched out in front of me. They come in contact with something solid and flat now. Fingers manipulate my hands, so that my palms are flat against what I assume is a wall. A short, sharp pain in my lower leg causes me to wince, as my legs are forced back so that I am leaning slightly. Again, no commands are given, and I am left in that position.

The sound of the white noise appears to have been turned up a notch or two. It is all around me and bounces off my whole body. It is like invisible fingers playing a beat on my exposed skin. I shuffle my feet a little to get more comfortable. The next thing I feel is a rough hard slap between my navel and sternum. I tense my muscles, but it is already too late. I feel physically sick from the blow and am left in no uncertain terms of the punishment if I move again.

I stand there alone and unflinching; for how long, I have no idea. My muscles are starting to feel the strain. How hard is it to lean against a wall? There is no concept of time in this place. When your senses are limited, it increases the inability to judge the passing of time. The continuous drumming of the noise, just adding to the scenario. I concentrate and try and block out the sound, but to no avail. I can feel myself begin to move and prepare for another strike to my body. Instead, I am pulled away backward and I count another four paces, so I guess I am back where I started.

There is a pressure on my shoulders and I am forced down to my knees. Then I am pushed from the front, so that I am laid flat on the floor. Before I get a chance to get comfortable, I am pulled up to a seated position. My legs are pulled out, extended straight in front of me. Then my arms are raised above my head. Although there is no pressure on me, I feel an urge after a short while to drop my arms. The upper limbs are already aching from leaning against the wall. I lower and raise my ass cheeks from the cold, damp floor and receive a hard slap against my left thigh. I immediately cease any movement and send my mind to another place.

An overpowering sensation of helplessness surges through me now. If this is all part of the final test of graduation, I have never heard of it. Why have I been singled out for this special treatment? Were my scores not good enough and this was a final evaluation on whether I had the qualities to be an FBI field agent? Just as I think I can't endure the position any longer, I am moved. I am brought up to my knees with my torso inclined back at an angle of forty-five degrees. Even after a few minutes, the pressure in my stomach muscles is intense. My arms are pulled forward in front of me to what I can judge is the horizontal. These two positions, and being placed against the wall, are repeated over and over, for I don't know how long.

As I endure these techniques, I question myself. How much do I really want to be in the FBI? Surely, all of this is not worth the sacrifices I have made. I contemplate giving up, but something deep down inside me, urges me to continue. My whole body is quivering by this point and I cannot concentrate. In between the stress positions, I was given sips of water. Then, I am pulled away from the wall and my hands placed down at my sides. I am left alone with my thoughts. The blood rushing from my upper arms to the tips of my fingers, makes them tingle.

Cold, hard steel encircles my wrists and a pressure is applied which pinches my skin. I am dragged forward a few paces and then my head is pushed down. The squeezing of the noose or leash around my throat lessens and the hood is pulled off. A hand keeps my head facing downwards. As I blink to try and focus against the blaring white light surrounding me, I can see my dishevelled reflection in a pool of water at my feet. The colouration of my toes is white from the lack of circulation. I take deep, long lungsful of air and savour the sweet taste, then I am pulled forward until my feet make contact with something solid.

A hand appears and pulls one leg at a time upward, and they aid me to step into something. As I take the last step, I can see it is made of wood. I am forced to lay down in it and as I look up, the last thing I see is the figure of one of my captors. He or she is wearing a balaclava hood. There are slits cut out so that all I can see are a pair of merciless eyes. Then once more everything turns black.

I am curled up in the foetal position, my knees touching the side of the box. The walls close in, and I want to curl my hands into fists and punch right through them. I know they aren't moving, but my brain is telling me different. I have always detested enclosed spaces and it is one of my biggest fears. I once climbed into the refrigerator when my mother was defrosting it. Unbeknown to her, she closed the door and I was trapped inside. Only the sound of my voice, a short while later, alerted her to the fact. For many years after, I always fell asleep with the light on. It took me a long time to break the habit. Now the memories of that experience return with a vengeance. My stomach lurches, adrenaline pumps and I want to scream to let out all the fear that's building inside me.

I convince myself that this is just a test and it will soon be over. Panic sets in, and the longer that I am imprisoned, the more it feels like I will lose my mind. They will not break me. I mutter this sentence under my breath, again and again. Thoughts and visions of my wife and child a lifeline, something to hold onto. At last, just as I am about to lose my mind and self-control, the lid of the box is opened. The glare from the lights make me squint my eyes and I briefly see the hooded faces of my two captors. They aggressively haul me from the container and frog-march me to a chair. I am forced down into it and one of them moves around the table. The figure takes a seat opposite me and rests its elbows and forearms on the surface.

I can sense the other standing close behind me. The white noise has ceased, but my mind is still in turmoil. The cold, steely eyes stare at me from the slits in the balaclava hood.

"How long have you been a member of "The People's Temple?" The voice is guttural, with the same British accent as the man who introduced himself as the "Umpire".

"I'm sorry, I don't understand the question. My name is David Silver. I work at the Virginia Times newspaper. I'm a journalist." I give the cover story and alias we all were given at the beginning of the course.

"We know who you are, but that was not the question." There is a snarl and aggression to the hooded figure's tone.

"How long have you been a member of "The People's Temple?" This time it is a female voice and comes blasting into my right ear. Now I feel really uncomfortable.

"When did you meet Jim Jones?" The male voice makes me swivel my head so I am facing front once more.

"I have no idea who Jim Jones is!" I have heard the name, of course I have. Just about everyone in the country knows Jim Jones and *"The People's Temple"*.

"Look, son, this isn't a fucking game! Just tell us when you met!" There is real anger now in the stranger's voice. He grips my jaw on both sides and squeezes hard. It feels like it is going to shatter.

"I'm not playing a game." I sound desperate now, and to tell the truth, I am.

"Hood him!" is the last words I hear before the white noise returns even louder now.

I scream out loud to myself under the hood. Please let it stop! This was only the beginning of what was to be the most testing part of my life so far. I am moved from stress position to stress position. As soon as I begin to show signs of weakness, I am moved again. My body is weakening, and I don't know how long my resolve can last. I am laid face down on the floor, my head in a pool of water. I have to lift my head to keep my mouth from being submerged. My legs and arms are trussed up behind me, like a turkey on Thanksgiving. The bindings cut into my wrists and ankles if I move. Every fibre and muscle of my very being is on fire. Once more, the hood is removed, and I am placed inside the box. As the lid is closed, I wail out loud, but it remains shut.

This is my third time in there and I don't think I can take a fourth. Finally, the lid is opened and I am hauled out of there and thrown down into the chair. The scraping of the stool opposite makes me lift my head in preparation for the next line of questioning. Instead of the hooded balaclava, I am looking into the eyes of the man in the Director's office. There is not a hint of compassion in those eyes, he merely looks me up and down before speaking.

"Who am I?" He speaks in a slow, methodical way. His words clear and precise.

The room is deathly silent and all I can hear is the tick-tock of the analogue clock, hanging on the wall behind him. The second hand moves in slow motion, as I collect my thoughts and composure. I lick my lips, which are parched, and a glass of water is pushed across the table towards me. As I pick it up, my hands are trembling. It is only then I realise, that for the entire time, I have been completely naked. The time on the clock says

4:20. I have no idea if that is AM or PM. In fact, I have no time reference for even what day it is.

"You are the Umpire." I struggle to get the words out and take another sip of water.

"Yes, I am the Umpire and this phase is over. Your training will begin in the morning once you are rested."

I am helped to my feet by a plain faced, middle-aged woman. She is dressed in a green t-shirt and camouflage trousers. Her body shape is more masculine than feminine. She holds a pair of combat fatigues and a t-shirt in her hand and passes them over to me.

"Put these on." Her voice is gentle and calming. I take the offered clothing gratefully and pull them on. It is amazing how comforting clothing can be when you have been without for so long.

Once I am dressed, I am taken from the room. I am unsteady on my feet, obviously weak from my ordeal and the lack of proper nutrition. The woman steadies me by placing an arm around my shoulder. I peer back over the room and the Umpire gives me a nod of his head. With that one simple action, I feel a great sense of pride. I came close to giving in but endured until the end. I may not know what they have in store for me, but I am intrigued by the prospect.

I spent the night in the deepest sleep that I can remember. The trials of however long my interrogation lasted, having taken more out of me than I thought. I was not taken back to the dormitory, but a single room in the administration block. I would imagine that my course buddies would be wondering where the hell I was. It seems like an eternity since I was called to the Director's office. I have no idea how long ago that was. Perhaps this morning will throw some light on the whole thing, and the reason for undergoing such a harsh test.

I get out of bed and shower quickly. The female who escorted me to the room said that I was to report to the Director's office at 8am sharp. I glance at the clock as I towel myself down. It is 7:45 and I better get myself dressed. I was not told the dress for the meeting, so I decide to put on a pair of jeans and a sweatshirt. There is no point in me getting a perfectly good suit ruined, if I am to be put through the mill like before.

I rush from the room and navigate my way through the labyrinth of corridors. At last, I find the Director's office and I take a deep breath before knocking confidently on the door.

"Come in!" The distinctive voice of Kurt Steinbeck bids me to enter. I push down the handle and step inside.

The Director is sat behind the large desk just as before. The Umpire sits on his right. There is a change to his demeanour and attitude and he smiles warmly as our eyes meet.

"Please, take a seat." Kurt indicates the chair opposite him, and I pull it towards me and sit down.

"I would like to introduce you to Captain John Mason. He is the Commander of the British Special Air Service Counter-Terrorism Wing." The Umpire reaches over and extends his hand to me.

"I'm sorry for putting you through the ringer yesterday. We just wanted to see if you were up to the task, if things get messy. I would like to congratulate you on the way you conducted yourself. Not many people last a full 48 hours without cracking." Some of the words he uses are alien to me, but I get the general picture. Wow, I had endured that shit for two days!

"No apologies needed." I release his hand, which has left visible marks on my skin due to the strength of his grip.

"You are probably wondering why we put you through that.?" The Director raises an eyebrow as he poses the question.

"It did cross my mind, Sir."

"Before I go on to explain, there is some video footage I would like you to watch." Without any further explanation, he presses a button on a VHS recorder in the corner of the room and retakes his seat.

The TV springs into life and is filled with images of inside what I think is a Pentecostal church. A man stands centre stage and I recognize him from news coverage over the past few years. It is the same man that I was questioned about again and again during my interrogation. His dark, almost black, slicked down hair gives him the appearance of a salesman. Yet there is something about him. He has the room in raptures, hanging on every syllable that spills from his mouth. It is as if some of them are in a trance, swaying with their eyes closed, arms raised to the heavens. His rise in popularity, even to the black community with his forward vision of equality, was meteoric. He established churches from Utah to California and his movement was growing.

The clip ends, and another begins. It is the same sort of scene, except this time it is outside. A mass of devout followers are chanting someone's name. I don't know the person, but he has the same charismatic personae as Jim Jones. The crowd has been built up to a fever pitch and the figure stalks up and down the stage, where he is delivering his message. One piece of footage follows another for the next twenty minutes or more. Finally, the Director gets up from his chair once more, and turns off the TV.

"There are cults like these all over the world. Some of them are innocent enough. Yet, there are others here in the United States, who are a threat to National security. We have taken an interest and launched investigations and operations on a number of them." The Director's tone has taken on a more serious timbre. He clasps his hands together as he speaks.

"We are constantly on the lookout for any emerging groups, or individuals that may be perceived as a threat." He rises from his chair and moves to a flip chart and pulls over the first page.

"This is such an individual. His name is Curtis Stewart. He came to the attention of a team that are working out of the California office." The lone photograph of a rather handsome young man, stares back at me. He looks innocent enough, but there is something about the eyes that scream danger. They say that the soul is revealed through the eyes.

"He popped up on the music scene in a few of the bars that the rich and famous frequent. The folk singer Milton Rogers has taken him under his wing. You may not know this, but Rogers and other people in his circle, have been on our radar for some time. Their songs and subversive speeches, about the war in Vietnam, have given them notoriety among the young, impressionable people of LA and surrounding areas." My interest is suddenly pricked as I adjust myself in the chair.

"We believe that Curtis Stewart is building a similar sort of following, but we don't know exactly what his intentions are. That is where you come in." I shuffle forward in my seat, anxious to hear the reason for me being there.

"It will be your task, if you are in agreement, to move to LA and to get to know this guy. We want to know how he ticks. Any plans he may have and if you think he could be a threat. The reason we have chosen you, is that you are a new face and would have less chance of being compromised. Are you willing

to undertake the task?" He sits back and lifts his hands in front of him, his fingers forming a steeple.

"Absolutely, Sir." I cannot hide the excitement in my voice. I have not even graduated, and I am being given my first mission and it's an undercover one.

"There is a drawback to this. No one can know that you are undertaking this job. You will graduate with your course and go on leave to see your family. You must explain to them that you will be going away, but do not mention anything about what you will be doing. Are you still prepared to take the job?"

"Fuck yes, Sir!" I don't believe I just swore in front of the Academy Director, but he seems to like my enthusiasm.

"Good man. Now get out of my office and re-join your course. You will tell them the reason for your absence was an illness in your family. We will see you back here in two weeks. Captain Mason will be taking you through your covert training." The big British guy gives me a wink as I stand and shake the Director's hand and then his.

I turn around and walk from the room. I don't fucking believe I am a fully-fledged member of the FBI!

CHAPTER ELEVEN - CURTIS

I begin to process my feelings and thoughts over what I witnessed between Magdalene and Milton. Yes, I know he was doing it to hurt me. A way of him getting back at me for using his place as my own personal fuck palace. The guidance I have given and preached to my followers on how to live their lives, comes back to haunt me. I should not feel this way. Magdalene was only fulfilling my wishes of sharing herself as per my dogma. Yet, I feel a pang of envy as I watched her being pumped by that fucker.

Jealousy is a complex emotion that encompasses feelings ranging from fear of abandonment to rage and humiliation. It is something I have never dealt with in my life. Why would I? I'm quite a selfish, self-centred person really. My upbringing made sure of that. Now that I have the attention I desire, I intend to make full use of it.

Human thought is an amazing thing. It has given us science, literature, morality, and last but not least, philosophy. Thought even has the power to create new realities. Just as I am doing building another world, purely by the power of thought and suggestion. Using the tools that were forced on me by the monks at Upton Abbey, I will have my revenge. I will build my own society built on love and passion. Not the same as preached to me within those hallowed walls.

Every society is a creation of the human mind, of human thought in particular. They all exist because we simply think them into existence. I took up reading philosophy when I began to realise that the Bible was a book full of lies. Yes, the philosophy behind the stories it contains were valid, but the selection of what was included in it was contrived. More to the point, the passages that were omitted because they didn't serve the male dominated clergy and priests.

Of course, the mind is not all sweetness and light. It has also given us superstition, slavery, and war. We all have different kinds of thoughts, but those linked to desire are the ones that I am fascinated with. The other type of thought is what I would term a belief. Beliefs represent or misrepresent, how things are in the world. To me, they are true or false. The rational thing to do is change our beliefs to match the world. Desires, on the other hand, don't represent how the world is.

Unlike a belief, a desire is either satisfied or unsatisfied. It is my intention that every desire I crave, will be satisfied before I leave this mortal coil.

Beliefs, desires, and intentions are like building blocks. It is how we arrange these and put them together, that will result in my concept coming together. I look around at the group who are now seated all together once more. Magdalene glances in my direction and I give her a reassuring wink. She is like a lost child, eager for my approval over what just happened. It is time that I leave this drunken slut, who is clumsily fondling my cock and balls, and return to my flock. I cast my gaze towards the sofa where Milton is laid fast asleep. The sedative I slipped in his drink worked quicker than I expected. He will be comatose until at least midday, plenty of time for me to bring my plan into action. Before that, I have needs that require fulfilling.

I pull the drunken girl's hand away from my genitals and leave her mumbling something in my wake. I haven't got time for two-bit whores, who will sleep with anyone as long as they are famous. Yes, I include myself in that statement. I have attained a certain gravitas due to the sponsorship of the sleeping Milton. Now, it is time for me to spread my wings and forge my own path. I have made it public that it is a righteous one. Little do my new-found family know the deepest, darkest depths of my desires.

"Good evening, brothers and sisters. The party seems to be warming up. I see our host has started a little early, though." I can't supress the smirk that is emerging on my face, as I look across at Milton sprawled on the sofa.

"Good evening, Teacher." They all answer me in unison, except Peter, who simply nods his head in greeting.

"We have work to do later. I think we have outstayed our welcome in this place. Before I tell you of what I have in mind, let us enjoy the rest of the evening." I take Bethany, who is sitting to my right, by the hand. I pull her up and embrace her with a long, slow kiss.

She responds eagerly and her lips press against mine. Her hands encircle my waist before dropping to my buttocks, squeezing them firmly between her fingers. She pulls me close and my now stiffening rod, pushes against her. Her lips taste sweet, like cherries warmed by the California sun. The thin top she is wearing allows me to feel her hardened nipples as she presses herself against me. I open my eyes and catch a glimpse of Magdalene. There is a definite look of disappointment on her face that I have not chosen her from the flock. I must try and distance myself and not allow my personal feelings to influence what I am trying to build.

Our actions galvanise the others and there is a distinct atmosphere of sexual excitement in the air. As usual, Peter seems to hold himself back and waits for someone else to make a move. Tabitha, who is sitting next to him, leans over and kisses him gently on the cheek. She is quickly joined by Lydia, who takes up a position on the opposite side of him. She runs her hand from his knee, along the length of his thigh. It lingers over his crotch, her fingers stroking the protrusion of his dick as it increases in size under her expert touch. Her time on the streets, giving pleasure to countless clients, is very apparent. She knows exactly which buttons to press.

Martha and Priscilla pair off with Luke and Thomas, leaving just Magdalene on her own. She looks forlorn and lost. Just like a girl at the prom waiting to be asked to dance. My heart goes out to her and I want to wrap her in my arms. I make to move my lips and call out to her, but I am too slow. Luke has already spotted that she is free and calls her to him. I know that this soon will end up a down and dirty fuck-fest. It would be expedient that we take it somewhere a little more private. Also, we need a secluded place to discuss what I have in mind for later.

"I think we should retire to the games room." My suggestion is welcomed with a series of agreements and giggles from some of the girls.

The party is in full swing and the room is a little overcrowded. In our twos and threes we navigate our way through the crowd. I stop by the sofa on which Milton is languishing. His chest rises and falls, indicating that the drug has him fully in its grip.

"Sleep tight, sweet Prince." I give him a friendly pat on the head, but he does not flinch. Perfect, we will soon be free of this place. He has outgrown his usefulness to me.

I lead the entourage through the reception room and through a door to the right of the entrance. The recreational room is spacious and there is enough room for us to pick a spot and not be too overcrowded. It is like a perfect magazine cover. The kind of place where you are afraid to sit in case you wrinkle the fabric or stain it with something. It is Milton's private retreat.

A place reserved for his special guests and where we have enjoyed many a happy time. A pool table takes centre stage in the room, with a number of pinball machines along one wall. A basketball hoop is suspended at one end with the shooting "D" marked out on the hardwood floor. It is a teenager's paradise, but the games that it contains are not the ones predominantly in my mind. The couples and trios pick their places and I watch with great amusement as there is a jostling for the best positions.

I take Bethany by the hand and lead her to the pool table. It may not be comfortable, but it gives me the perfect vantage point to see what is happening around me. The sofas are cream, but inlaid with a fine green silk. Leaves embroidered so delicately that they might have landed there in spring and just sunk in, but I know they took hundreds of hours to sew. They seem slightly out of place for a man's taste. The white curtains are linen, the kind of white that is untouched by hands and devoid of dust. There are hidden cords that are used to open and close them. It must have been Milton's intention to use the room as they were already drawn.

The floor is a high-polished wood, dark and free of either dust or clutter. An ornate bookcase stands against one wall. It was as if it was carved by a person with a profound love of literature. The engravings were of leaves, of autumn berries and birds on the wing - so sublime as to invite the fingers to take it in just as much as the eyes.

I turn my attention from the room to the beautiful creature standing before me. I could see a reflection of the same amorous stirrings that I was feeling in those deep blue eyes. A look came over her face that I can only describe as like watching a fire grow from a spark to ember and then to licks of burning flame. She looks at me with hunger and I know I must look the same to her. We almost launch at each other in a deep kiss and grasping hands. I reach my hand around Bethany's back and pull her towards me. Not close enough, though. I need to be pressed against her. I need her to feel how aroused I am. To feel my hard cock against her and know that it was for her.

Every person in the room was either kissing or fondling, removing articles of clothing in anticipation of the fuck-fest to come. The dark thoughts invade my consciousness. I see naked bodies strapped to racks. The flesh being mortified by leather throngs. My past is something that has shaped the person I have become. The need to feel and induce pain is an emotion that excites and terrifies me. I am not sure that I can control the rage within me for what happened over my life. An irresistible urge to transmit those desires on another person, male or female, to me, is irrelevant.

Bethany pulls at my shirt, grasping as if her hands were not controlled by her mind. They pull and then push and eventually her hand makes contact with my skin. She puts her hands on my chest and scrapes her fingernails over my tense muscles. The sensation they provide is exhilarating and I push my stiff cock hard against her. Her fingers move down to the waistband of my trousers, flicking open the button with one hand. Her hand descends until she grasps around my throbbing dick, feeling it pulsate against her fleshy palm. In reaction to this, I reach my left hand behind her neck and grab her by the nape, pulling her hair to expose her neck to my kiss.

I nibble gently against her neck at first, my other hand reaching down to just above her knee. I slide it upwards along her silky, soft, inner thigh. She murmurs as my fingers trail closer to her pussy. My pulse quickens as she parts her legs and pushes forward so I can find her mound and move down to firmly, insistently, but softly rub her now obvious wet folds. I glance to my left and observe writhing, naked bodies. They make no pause. They are just beautiful animals devouring each other.

Luke's head is buried between Martha's legs and her head is thrown back in ecstasy. At the same time, she is sensually licking and sucking on Thomas' balls as he drives in and out of Priscilla's cunt. Everything seems to be in slow motion, the very sight of it making my blood simmer in my body. Magdalene is laid beneath Priscilla, her legs open wide to allow her sister to give pleasure with her tongue. She is oblivious to my stare, as she writhes under Priscilla's touch. Her hands grip behind her sister's neck, pulling her down further into her opening.

The scene has me at fever pitch and my breathing comes in short, ragged bursts. I return my attention to Bethany. She was looking in the same direction as me and her breathing seemed to have stopped. Her eyes were wide and a smile was painted on her face. It was as if she was waiting with bated breath, as the saying goes. We turn to face each other and I make short work of tearing off her flimsy dress and cast it to the floor. She is completely naked beneath the garment. I reach around behind her and my fingers squeeze her ass cheeks firmly. In one movement, I have lifted her off her feet and placed her on her back on the table, with her feet flat on the red felt surface.

I can smell her fucking amazing aroma and it near drives me wild. I don't know if I had a plan before then, but when I catch her scent, there is only one thing I want right now. With one hand, I push her down. With the other, I spread her legs a little further apart. I restrain myself for a moment and I want to savour every moment. I kiss her inner thigh and the crease next to her pussy, driving myself fucking crazy with the desire to thrust my rampant tool deep inside her.

I tease her with my tongue and lips, making her squirm against the cloth of the table. The juices have already begun to flow down her outer lips. I grab both her inner thighs from below and push her legs back and lightly lick her folds, from her incredible wetness to her waiting clit. Then I lick deeply, truly tasting her. I use my tongue to probe in and out of her, again and again. Then I use my tongue to separate her lips and trace a line upwards, until I reach her swollen bud. Bethany arches and moans and grabs my hair. She holds me tightly there and I take her clit between my lips and pushing back her folds, I suck on it. A low murmur escapes her lips and her lower body quivers. I can feel her building already to climax, but I am not finished there.

I take one, then two fingers and insert them into her opening, the silky juices coating the surface of my skin and running down to the joints of my hand. She wriggles and writhes as my fingers move vigorously in and out. I can tell that I need to quicken. Bethany grabs my head as I finger-bang her and my tongue circles around her clit. She moans deeply and bucks with the pulsing orgasm that runs through her. Her hands fall away from my hair and she lays there panting and occasionally quivering. Watching her makes my cock even harder, my eyes bulging in their sockets. The sounds and smells of couples fucking like demons, fills my senses.

I gently explore her whole pussy with the end of my dick. I was in no hurry, I love every millimetre as I traverse and experience every slippery sensation through my rock-hard tool. Bethany lifts her head from the table and looks at me with a satisfied look. She reaches down and grips hold of my shaft and takes over where I have begun. She directs me around and down, up and down again until she hovers my head over her wetness. I cannot hold back any longer; with a lunge of my hips and grasping both her hips in my hands, I enter that warm, wet, lush cavity. The lips part with ease, lubricated from her climax and I push myself until I can go no further. Her eyes gape wide, as the tip hits the back of her cunt. I hold it there for a moment, watching the look on her face. She gasps when she feels the complete fullness of me.

"God, yesss! Fuck me hard, Teacher. Inject me with your heavenly seed!" Her voice is that of a banshee. A woman possessed by demons.

I draw back and then slowly move back and forth. I want to feel everything down the whole length of my cock. I want her to feel every movement of me inside her. I speed up and drive deeper. Bethany looks into my eyes with an expression of deep, animalistic hunger. The kind of look that dates back to our prehistoric past. I move my hand behind her head and firmly grip her hair as I slide harder and deeper, and I can hear myself slapping against her gorgeous skin. Her hungry look deepens as we ride each other together. Her hips rise up to meet my thrusts, ensuring she takes every last inch of my shaft. The sound of balls slapping against bare flesh echoes around the room, from the rest of my flock. It is like rapturous applause to our carnal celebration.

Magdalene is now on all fours facing towards me. Peter is pounding in and out of her, forcing her forward with each stroke. Her gaze meets mine and I see a hint of regret as I watch her being ridden like a rodeo steed. It only fuels my need to be sated. I pull myself clear of Bethany and roughly turn her over so her ass is sticking up in the air. I clamber onto the pool table so that I am towering above her. I look down at the gorgeous ass, the rectum almost winking at me invitingly. I grasp my shaft and angle it so that it is pointing down. I use one hand to steady myself on her right buttock and lower myself gently down. As the tip makes contact with her anus, it makes me shiver with delight.

I feel an uncontrollable urge to cum and force the entire length deep inside that tight hole. She catches her breath as her muscles tense, relax and tighten again round my iron- hard dick. A sigh follows quickly after and I know this is exactly what she wants. That is immaterial, as it is what she is going to get!

"You like this don't you, my child?" I lean over her and hiss the words in her ear.

"God yes! Make me cum, Teacher!" The blasphemous use of the Lord's name causes me to strike her ass cheeks hard with the palm of my hand. I repeat it in time with every thrust.

"Never take his name in vain, sister!" I fuck her hard and without mercy, her tits squashed firmly against the surface of the table.

The sight of Magdalene being given the same treatment only spurs me on. Her eyes are tightly closed as she is ridden over the edge. Her whole body shaking induces the same feeling in me, as my orgasm reaches its zenith. There is no turning back now. Wild horses could not pull me away from that delicious ass, waiting for my creamy cum to fill its cavity. My ass cheeks clench and abdominals tighten, as I spill my seminal fluid deep inside her. At the same time, there is a wail from Magdalene as she reaches her own climax. As if it was an echo, the same reaction spills from Bethany's lips as her body quakes beneath me. A bead of perspiration drips off my forehead and splashes against the curvature of her spine. I pump my last remaining drops of cum into her, before slumping spent and sated against her.

We take a moment to recover and I watch with interest, as the others reach a similar conclusion. Every face in the room is a picture of joy and happiness, as they all pleasure each other until the final inevitable moment of release. It is a sea of naked, writhing flesh. Almost like a picture from Dante's Inferno. If this is what hell looks and feels like, you can keep your God! I will let them get their breath back before I impart the next part of my plan. We need somewhere that we can call our own. To flourish and develop even further as a group. A place that I can shape to my own particular brand of depravity, in the Lord's name.

CHAPTER TWELVE - CURTIS

It took some time for me to persuade the guests to leave the house. Milton's parties were famed for lasting until dawn. I made the excuse, with the host incapacitated on the sofa, it wasn't right that we abuse his hospitality. I was met with a series of groans and remonstrations, but as ever, my powers of persuasion won through. I bid the last guests farewell and closed the door behind them. My flock left over an hour prior, just as we agreed, when I explained what we needed to do. If we were to get a place of our own, then we would have to finance it somehow. One thing I have learned over my time staying with Milton, was that he was very mistrusting of banks and financial institutions. He once showed me several places in the house where he stashed large sums of cash. He never told me where it came from, but I am sure that it was more than just music royalties.

His main hoard was kept in a safe in his bedroom. He also secured his more expensive drugs there. On more than one occasion, I was present when he retrieved some for our use or for a party that was going to be hosted. I may not be super intelligent, but I have a gift of being able to recall things. I can see in my mind's eye, his fingers nimbly turning the dial of the safe. The numbers locked firmly in my memory. This information was now in the hands of the Seekers of the Way. When I revealed my plan to them earlier, there was a look of apprehension at first, which quickly turned to excitement. They were all high on drugs and the euphoria of our combined love-making.

I went on to explain that I could not be involved, as this must look like it was an outside job to any man. They all agreed wholeheartedly. However, I noticed that Peter was a little less exuberant than his brothers and sisters. He seemed to be weighing up options, scratching his chin deep in thought. To my surprise, his doubts quickly turned to an acceptance, so much so that he agreed to formulate a plan. I have known him for a number of months now, but in all that time I never really asked what he did before he decided to drop out of society and move to California. I do know from his accent that he was not raised in these parts. All I know, is that he has the attributes to be a good leader. If this were a wolf pack, he would definitely be one of the Alpha males.

I check that Milton is still in his drug-induced sleep and make my way upstairs. On passing his room I check the door handle to make sure he hasn't locked it for any reason. Not that I have ever seen it locked, but paranoia seems to be setting in. Satisfied that there is easy access, I make my way to my own bedroom. I feel a tingling sensation down my back from where my morning flagellation tore the flesh. It gives me the urge to mortify my skin one more time before sleep. I force it to the back of my mind and undress and jump into bed.

I place my hands behind my head and stare up at the fan that provides a little draft of air to run over my body. My mind begins to wander about the path I, and the others, are about to embark on. Am I fleeing from reality, or just building my own twisted version of it? To a vast extent, we humans are great at masking the real world around us. We want to ignore the facts, shun any opposing criticism or feedback, and we hold dearly onto our beliefs, attitudes, and choices. I have always been quite an obstinate person. When my mind is made up, that's it. In short, I'm only human.

We are all fallible in some shape or form. One of these failings is the impulse to justify ourselves and avoid taking responsibility for any actions that may turn out to be harmful, immoral, or stupid. I am far from stupid! I know what I want and will take any steps necessary to achieve my goals. Most of us will never be in a position to make decisions affecting the lives of a group of people, or in fact, shape the destiny of a much larger population. God, and through his son Jesus Christ, have given me that opportunity. The use of their teachings is a perfect vehicle to bend people to my will. That is how it worked at Upton Abbey. The monks using the scriptures for their own evil, depraved devices. A justification for the abuse of hundreds of young boys that passed through those hallowed halls.

Self-justification is not necessarily a bad thing. It helps us sleep at night. Without it, we would torture ourselves over the decisions and choices we make. Or, regret the road not taken or how badly we navigate the path we did take. Without it, we would agonize in the aftermath of almost every decision. Did we make the right choice or correct decision. On the other hand, mindless self-justification, like quicksand, can draw us deeper into disaster. It blocks our ability to even see our errors, let alone correct them. It distorts reality and keeps us from getting all the information we need to assess issues clearly.

I know all this, but am still powerless to prevent my decision. There is an invisible force driving me on. Either consciously or sub-consciously, I submit to its will and to whatever fate may hold. I turn on my side and force my eyes shut. Sleep will not come easy, I fear. My mind is full of plans and visions of my new utopia. I see green fields, a lake and it all being surrounded by pine forests. It is the perfect location for building my new community. Remote enough to be private, yet close enough to habitation to find new members. As the images flicker before my eyes, I finally succumb to sleep.

The flashing red and blue lights illuminate my bedroom. I am dragged from my slumber by the sound of voices below my bedroom window and the rapping of a heavy hand on the door. I rub the sleep from my eyes and drag my ass from the bed. Peering down through the drapes, I can see two heavy-built police officers. One of them is using the end of his flashlight to hammer on the door. The other glances around the property for any sign of life. Milton must still be unconscious from the drug I slipped in his drink. I pull on a t-shirt and a pair of jeans and head off down stairs.

As I reach the hallway, I glance into the living room and Milton is laid, unmoving, on the sofa. I move towards the front door and, as expected, find that it is unlocked. There is no evidence of any forced entry and I wonder if Peter and the seekers have put their hastily laid plan into action. I push down on the handle and pull open the door. The end of the flashlight almost strikes me in the chest as the officer attempts one more time to awaken the home owner.

"Good evening, Sir. Are you okay?" The first officer addresses me, looking past me into the hallway.

"Yes, I'm fine officer. What seems to be the problem?" I attempt to look as confused as possible, but I suspect I know why they are here.

"One of your neighbours noticed a group of people acting suspiciously around your property. Are you the homeowner?" The second officer takes over from the first.

"No, I'm not. He is sleeping on the sofa. We had a little bit of a party last night." I begin to worry, as I can't remember if there were any signs of drug use inside.

"Do you mind if we take a look around?" The second officer continues.

"No, of course not." It did not sound like a request, so I don't bother trying to dissuade them.

I take a pace backwards to allow them to pass me. The older looking of the two, and who I regard as being more experienced, takes in the scene. The glasses of alcohol still half full from where they were left. A sweet pungent smell still hangs in the air from the copious amount of weed that was continually smoked in the house. To my relief, there does not appear to be any left-over evidence of drug paraphernalia. The two cops wander around the place as if they are looking for something, or someone. They disregard the ashtrays full of roaches and the remnants of white powder on the glass coffee table. One of them checks the security of the doors leading out into the garden. The other makes his way to the sleeping Milton.

"Mr. Rogers, Mr. Rogers? It's the police!" He shakes the comatose Milton into life. They knew all along that this was the homeowner. The homes of the rich and famous well known to the police.

"Mmmmm, what's happening? Where is everyone?" Milton looks around the room through bloodshot eyes. He is still not fully compos mentis. The effects of the drug still running through his veins.

"We received a call from a neighbour. They reported some suspicious activity around your property. Could you check that everything is okay?" Milton stirs from his position on the sofa and struggles to his feet.

He does not acknowledge my presence and begins to look around the room for any signs of disturbance. Quite a feat, as it would be difficult since the place was in disarray from his departed guests. He finally seems satisfied that everything is in order, before turning to the cop.

"Nothing seems to be taken, Officer." He rubs his face in an attempt to gain some form of lucidity.

"Are you sure? Do you have any valuables in the house, apart from down here?" The policeman seems a little confused. The information they received must have been enough to warrant them being here.

"I do have valuables upstairs in a safe." Milton mumbles his reply.

"Could you check for us please, Sir?" The second officer speaks this time, joining us after checking the security at the rear of the house.

"Of course, follow me." He leads them up the stairs and I follow on in their wake.

I am beginning to feel apprehensive as we draw closer to the bedroom. We enter and my view is obscured by the officers and Milton. I step to the side and on the wall just above the bed the safe door is open wide. Mission accomplished. I am impressed by the stealth of the group as I never heard a thing. It was just a pity that they were spotted by an all too vigilant onlooker.

"What the fuck!" Milton wails out loud and rushes to the safe. He peers inside and turns to us.

"Everything is gone!" He addresses the officers and at the same time acknowledges my presence. I am probably one of the very few people who know of the safe and that he holds quite a bit of cash in there.

"How much was there, Mr Rogers?" The heavier-set officer asks the question.

"I can't say exactly, but somewhere in the region of one hundred grand! I also had some family heirlooms in there. They have been taken as well. I can give you a list. I want these fuckers caught!" He looks at me accusingly, as if he has guessed that I have something to do with the crime.

"You can rest assured, we will do everything in our power to catch the perpetrators. The witness did not give a description, only that there were at least four or five of them. From what was said, they would guess at least two of them were female, from their builds." Once more, Milton glares at me and I can see the rage boiling inside him.

"You will need to leave the room so we can preserve the crime scene for the investigators. I will need to take statements from both of you." They look at us both in turn and I nod my head in supplication.

That was the last time I exchanged words with Milton. It was not a pleasant conversation and full of recrimination. I held my nerve, as he did not have any proof to his accusations that I planned the whole robbery. It was inevitable that he would ask me to leave. Even if he didn't, I already made that decision for myself. I am not a user, but he was quite useful when it came to me being accepted in this show business community. He gave me the chance to mingle with the rich and famous and to acquire a following of my own. It was a shame it was not in the music industry, but I knew, in my heart of hearts, that I was not good enough to survive in that arena. What it did provide me with, was access to the impressionable young people in his circle. I have found my own particular niche, and it is time to build my own new world.

I gaze down on the vista laid out before me. I stand in awe as the great mountains loom up before me, their cold, grey crevices capped with snow. They are covered with a rug of trees, green, yellow, scarlet and orange, but their bare tops were scarfed and beribboned with snow. From the carved rocky outcrops, waterfalls drifted like skeins of white lawn, and in the fields we could see the amber glint of rivers.

It was a warm, sultry August day in Sonoma County, California. The lake is as flat as any mirror. It lies without a ripple in the silver-blue water, as if time itself has been frozen. Tall pines surround its edge. Not a sound can be heard. No movement of branches, no birds calling. The lakeside air is pungent with the fragrance of jasmine. It drifts up the valley towards me, as I sit and observe nature's raw beauty. The lake is clear enough to see the plants and life below the surface. Brightly coloured fish dart this way and that. Some of them are huge and I estimate they are half the length of my arm.

I inhale slowly and savour the peace and tranquillity. The meadow is thick and lush, growing in dense tussocks. White umbrellas of cow parsley becoming tinged with brown, as the summer days draw towards fall. The meadow is carpeted by petite, fragrant daisies. Their sunshiny centres grinning at me, while a soft breeze ruffles their white petals. An oak tree providing sun-flecked shade, a cool and refreshing respite from the late summer sun. The group sits under its sprawling canopy and the sound of laughter and joy rolls across the meadow towards me.

The location I have chosen to build my community is perfect. The Russian River off in the distance, winds its way through the heart of Sonoma Wine Country. The area is a magnet for families and those who adore the opportunities of outdoor life. The piece of land that I have acquired is far enough away from the main tourist trails to stop any snoopers poking their noses into our business. Yet, it is close enough to areas of habitation so we can continue to grow as a community. The nearest town is Forestville, with a small population of around three thousand people. The closest city is that of Sebastopol, which is only a twenty to thirty minute drive away from where we will build our new home.

The idea behind building a new life together, cut off from mainstream society, is not a new thing. I have thought about it many times. It is not simply to make improvements, or to sweeten our lives with a sense of spiritual meaning, or to condone your thoughts and beliefs or past actions with some kind of blessing from above. There came a point in my life where I realized that the life I was living really was not appropriate for me. I needed something more. A sense of purpose, where I could explore and embrace my inner dark thoughts and desires.

I know it will be a series of compromises and learning experiences. It is a compromise with how I regard myself, how I regard others and how I regard the world. God knows that without Knowledge, the deeper intelligence that has been placed within me, I would live a life of concessions. Yet, am I ready to seek alternatives in order to avoid ridicule or criticism or condemnation or even social rejection? I am my own man and a single, self-centred one at that. I know all these things, and it will be a hard and rocky road to travel.

During my brief life as a musician and the fame that went with it, I became a product of society, a product of the expectations of society and a product of a collective mind-set of what is right and wrong. Even if I achieved my goals of reaching stardom and fame, my life would have been empty. The joy would have been short-lived, and they would come at a great price of time, energy and effort. The rewards would be momentary and fleeting. Here I have the chance to reap the rewards as much as I design. It is what my heart has been yearning for so long. It is not just the act of adoration and blind loyalty. It is a physical need that has been denied me for so long.

I have always found relationships difficult to maintain. At first it was relatively easy, things unfolded pretty well, I wouldn't fight or disagree. But, as life has a tendency to do, sooner or later stuff tends to get real. Intimacy was one of my biggest stumbling blocks. The amount of closeness, emotional, physical, spiritual, and even mental that is needed in a relationship, is overwhelming to handle at times. This was more so for a person with my particular traits, qualities and background. It was as if I was wound up tight like a clock spring. My idea of creating a world where there was no need for this intimacy, was a definitive part of the whole concept. Wrapped up in the teaching of Jesus and the Bible, the perfect shroud to mask my true intentions.

The hand that life dealt me, has only heightened and magnified my true self. From the monks with their sadistic methods of their own divine teaching, to being brought up without a stable father figure. Yes, these were all factors that would shape the man I have become. When I lived for that brief period with Glenda and Tom, I came to realise that I myself was dominant in nature. I admired the way that my guardian ruled the roost. I allowed him to think that I submitted to his will and rules, but inside I was burning to have our roles reversed.

As I look down the slope at my flock, gathered at the water's edge, I smile. I rise to my feet and begin the short journey towards them. I am usually quite adept at hiding my feelings and emotions. Not today. I can feel the excitement pouring out of me like sunshine through fine white linen. I am glowing from the inside out. All the mundane thoughts about my past life have been muted and predominantly in my mind, is this moment. No worrying about the past, no anxiety about the future. I reach the group and, as one, they turn to look at me. They all appear eager to hear what I have to say, even Peter. The stoic, reserved look has been replaced with one of anticipation.

"Brothers and sisters. Gather round. Tomorrow will be the start of a brand new way of life. Just as King Solomon of old, we will build a magnificent temple where we may live in peace and harmony and where the glory of the Lord may reside forever." It has begun.

CHAPTER THIRTEEN - PETER

I cannot help it, but just like the others, I hang on every word that falls from his lips. He has a magnetism about him, which is almost impossible to explain. Everything from the way he held himself, to the way he spoke, to that look of unassailable confidence in his eyes, exuded self-belief. That conviction and delivery of his words was effortless. The man is a charm to be sure. He has the right twinkle in his eyes and a voice that is warmer than sunlight on amber.

Not contrived or pausing for what he would say next. It gave the rest of the group the feeling that they would do anything for this man. In fact, we have already committed a crime just to please him. It came out of the blue and I was not prepared for it. I knew that there might come a time when my cover would be tested. I managed to pull it off without actually being involved to the point where I took the money. As he goes on to explain his plan for the coming weeks and months, my mind drifts off to leaving my family behind.

Leaving home is so hard, so many memories, and now all of them balled up in my chest. The time I spent at home after graduation was something that would strengthen my resolve over this operation. You just can't put a price tag on family. They are truly the one present we all can't wait to see when we run down the stairs on Christmas morning. Family isn't defined only by last names or by blood, it's defined by commitment and by love. It means showing up when they need it most. Yet, I made the decision to take the assignment offered to me by the Director of the Academy. The love of family is one of life's greatest blessings and I have spurned that fact. I explained to my wife that I was doing it for our future. When she asked what it was I would be doing, and where I was going, it was heart-wrenching to tell her that I couldn't say.

We were childhood sweethearts and have never spent more than two days apart in our whole lives. Parents believe that a young child is incapable of feeling true love. Adults refer to these relationships with demeaning language, calling them "just puppy love" and these romantic bonds are not taken seriously. They're of the opinion if a child is moved to another community, he or she will soon make new friends. It was as if they treated these relationships as exchanging one toy for another. That was definitely not the case between Emily and myself. My parents came to accept that fact, and over the years, we grew closer and closer together. We married at the age of nineteen and our son, Liam, was born only two years later. My father was proud that I had named my boy after him. I was raised a good Catholic boy and believed fervently in the teaching of Jesus Christ. Never in my wildest dreams did I believe my faith would be put to the test. Perhaps that was one of the reasons I was chosen by the Director of the Academy.

The image of me walking away from my family home, and opening the white picket fence gate, is vivid still in my thoughts. I turned back and looked at Emily, who was holding Liam in one arm. His legs wrapped around her waist resting on her hip. Even from that distance, I could see the tears that have misted her eyes. My stomach began to heave and I felt physically sick.   When you leave your family home, you leave a piece of yourself behind. You may try forget all about it, or you may let it grow inside of you as a small wound, that kind of acts up when the weather gets bad. This will be my greatest challenge in my life so far. I take a deep breath, blow Emily a kiss and silently mouth the words "I love you". That was the last time I saw them.

The first day back at the Academy seemed so strange. I was met by Captain Mason and the female British operative. They seemed genuinely pleased to see me and to get on with my training. We spent the first day discussing what it was like to work undercover. Both of them were seasoned veterans when it came to that kind of work. They had taken part in assignments all over the world, which were perceived to be possible threats to the United Kingdom. They began by explaining undercover operatives and the stressors inherent to undercover operations based on their own experiences.

Society is fascinated by, and romanticizes, undercover operatives. These operatives are often portrayed in high-risk situations which they usually take on and survive triumphantly. Nevertheless, what most of the news headlines miss, is the very complex and difficult work that make up most successful undercover operations. In fact, the public rarely, if ever, hears or reads about the impact that undercover operations have on the operatives and their personal lives.

With the increase in the numbers of Federal Bureau of Investigation (FBI) agents working undercover, the FBI administration became concerned with the detrimental aspects of the personal commitment required for undercover operations. We are joined by Kurt later that morning, who highlights some of the issues facing undercover operatives working in the FBI.

"As the numbers of FBI agents and task-force officers conducting undercover work continues to increase, so do the numbers of psychological assessments that we need to carry out. These will not only be part of your training assessment, but will be re-evaluated post operation and throughout your time with the Bureau." His voice sounds reassuring, even if the statement is quite alarming. It brings home the enormity of the task that I have decided to undertake.

"I understand that, Director, and know that you will have my best interests at heart." Although I give what I perceive to be a satisfying answer, he does not seem convinced.

"Sometimes to gather intelligence from the inside, it is necessary to put ourselves in danger." Now it is Captain Mason's turn to interject.

"Yes, I understand that." I immediately go on the offensive and my tone draws a slight smirk from the British Officer.

"I will make one thing clear from the start, Patrick. Officers who participate in covert operations are not born with the talents needed to perform effectively and safely in undercover situations." He stares deep into my eyes as if he is looking for a reaction.

"Can I ask why I have been chosen then?" I look from him to Kurt, who is sitting inclined in his comfortable leather chair.

"You were chosen because of your religious background and because of the scores you attained during training. We will see in the coming weeks if you have the temperament to be a successful covert officer." So, it is not cut and dried. I still might not make the grade. I feel a little down-hearted, but it gives me even more resolve to succeed.

"These talents we speak of are developed from experience, hard work and training. This program will provide you with the techniques and survival tactics necessary to develop and compliment your task." Mason has now begun to get serious and I know that this is not going to be quite as simple as I first envisaged.

"How will I know if I'm made of the right stuff for this kind of work?" I am beginning to sound apprehensive and wonder if that is a good thing.

"The fact that you are questioning your ability is a good starting point. None of us know if we are compatible with this kind of life. We will know in the coming days if you are suitable or not." There is a finality to Mason's reply and a wistful look as he rubs the facial growth on his chin.

"Meet myself and Jenny at 10 o'clock in the administration block reception." With those final words, Mason gives a gesture for me to leave the room. As I close the door behind me, I feel compelled to put my ear against the door and listen to their assessment of me. I decline the urge.

I was not given any instructions on what I should wear for our meeting so I dressed in a t-shirt and jeans. As I enter the building, both Mason and the female, I now know as Jenny, were already waiting for me. Both are dressed casually and I give a silent sigh of relief. I have no idea what they have in store for me as I was not given any timetable as yet to what my training would involve.

"Good to see that you are punctual." Mason lifts up his arm and glances at his wristwatch.

"I'll bring the car around front." Jenny immediately makes her way to the parking lot out the back of the administration building.

"We are going into town to meet up with an operative. For this exercise I am his handler. All you need to do is observe. We will do a little question and answer session after the meeting. Do you have any questions?" He raises an eyebrow inviting me to speak.

"So, this is just an exercise then?"

"Yes it is, but I want you treat is as though it was the real thing. Be aware of your surroundings, I may ask questions later." With that rather vague statement, he turns on his heel and heads towards the front of the building. I follow on a few paces behind.

By the time we reach the bottom of the steps of the administration building, Jenny pulls around the corner and brings the black Buick to a silent halt. Mason takes the seat next to her and I clamber into the rear. We pull away from the sidewalk and head down the main street towards the gates of the facility. The journey is taken in total silence, but I heed Mason's words. I *occasionally check behind us to see if we are being followed. I am not sure if this would be one of the questions later, but I thought it prudent to do so. Or was I being just a little over zealous? By the time we reached the centre of town, I began to relax. Jenny pulls the car into the parking lot of a bar. She turns off the engine and gets out. She is quickly followed by Mason, so I guess we have reached our destination.*

"I want you to go into the bar and take a seat somewhere at the counter. Jenny and I will enter in about five minutes. If you notice anything suspicious or are uncomfortable with anyone, you are to leave immediately. Once we have engaged with the operative I want you to be able to observe the whole room. If necessary, move to a position where you can oversee any threat to us and the undercover officer. Is that all clear?" Mason makes this sound as if it is for real.

"Quite clear." I reply immediately and turn around to make my way to the front of the building.

The increase in my heart rate is involuntary. The adrenalin that is pumping through my veins makes me alert. I think of the qualities that make up a good FBI agent. The one that springs to mind is to have a high level of intelligence and deductive reasoning. I am hoping that this particular quality will assist me during this morning's exercise. Only time will tell and I push my weight against the door of the bar and it swings open with a creak.

I step into the dimly lit room. Tobacco smoke hangs heavy in the air and I cough to clear my throat. Bad move. Although it is only 10:45am, the place is half-full. The sound of my coughing caused heads to turn around in my direction. I feel about as welcome as an African American in a "Whites Only" bar in one of the Southern States. I glance around checking out some of the faces that are looking me up and down. Some appear to be hostile. While others are merely inquisitive about this stranger that has stepped into their own little world. None of them I perceive to be a threat as the alcohol is more of an attraction than my presence. It does not take long for the muttered conversation to commence once more. I stride confidently to the bar and pull up a stool.

I have been lucky enough to find a seat at the corner of the counter which gives me a full view of the bar, the door and the exits. I settle down on the stool and once more check out my surroundings. My inspection of the room is soon interrupted by the sour-faced looking bartender.

"What can I get you?" His question is loaded with venom as if my custom is not really welcome.

"I'll have a beer and shot of Bourbon." I answer as curtly as the question was framed.

"Coming right up." My rather discourteous reply is met with a nod of approval by the bartender.

"That'll be two bucks!" He slides the beer and shot of golden liquid towards me. I return the action by slapping down two dollar bills on the counter.

"Thanks!" I take a deep draught of the beer and follow it with a swig of the fiery liquid.

At the other end of the counter, a guy glances in my direction. He gives me a cursory inspection before returning to his drink. The sound of the door opening and the hush of the room draws my attention to the figures of Mason and Jenny. Just as I did, they do a quick head count of the room. They do not break stride and continue to walk towards a booth in the corner of the room. A man has his head hung low, staring into a glass of beer. He lifts it only when they are a few paces from him. No words are spoken and the two newcomers take a seat opposite him. An ashtray is full of discarded cigarette butts. The rather dishevelled-looking guy is puffing vigorously on another, which is quickly stubbed out into the receptacle.

From his appearance, with his long, lank hair and beard, I would have taken him for a local drug addict. He was fidgeting in his seat. His fingers raking his arms as if he was in need of a fix. He shifts his position so that his face is only inches away from Mason's. I see his mouth move but cannot hear what is being said. It is only then I remember my task is to observe and make sure that the meeting goes without incident. The guy at the end of the bar gets up from his stool and takes his beer with him. He disappears through a door to the left of the counter. That is one less customer to worry about, I think to myself.

Jenny approaches the counter and orders a round of beers. The bartender does not give her the same look of disdain as he did me. Perhaps this is not the first time they have visited this place. I do not make eye contact with Jenny, just sit there drinking my beer and Bourbon. She takes the beers and returns to the table. As she places down the glasses, I notice the long-haired guy slide a piece of paper over the table. Mason slips the *paper surreptitiously into his pocket. Jenny takes her seat and the three of them sit drinking.*

I return to my own drink and begin to watch the football game that is being shown on the TV. I glance at my watch and notice I have only been sat there for a little over twenty minutes. The guy that disappeared from the end of the counter returns and places his beer down in front of him.

A movement and scraping of feet causes me to swivel on my chair. Mason and Jenny are already on their feet. Mason leans forward and pats the dishevelled-looking guy on the shoulder. I give them a moment to leave, not wanting to follow immediately after. As they depart, Mason's path is blocked by a gigantic figure. He is dressed in leather chaps and waistcoat. His shoulders are huge and the massive biceps and arms are covered in colourful tattoos. He has a black and white bandana wound tightly around his head. Mason sees him at the last moment and stumbles into him. There is, what I assume, a brief apology and the big guy seems to be placated.

I settle back down into my seat and allow them enough time to exit the building. When I think I have allowed enough time to elapse, I drink the remainder of my beer and finish my shot. I slam a dollar coin on the table as a tip and give my thanks to the bartender. The guy at the end of the counter has disappeared. Due to the commotion with Jenny and Mason, I had not noticed his departure. His beer still sits there and it is only then that my attention is drawn to its contents. I look at my watch again and calculate I have been there over half an hour. The bottle is still three-quarters full!

I leave my stool and head out into the Virginia sunshine. The motor of the Buick is already running and I climb into the back seat. Jenny puts her foot on the gas and we speed out of the lot and re-join Main Street in the direction of the freeway.

"So, give me your conclusion to what just happened." Mason begins my de-brief.

"Well, it was obviously an exchange of information between you and the operative. I saw him slip you a piece of paper." A wry grin crosses Mason's face as he exchanges looks with Jenny.

"What did he look like?" Jenny speaks this time.

"He was about 6 feet two inches from what I could guess. I couldn't swear to it as he was sat down. He had long, dark hair, with blue eyes. No distinguishing marks that I could see, but a

pair of well-worn sneakers." I feel pleased about my description, but not the reaction from Mason.

"You see what people want you to see. Like I said, be aware of your surroundings and environment. That guy was a local drunk that we have met a few times when we have visited that bar. The piece of paper you saw him give me, was a tip on a horse race. The exchange of information happened as we were leaving." Now I feel really stupid, but that was the intention. We should learn from our mistakes.

"So, the big biker dude was the operative?" Now both Jenny and Mason burst into laughter.

"Yes, indeed he was. Did you notice anything else?" It was time for me to make amends for my stupidity.

"I think so. The guy that was sitting at the opposite end of the counter disappeared for around fifteen minutes while we were there. He took his beer with him, and when I left I noticed it was still almost full. That was to me a little out of the ordinary. Who takes twenty minute to drink a beer?" I wait in anticipation for Mason to reply.

"Okay, that's a plus mark. He was a member of the training team placed there to see if you would notice. As your training progresses you will learn more of this kind of field craft, but I think you will have no problem at all fitting into this type of work." Although I am still annoyed that I didn't see the real exchange, I feel better that I had redeemed myself.

For the next couple of weeks, I underwent a series of interrogations, followed by psychological evaluations. Days were interspersed with firearms training, physical fitness and unarmed combat. To my surprise, it was Jenny who taught the unarmed combat. At the beginning of the course, Kurt handed me a thick buff folder. I spent all of my spare time going over the contents it contained with a fine tooth-comb. He stressed to me how important that folder was. It contained my cover story. Who I was. Where I was from and all aspects of the life that may come into question during my time on this operation. I read and re-read it from cover to back until I believed I was the person those pages portrayed. During my interrogations I would recite the answers that reflected my legend.

That was some three months ago now. As the warm fuzzy feeling of the cannabis seeps once more into my bloodstream, I listen to Teacher's vision of our future. He scans the whole group looking for signs of approval or rejection. He seems to be satisfied at the murmur of excitement that greets his plan. Finally, his eyes bore into my own. There is a look of suspicion in those eyes. The intense glare turns to warmth as he smiles. For just one moment, the first time since our little community was formed, I feel apprehensive. I have managed to earn his trust and confidence to such a point, that I believe he almost sees me as his equal. I have never tried to oppose or question his beliefs and in fact, I agree with a lot that he has to say. From what I have learned so far, I do not see him as a threat to National Security or the need for FBI investigation. Yet, there is something about him that is elusive. It is as if he is harbouring some secret that he is not yet willing to impart. Only time will tell.

CHAPTER FOURTEEN - MAGDALENE

I am not asleep, but it is as if I am in a trance-like state. His voice is addictive and the more that he speaks, the more that I want. As I look around the group, I notice that he is having the same effect on the others. Even Peter, who is normally quite reserved, hangs on every syllable that spills from his mouth. My mind is in turmoil with the intensity of the emotions I am feeling. All my young life, my heart has been hungry for intimacy. A natural yearning for a close relationship with someone I can trust and devote myself to. It is something I have been denied due to my strict religious upbringing. A freedom to love was the reason for me relocating to Los Angeles. I was away from the strict guidelines of my parents. I was able to make my own mistakes without fear of retribution.

We are free to love only to the extent that we aren't forced into it, in vain attempts to relieve guilt, shame, or fear of abandonment. It was not a misguided effort to make up for past mistakes. It was an emotional need, a preference or desire to make my life whole and complete. We all have an intense desire to be loved and nurtured. The need to be loved could be considered one of our most basic and fundamental needs. This is what makes us different to other creatures that God created.

As I continue to admire and explore Curtis and his rugged, yet handsome, chiselled features, I feel jittery in my stomach. My palms are sweating and a flutter of electricity runs through my body. I am confused. Is this merely infatuation or love that I'm feeling? The butterflies and the giddiness I am sensing only really happens when you're in love. Or so I am told. I have never really been in love so cannot confirm this opinion. All I know is that, this euphoria of combined emotions is something that I cannot explain, nor do I want to.

There's something about Curtis, a slight confidence and inflated ego, which has me muddling my words and blushing uncontrollably whenever he's around. He has a natural drive and ambition, masculinity and strength, which only enhances my desire for him. That sparkling, beaming smile and perfect white teeth makes me damp between my thighs. Along with his husky voice, it is the ultimate drug which induces an almost hypnotic quality. The soft lilt of his voice causes my eyes to close for just a moment.

"Do my plans not excite you, sister? It is late. Maybe you wish to retire for the evening?" There is a sarcastic and malicious tone to Curtis' voice that makes my eyes flutter open immediately.

"No, Teacher! I was just imagining the beautiful structure and loving community that will fill its walls." I lie, and the look in his eyes tell me he knows it.

"I would love to hear your own personal views on that after I have finished. Stay behind and we can discuss it in a more relaxing environment." My cheeks continue to warm as my embarrassment is complete.

"Yes, Teacher." I concentrate on his face and how his lips move effortlessly, not pausing for thought.

I have the deepest respect for him and everything he is trying to achieve. He treats everyone with the same respect in return. That is one of the attractions to him for me. Behind his confidence and emotional strength, I sense a vulnerable side to him. There is also something else. Something dark and foreboding. I have observed it on only a few occasions. One was when I was being fucked from behind by Milton at the party. The other was just moments ago when he silently chastised me with just one look.

Everyone has a part of them that they want to keep hidden from the world, and I put those thoughts to one side. This man makes me laugh and I feel safe and protected in his company. He is not old fashioned, but will still hold a door open for you, or pull back your chair for you to sit. Those little touches that make a woman feel cherished and special. As I try and make sense of my mounting feelings, I come to the conclusion that it is almost impossible to do so. Falling for another person is an illogical process. There is no set pre-made list that we tick off in our heads to match ourselves to a potential mate. It is like throwing yourself from an aircraft without a parachute. You are raw and exposed and unable to breathe. You see your entire life stretched out before you and your past is banished.

My breathing is ragged; I am excited and frightened in equal measure. What is happening to me? How can one person make me feel this way? Whatever the reasons, I want more of it and would do anything for him. So much so, I have given over $20,000 from my trust to help the community build this new life. Of course, I have reasons for doing that and he stands right there before me.

"So, brothers and sisters, my Seekers of the Way. At dawn, we begin to build our new home. You will need rest. Go now and we will start out on our journey as the sun rises in the East." The group stands as one and begin to drift off to their tents and recreation vehicles.

"Magdalene, come here, child." His voice is soft and gentle and he beckons me to him with a crooked finger.

The increase in my heartrate comes from excitement as I draw closer to him. Yet, there is something else that makes my chest pound under its beat. It is the slightly devilish look in those normally kind eyes. A hint of malice and aggression, but as his fingers reach out and take mine, the sensation vanishes. He pulls me close and feathers my neck with soft, downy kisses. I bite down on my lip and cross my legs as he runs his tongue across my shoulders and up my neck. He lingers around my ear lobe, nibbling on it at first, then his tongue flicks it until I squirm. He knows exactly what makes me hot, as if he can read my mind.

"Now, come and tell me of how you see this community of ours developing. I am intrigued to know what you were thinking just now." He breaks contact with me and whispers in my ear. Once more, the sarcastic tone has returned and I shiver in the warm evening breeze.

With his arm around my shoulder, he guides me in the direction of my recreational vehicle. It was a gift from my parents when I left home for Los Angeles. It was somewhere to stay until I found a place of my own. Out of the caravans and different vehicles in the group, it is the most spacious of them all. If envy was allowed, then I am sure some of my brothers and sisters would succumb to it. Curtis slips his hand from my shoulders and places it in the hollow of my back. With a gentle but firm pressure, he pushes me up the two steps to the door of the RV. I hastily, with trembling fingers, open the door and step over the threshold. In two steps Curtis is right behind me.

His hand returns to the centre of my back and he pushes me further into the inside of the vehicle. He seems eager to get to hear my views on his plans and vision for the future. I take a seat on the cushioned bench that is built into the side of the RV. A small table is perfect for meal times and it lies between myself and Curtis, who has now taken a seat directly opposite me.

"Can you remember what I said in the beginning, about how this family will run?" He raises a quizzical eyebrow, the indentions in his cheeks heightened, which makes him look even sexier than usual. I love that smile so much.

"Yes, we were to follow all rules that were set out by you and to agree to any punishments that you saw fit for any transgressions." His question has me confused, the change in demeanour even more so.

"That is correct and it seems that I will have to remind the family of that fact. This community will live in peace, love and harmony, according to the laws laid down by me. Just as Jesus created his community and expected his followers to live by his divine rules, so will be the foundation of our new lives here." He seems to be having some type of out of body experience, as if he is listening to a voice only he can hear.

"I must punish you for your disrespect earlier. You do understand that, do you not?" He sounds almost apologetic, but the grin on his face reveals his true feelings on the matter.

"Yes, Teacher." I simply nod my head.

"Then stand up and come here!" He commands me in no uncertain terms, pointing at his feet. I stand and step around the table.

He takes me by the hand and places me so that my thighs are touching the table. Once he is satisfied, he disappears out of my peripheral view; only to return clasping two of my scarves and a couple of clothes pins. He stands directly in front of me and without speaking, he slips the thin material of my dress over my shoulder so that my breasts are exposed. He lifts one of the wooden clothes pins up so that I can see it. He applies pressure with his thumb and fingers so the jaws open and close. I am mesmerised by the action, but before I know what is happening, he has attached the first to my right nipple.

"Owwww, that hurts!" I exclaim out loud and my voice must be able to be heard from outside.

"Pain is all part of confession and absolution of sin, my child." There is a leer on his face and he licks his tongue over his lips and applies the other peg to the opposite nipple.

This time, I curb the urge to scream out and ride the stinging pain it produces on the sensitive surface. Curtis waits for a moment, examining my reaction to the crude clamps. It is as if he is enjoying my discomfort. Surely not? It is not long before the pain becomes much more bearable and I settle down to whatever other punishment he has in store for me.

"Give me your wrist." He lifts my left arm and I extend it towards him.

With gentle but firm hands, he ties one end of the scarf around the wrist. He does not pull too tightly as to cause any great discomfort. He runs his fingers along the length of the material delighting in its silk properties. At the same time his eyes never leave mine, gauging my thoughts. On reaching the end of the silk, he runs it around the leg of the table and pulls it into a loop. Threading the end through the loop, he pulls so that my arm is drawn towards him and my body is forced down onto the wooden surface. Once I am in position, he retrieves a cushion from the sofa and places it under my stomach so that my hips are raised. Then, as before, ties my other wrist and secures it to the other table leg. I am laid across the table prostrate and unable to move my upper body. My breasts are pushing against the pegs pulling on my taut nipples.

Curtis disappears from my view, moving I assume behind me. I can sense his presence, but for a moment he does not speak. I can hear items being moved about, but it is not until I feel a gentle hand on my waist, am I alerted to him standing behind me. His hand slips down to just below my ass cheeks and in one movement my dress is thrown up on my back. The space is deathly silent, but I can hear his breathing coming faster and deeper now.

Then all of a sudden, a hand softly caresses my left buttock. He moves his palm flat over the skin moving from one cheek to the next. He builds up the pressure until he is squeezing the flesh between his fingers and the sensation is not at all unpleasant. I can feel the heat rising in my pussy, my lower back sags and my ass pushes back a little. Curtis requires no further invitation and his fingers run along the inside of my thighs until they meet the sweet juices now emanating from my cunt. It is my turn to attempt to regulate my breathing, which has become elevated under his touch.

I hear him say something, but so heightened am I in anticipation, I cannot make out the words. His hand runs up to my pussy and plunges deep in between the folds, covering himself in my wetness. Once more he speaks and this time I hear him.

""I asked you a question; I expect an answer." He says in a flat but firm tone.

"I'm sorry, Teacher. I did not hear you." My voice is but a whisper and is shaking slightly.

"I said that ten swats should be an adequate punishment. Although, as you were not paying attention again, I will add a further ten!" He snarls between curled lips and a little spittle from his mouth hits my back. I have never seen him like this, but I am still not afraid.

He moves around the table so that he can see my face and he asks me out loud.

"What is it you are being punished for?" He lifts up my chin so that he is staring into my eyes.

"For not listening to you, Teacher." I murmur my reply and can feel his hot breath against my face.

"How many swats are you to receive?"

"Twenty, Teacher!" I immediately reply.

"Well done, my child. I seem to have your attention. Now let us begin."

He returns once more to a position behind me. The weight of his body, as he places his hand on my back, is enough to make me shift my position. The expectation in me is building as I prepare myself for what is to come.

"Ask me to spank you. Tell me why you deserve to be punished and ask for your spanking." Curtis calls out to me to confirm that I am willing to take the punishment and I know why it is to be administered.

"Spank me, Teacher. I deserve everything you give me." My reply is loud and confident, but I don't feel that inside.

My pussy begins to twitch as his hands now begin to roam once more around the flesh of my buttocks. Then his fingers run along both inner thighs from my knees upward to the lips of my now soaking cunt. I shiver and adjust my feet so that they are a little more apart. This action is met by the first of my smacks aimed flat against the right ass cheek. The pain is more from shock than the sting. The next one I am ready for and it comes in quick succession. The flesh of my buttocks begins to sear with a glowing pain from the inside out. This is not like any chastisement I received from my parents as a child. I am actually enjoying it. I want to cry out for him to do it harder but think better of it.

His fingers alternate from spanking me, to my now swollen pussy lips. He finds my clit, which is throbbing from my arousal and massages it, while his other hand continues to strike my ass. The sensation of both at the same times causes me to buck my hips slightly. Cutis removes his fingers from my opening and with both hands pulls me towards him. I instinctively open my legs a little further apart.

The contact with my hips is broken for a moment and I eagerly await his touch once more. Then, I feel something just above my left knee. It is a feeling I cannot quite put my finger on. It is familiar, only not on that part of my body. The electricity runs through my body as the implement is drawn over my skin, upwards along my delicate inner thigh. It does not take me long to work out that this wonderful sensation is coming from my hairbrush. The black, stiffened bristles pricking my flesh ever so slightly as it transits closer to my cunt. As it touches my mound, Curtis applies a little more pressure and in a circular motion, massages my clit. I think I am going to cum right there. I exhale deeply, which is greeted with another slap from Curtis' free hand. If this is punishment, I will be a sinner every day.

My lips are pushed apart from what I assume is the handle of the brush and inch by inch, it is inserted in my vagina. The smooth wooden handle slips effortlessly inside my soaked opening. He pushes it as far as it will go, then in a deliberate push and pull, begins to fuck me with it. Even though it feels divine, all I can imagine is his shaft buried deep inside me in its place.

"Teach me to listen to you better, Teacher. I need to be punished for being selfish." The words come out before I even realise I have said them.

The handle of the brush stops its forward and rearward action. I can sense the pressure ease on its grip. All of a sudden, I open my eyes and find Curtis stood in front of me. That same leer is painted on his face as earlier. He is completely naked and his cock is erect at an angle of forty-five degrees. I am only about ten inches away from it and can see every throbbing vein that covers the shaft. He leans forward and with both hands removes the clips from my nipples. The instant rush of blood to the buds gives me a tingling sensation which is replaced with a sting as he pinches each of them between his thumb and finger. I lift my head to try and ride the pain and my lip makes contact with the head of his cock.

"Let the Lord's divine rod purge you of your indiscretions!" His fingers let go of my nipples and grasp me firmly at the back of my head.

The muscles in my jaw relax, as I open my lips to allow his cock entry to my mouth. This time, he is no longer gentle and he forces his meat deep inside me until it will go no further. His lower stomach presses against my nose, blocking off my airway and I gag out loud. This has no effect on him and he merely pushes himself harder inside, his hands pulling my head against him. I fear I might blackout from the lack of oxygen, only for him to relax the pressure and pull his cock back. I have time to catch my breath before he forces himself back inside me. His hips buck to and fro as he slams his throbbing dick in and out of my mouth.

The saliva builds up at the corner of my lips until we are attached by a single silver thread on his stomach. It is only broken as the intensity of his thrusts increases. I have the compulsion to caress and squeeze his balls, but cannot move my arms due to the restraints of the scarves. That, in itself, is punishment enough. I would love to milk him dry of that sweet seminal fluid and feel it coat the back of my throat and tongue. My mind is in a euphoric state, only to be brought back to earth as he pulls himself clear. I open my eyes once more and he disappears from view.

The pressure on the brush is taken up again and he pushes it back deep inside of me until it will go no further. Then, I feel his hands running down the inside of my thighs again. They are joined by a warm soft sensation as he blows gently over the skin. Then in the tenderest of moments, he feathers my sensitive flesh with his lips. Oh my fucking God, I need to cum so badly! His lips are exchanged for his wet tongue as it traces a line northwards. It touches my clit and the tip eases it out of its velvet hood, lapping at it fervently. I squirm under his ministrations, pushing myself back against him.

The next thing I feel, is my ass being pulled apart. His tongue leaves my pussy and is inserted deep between my cheeks. He probes and darts in and out on my ass bud. The feelings it produces is like nothing I have ever experienced. I murmur out loud in pleasure and he increases the speed and pressure with his tongue. He eats my ass for the next five minutes not breaking at all. I can feel my juices, combined with his saliva, running down my ass crack and pussy. His tongue is replaced by first one, then two fingers, forcing open my now well-lubricated anus.

I concentrate in relaxing my sphincter and allow both of his fingers to delve deep inside me. He stretches the skin a little more on each forward thrusting motion until I am comfortable with the feeling. With his fingers still inside of me, one hand is placed on the centre of my back. He holds my body down forcing my stomach into the pillow beneath me so that my back arches and hips raise with my ass cheeks. Without warning or speaking at all, he plunges his cock deep into my open pussy. The force of it rocks me forward, pushing my face against the table. He pumps once, twice and three times before pulling clear again.

Curtis removes his fingers from my ass and slams his, now naturally oiled cock, in their place. His pubic mound grinds against my buttocks until the base of his shaft is against me up to the hilt. The pleasure mixes with a throbbing pain as he begins to drive in and out of me. He is like a wild beast and I am loving every second and every sweet thrust! He fucks me hard and fast, rebounding off my now tender ass cheeks. I begin to moan as he slides in and out of me, each time harder than the last. My legs begin to quake as I reach climax and his hand reaches down around my waist. His fingers find my clit and he rubs it as he continues to pound into me. I wail out loud now and he doubles his efforts.

"Let the sins flow forth from you, my child!" Curtis throws his head back, but continues to strum my clit as if playing his guitar.

He pinches my pearl between his finger and thumb. The sharp pain and sudden sensation sends me over the edge. I buck my hips and cum like a fountain. That is all he needs and with a few final thrusts, he fills my ass with his hot, sticky juice emptying every last drop into me.

Spent, he collapses on top of me. Still joined, both of us catch our breath. He waits until I feel his cum drip from my ass, before pulling his dick from it. He wanders around the table and unties my wrists and I rub them to get the circulation going. He reaches forward and gently strokes my reddened ass, soothing it lovingly, the look in his eyes now returned to normal. He takes me in his arms and softly rubs his fingers over my back and I melt into his embrace. We stand there for a while, holding each other, before he looks me in the eye.

"Let that be a lesson to you, my child."

"Yes, Teacher!" I murmur my reply and our lips meet in the sweetest kiss imaginable.

CHAPTER FIFTEEN - CURTIS

When I was a young boy, I always tried not to inflict pain on others. On occasions when it did happen, I would feel guilt and remorse. It was life that taught me for some, cruelty can be pleasurable, even exciting. The act of inflicting pain on others, for personal enjoyment and sexual gratification, was introduced to me at Upton Abbey. I watched in wonder on passing by the monk's cells as they flayed their skin bare, with whips and chains. The abuse of nubile young flesh on a daily basis, seared into my memory.

Over time, I honed my skills and mastered the art of deception. On the outside, I could appear respectable and sincere, but often that's just a façade. A way to draw people into my confidence, or ensnare someone in a relationship before I would reveal my true colours. People like me are really not interested in others, except as a vehicle to allow me to gain control, so that they become willing participants in my plans. I have designed several ways of doing this. I have a natural ability to turn and twist what people say, so that what they have said and done becomes barely recognizable to them. I have distorted the scriptures to fit in with my own idealised version of life. It is all a matter of smoke and mirrors, let people see and believe what you want them to.

In my youth I became quite adept at lying, if it served my purpose. This was well-known to my wayward mother and uncle, who chastised me for it. I would play the victim, blaming others for my wrong doing. It did not take people long to work out that this was all a game. It became more difficult for me to get away with my lies. I have always avoided taking responsibility for my conduct and would simply blame others for it. I just see nothing wrong for not taking responsibility for my actions when there were others to blame. It guess that is just the way I am wired.

If I am to convince my flock of our purpose, we must have a common enemy. As in the Bible, the villain was portrayed by the Devil, the arch-enemy of Jesus. He stood against anything that was good. If there is light, there must be darkness. That is the natural order of things. We all look for someone to blame when things don't go our way. At least that is my view on the subject. Just like Lee Harvey Oswald, a fall guy for the assassination of President Kennedy, I would need to find such a character.

I have given it much thought over recent years and have come to the conclusion, the answer lies in not one single person. Over history it has been groups, rather than individuals, that were radicalized for their beliefs or acts. We only need look at the Old Testament to see how the Jewish people were subjected to slavery and oppression for thousands of years. I don't even have to search outside of our own country to see evidence of this much closer to home. Catholics have been targeted by the Ku Klux Klan and in states like West Virginia and Indiana, have been attacked and harassed. Only with great controversy was John F. Kennedy elected the first Catholic president of the US, and only after he made a famous speech announcing his independence politically from the Vatican. Just as Jews and African-Americans, Catholics have been historically excluded from some exclusive clubs and organizations. The fact that many US Catholics were of Irish, Italian, Spanish and Polish descent became part of the prejudice against those groups.

Up until 1965 Jim Crow laws, which were state and local laws that enforced racial segregation in the Southern United States were slowly being lifted. This was due to a rise in the black civil rights movement. Since the actions of a simple woman, by the name of Rosa Parks on a Montgomery, Alabama bus, things were rapidly changing. It was late in the year of 1955 and segregation laws at the time stated blacks must sit in designated seats at the back of the bus. Rosa complied with this law, until a white man got on the bus and couldn't find a seat in the white section at the front of the bus. Rosa was instructed along with three other black people to vacate their seats. This, she refused to do and was subsequently arrested.

As word of her arrest ignited outrage and support, Parks unwittingly became the "mother of the modern day civil rights movement." Black community leaders formed the Montgomery Improvement Association (MIA) in recognition of where this event took place. Their leader was a charismatic Baptist Minister known as Martin Luther King. He would be placed, from that moment on, front and centre in the fight for civil rights.

Over the next decade, the civil rights movement gained momentum through various demonstrations, which were in general, mostly peaceful affairs. By the latter half of 1965, President Johnson signed the Voting Rights Act, bringing it into law on August 6 1965, which then took the Civil Rights Act of 1964 several steps further. This was not without cost to certain prominent leaders of the civil rights movement.

Earlier in 1965, Malcolm X, former Nation of Islam leader and Organization of Afro-American Unity founder, was assassinated at a rally. Also, only a few years ago on April 4 1968, civil rights leader and Nobel Peace Prize recipient, Martin Luther King Jr. was assassinated on his hotel room balcony. This was to create an outpouring of emotions from both the black and white communities. Riots and lootings ensued and placed pressure on the administration to push through additional civil rights laws. Against this backdrop of political and ideological change, was the perfect shroud to hide my own twisted agenda.

As I sit and contemplate these issues, I look around at what we have achieved over the past few weeks. The sound of hammer, nails and other metal tools can be heard above me. The whole of the group was involved in the excavation of this subterranean space, while I have spent more time making sure it was to my design and plan. I used the idea of the catacombs which originated in Rome in the second and the beginning of the third centuries A.D. This underground labyrinth would be where the most important pontiffs of the third century would be buried. The custom of burying the dead in underground areas was already known to the Etruscans, the Jews and the Romans, but with Christianity much more complex and larger, burial hypogea originated in order to welcome the whole community in only one necropolis.

The actual term referring to these areas is *coemeterium*, which derives from the Greek and means "dormitory", thereby stressing the fact that for Christians, burial is just a temporary moment while they wait for the final resurrection. The monks at Upton referred to their own cells as dormitories, as a place of reflection and I have tried to replicate this in my design of this space. The choice of land on which to build our new home was not coincidental. Its location did not only mirror that of the Kidron Valley, where the first temple of Solomon was constructed, but the ground itself was perfect for the excavation of the catacomb area.

The soil is solid but easily removable. I have arranged a series of ladders which rise up to what I term galleries. In the walls of these galleries are built-in rooms, furnished or unfurnished. The unfurnished rooms are merely for reflection, privacy or meditation. The others I have filled with all manner of delights. They range from old-fashioned medieval stocks, to the black, shiny upholstered benches for administering flagellation, spanking and all types of sexual depravity. The throbbing of my penis is testament to how badly I crave and have missed such things. My mind returns to the cold, dark corridors of Upton Abbey and the sounds of pain and torment ringing around its hallowed walls.

At that time, it was not public knowledge how prolific sexual abuse in the priesthood was, and in particular, in establishments such as the Abbey. Even those of us who lived through it can never really quantify the level of abuse that was inflicted on those innocent boys and girls. It was not only the children that were at risk of the 70% of sexual attacks that go unreported, Priests were not averse to inflicting the same depravity on their own. It appeared, as in the wild, that predators seek out the most vulnerable.

As most Catholics consisted of large families, it was common for siblings of the same family to pass through the Abbey and leave a reputation behind them. I was lucky that I didn't have to live up to the reputation of a former pupil. I did see boys who were made prime targets for ridicule and contempt due to the past misdemeanours of their siblings. These were exactly the kind of kids the foul, malodorous, cassock or black robe wearing predators would prey on. Predators look for the weakest link. There is a reason jackals prey on the sick and wounded; they make great targets. There were a number of these beasts roaming the darkened corridors and niches of the Abbey, but none were as bad as the Abbott himself.

Almost everywhere the Abbott went, he was shadowed by his young protégé, Father Murphy. He was a young priest. He was cool and everyone, especially the boys, would do anything to be his best bud. He was the perfect predator. He blended into the background and was skilled in gaining people's confidence. There were rumours that his youthful looks were misleading and he had been in a number of establishments prior to Upton. The Catholic Church seemed to have a knack for ghosting its abusive priests to other parishes.

I have since found, to my horror, that the church became experts at moving their problem priests around to poorer parishes where their particular traits for young flesh would not be reported. Places like Latin America and places of abject poverty, sexual abuse would be tolerated rather than the fear of living on the streets. This was the worst case of musical chairs imaginable and I feel physically sick as I recall those abusive times.

The church even produced a manual on how to deal with abusive priests. When it comes to a time when you have to produce documentation to address such an issue, maybe that should in itself ring alarm bells. If there are guidelines on how to deal with paedophiles, then you'd think it might occur to you that you have too many paedophiles, and should perhaps address that problem?

Another act that the depraved among the clergy have refined, is the act of confession. It is about the most Catholic thing you can do, outside of making lasagna for the Pope! Talking about your fears and problems can be a wonderful way to get past them. That's the whole premise behind psychotherapy. However, the confession box also served as a snare for molesters to trap innocent, unsuspecting children. When you would confess your sins to a priest who was faithful to his sacrament, then he would simply absolve you with "Say two Hail Mary's and go with God."

The more nefarious of the priests, would ask questions that a young child would never have heard, let alone be able to answer truthfully. Things like ""Do you have impure thoughts?" Or the more direct approach of "Do you think of naked girls?" All of these things were a pre-cursor to something a little more sinister. The victims were often on the cusp of puberty, awkward and lonely. All some of them needed was someone to share their troubles and concerns with. A confidante, if you like. That is what I wanted all my life and Father Murphy had done his research well. After my first confession to him, I was told to meet him in his office to discuss these sinful thoughts.

I squirm against the cold, hard, stone step as the memory of the first time he raped me comes flooding back. After that first time, he wiped his bloody cock in my hair, telling me it was "The blood of our Saviour." That was just the beginning of what was to be two years of systematic abuse. Growing up in the seclusion of the Abbey, without any outside influences, meant that we could be made to think that our abuse was in fact not that at all. If a child growing up in the 60's was accused of doing something by an adult, it would generally be accepted that it was true. This was even the case if the child denied it. Even *more so if the accusation came from a man of the cloth. To me, it was one of those things where you don't want to say anything to your friends. Not that I made many friends at the Abbey. There was also the whole dirtiness factor about it. I thought there was something wrong with me as it was pleasurable as well as painful. I kept telling myself in later years that what happened made me a stronger person. That was not entirely true. All that it did was to set me down a road of vengeance that would lead to this place.*

The number of tolls from the bell above me alerts me to the fact that it is time for Vespers. I am transported back from the misty, murky rooms of my past and rise from the cold stone steps of the basement. One by one, I trudge upwards and the ground floor is already shrouded in a falling darkness. The sun has already descended below the horizon, leaving only an orange glow to mark its journey to set in the west. The shadows have lengthened as I make my way to the small chapel room we have built onto the rear of the building.

As I enter the space, all turn to face me. I smile and greet each one silently as I pass down the aisle, to take my place in front of the Altar. I cast my gaze around the room and subconsciously do a head count. Our group has not grown as yet and it does not take long to realise we are one person missing. Once more, I scour both sides of the aisle and notice it is the young Martha that is absent from our prayer meeting. I laid out the rules quite clearly at the inception of our group and missing prayer was a punishable offence.

"Does anyone know why Sister Martha is absent from Vespers?" I look from face to face until my eyes rest on Tabitha, who attempts to avert my stare.

"My child, have you got something to say?" I do not use her name, but Tabitha's head lifts and looks at me.

"I last saw her in her cell, Teacher." There is a nervousness about her, as if she wants to tell me something, but is afraid to do so.

"Then I better see if she is okay. It must be something of great importance for her to miss prayer. Luke, will you take over please?" The confident young man steps eagerly forward to take my place in front of the Altar.

"Of course, Teacher." There is a smug look on his face that I have chosen him over the others. It was for no particular reason other than his were the first pair of eyes that I caught.

I make my way out of the chapel and through the main hallway. All of the dormitories are on the first floor. The males all share one room and the females are split between another two dormitories, although they still refer to them as cells, just as I have instructed. I wanted to mimic monastic life as much as possible. That was the reason for my constructing actual cells for meditation and reflection in the catacombs below the main building. The space had a dual purpose for which I am about to put to the test for the first time. I fight to control my breathing, which has now become ragged and my cock is throbbing, pressing against my lower abdomen.

I take the stairs, two at a time, bounding to the top. Martha shares a room with both Lydia and Bethany and it is the first one at the top of the staircase. I slow my pace, as I notice the door is open and murmuring sounds are coming from within. I draw closer and peer around the door frame. Martha is dressed in her simple cloth vestment, which is drawn up at her waist. Her legs are spread wide, with her feet resting against the bed and knees bent. One hand is held firmly against her chest, kneading the flesh beneath in a firm, circular motion. The other hand is running down the centre of her womanhood, her fingers covered in the juices of her obvious arousal. From the exertions and heaving of her body, and the ferocity and speed of her fingers, I guess I have arrived at a very opportune moment.

"What is the meaning of this? How dare you miss prayer to selfishly pleasure your body? I made the rules very clear from the beginning. All prayer meetings are compulsory! Now get yourself decent and come with me." Martha's eyes are wide with shock, as she hastily pulls down her robes to cover her modesty.

I wait patiently for her to come and join me. She scrambles off the bed and in four paces she is stood before me. The shock in her eyes has turned to one of embarrassment, having been caught in such a compromising position. This only adds to the thrill and adrenalin that is surging through my body right now. I take Martha by the hand and lead her back down the staircase and through the hallway. The sound of prayers being recited greets us as we enter the chapel. On our arrival, Luke stops mid-sentence and the congregation does the same and turns to look in our direction.

"I have found our sister, my children. Martha decided to deliver herself into Satan's care. I discovered, with my own eyes, how she plundered her body rather than attend Vespers. Our

Sister must be punished for her wrongdoings and you, my children, will assist me." There is a ripple of confused voices reverberating around the holy place. In tandem with the confusion, there is also a look of apprehension on some and excitement on others.

"Follow me to the catacombs." Still holding Martha by the hand, I swivel on my heel and turn around one hundred and eighty degrees.

I can hear the shuffling of feet as I lead Martha and my disciples down into the bowels of the earth. The air is notably cooler, with an almost damp smell to it. I place my arms around Martha's shoulders and pull her towards me. She inclines her head and her lips turn upwards in the form of a small smile. She knows that she has broken the rules and her face is a picture of acceptance. All of the females in the group are submissive in nature, it is one of the reasons they gravitated towards me. Even the guys, with the exception of Peter, were submissive. They needed someone to lead them, even Luke with his cocksure attitude. The only enigma was Peter. He didn't quite fit, but I like having him around.

We reach the bottom of the stone staircase and I make my way to one of the rooms which are carved out into the face of the rock. It is one of the larger rooms, with ropes and chains suspended from the ceilings. It is perfect for what I have in mind. It is spacious enough for all of my congregation to be able to observe and participate in today's punishment. I take Martha by the hand and guide her to the centre of the room.

"You're a submissive with a need for control. But, after all, that is what defines many submissive people." I grasp hold of her jaw firmly and lift her head, so that she gazes into my eyes.

"People are not alike. There is no mould that shapes a submissive person. I wouldn't presume to believe I know everything about you. Although, I do detect evidence of strong submissive tendencies. Not just in you, but everyone gathered in this room." I sweep my eyes over the assembled flock, who are waiting eagerly to see what I have in store. Some of them nod their heads in approval of my statement. As if I need their fucking assent!

"Our way of life here is all about discipline and control, my child. You must guard and control those urges that Satan implants in your mind. When he comes to you in the night, you will fight against it. You will only cum on my command, is that understood?" I whisper the words into her ear, but loud enough for the group to hear. I slide my hand down between her legs, at the same time applying pressure to her neck and pressing my lips against hers.

I can feel her body sag as she presses herself against me and her legs part slightly to allow me entry. I test how wet she has become at the situation and raise my finger and place it in her mouth, so that she can taste her own juices. Her eyes close as she suckles on my finger and I release my grip on her neck and step away from her. She sways ungainly for a moment, until opening her eyes regains her balance. I take a piece of black material which is rectangular in shape from a hook on the wall. I return to the waiting Martha and circle around behind her.

I use both of my hands to slip off the material of the robe she is wearing, and it falls unceremoniously to the floor. I peer over her shoulder, my erect penis pushing against her ass cheeks. Her breasts are full and voluptuous with a small, tight waist. I step back and admire her from the rear. Her long blond hair is pulled tight, braided and interwoven with leather strips. The ends of the leather hang loosely between her ass cheeks. My heart rate has increased and I am tempted to bend her over and fuck her senseless right there, right now. I hold myself back.

"Would you prefer the blindfold or not?" I lift up the black material in front of her face for her to decide.

"I would prefer to wear it, Teacher." Her voice is almost inaudible and I have to ask her to repeat it.

"I did not quite hear that."

"I would like to wear the blindfold, Teacher." Her answer is immediate and out loud this time.

"Good, that will add to the punishment." I slip the material over her shoulder and tie it off at the back of her head. I check that it is comfortable and will not slip.

"Peter, Luke and Priscilla will you join me, please?" It was an order, not a request, and they obediently step towards me.

"What would you have us do, Teacher?" Peter is the first to speak as they stand just one pace in front of the now blindfolded Martha.

"Take each of her wrists and secure them by these leather straps and chains. They are to be tight enough so she cannot move her arms, but not enough to cause discomfort." I offer the first leather wrist restraint to Luke, who takes it from me.

Peter follows suit and between them, they shackle Martha's wrists to the restraints. The chains are attached to a series of pulleys, and they adjust them so that her arms are stretched open wide and immobile. At the same time, I pick up a rigid metal bar which is approximately thirty-six inches long. At each end is another set of leather restraints and buckles. I motion for Priscilla to approach me and hand over the implement.

"Bind each of her ankles with this." I cannot hide the smile that emerges as Priscilla takes the instrument from me.

I leave Priscilla to her task while I walk over to a rack attached to the wall. It holds a selection of whips, floggers, paddles and other instruments of pleasure. The one I choose has a thick, sturdy, leather handle and the lashes comprise of thick cords with knots at each end. I pull the cool material through my hand and delight in the sensation it provides. I return to the now, trussed-up Martha, who is now visibly shaking. I run the length of the leather handles underneath her nose so that she can smell the leather. The falls trail over her breasts and the buds perk up with the effect.

"Brothers and Sisters, I want you to teach Martha the meaning of control. You will bring her to the edge of pleasure, but make sure you do not make her cum. I will leave it to your own devices how you wish to achieve this." I withdraw the flogger from under Martha's nose and bend the handle, feeling how pliable it is. The creaking sound makes her head shift in my direction.

"You will count for me. If you miss the count, I will start again. Are we quite clear on that?" There is only a small pause before her diminutive voice breaks the silence.

"Yes, Teacher." I step back and watch as her leg quivers. Priscilla runs her tongue along the inner thigh of her sister. Up and up she goes until she is just below that glistening cunt.

From my position, just to the rear and off to one side, I watch for a few minutes. Luke has cupped a breast in his mouth and his tongue is making circles around the swollen nipple. His free hand is resting on the top of Martha's pubic mound and the tip of his finger massages her clit sensually in time with his tongue. With Priscilla using her own tongue she laps at her swollen labia and Martha moans out loud. Peter is feathering her neck with butterfly kisses from her shoulders to the nape of her neck. I notice her skin raise in bumps at the excitement and arousal of being pleasured in three different ways. There is a pronounced gap between her thighs and I can see the glistening dew from her pussy in the meagre lighting of the room. Just as she is brought to an almost euphoric state, I deliver the first blow softly across her upper back. She murmurs under its touch and she drops her head slightly.

"One," She calls out. I then proceed down her back, alternating sides, my strokes becoming progressively harder.

She begins to moan louder with each one, but continues to count. All of the time, the other three are devouring every inch of her with their mouths, tongues and fingers. Luke is playing her clit like a bass guitarist and she licks her lips as Peter takes her other breast in his mouth. Priscilla is using her tongue in long, languished movements from the bottom of her opening to the top. Martha sways back slightly under the pressure.

"Teacher, please let me cum!" She is almost beyond the point of no return.

My rhythm is measured, and as I approach her ass, I pause a little. Just long enough to slide my finger between her buttocks and search out that tight little knot of her anus. To my surprise, it is also soaked with her arousal and my finger slides gently in as far as it will go. Then as quickly as it was inserted, I withdraw it and return my attention to the flogging. The next strike was delivered significantly harder on her right buttock, causing it to quiver.

"Ahh, twenty one," Martha wails, squirming in place. The next nine are delivered alternately on left and right buttocks with equal force. Both of her legs are shaking violently and I can tell she is close to orgasm.

"You have done well, my child. Now you can cum for me!" I drop to my knees and bury my face between her ass cheeks. My tongue probes deep inside and I feel the force of a finger inside her cunt, finger-banging her violently.

She is moaning loudly now and her pussy is dripping onto the floor, it runs freely down my chin as I drive into her ass with my tongue. She is almost delirious with desire, her words are unintelligible, just a series of wails, murmurs and moans. I pull my tongue clear and insert the handle of the flogger in its place. In a forceful thrusting motion, I fuck her ass and Luke and Priscilla concentrate on her pussy. Peter is alternating between her breasts which are swollen and red from the constant sucking and biting.

Her whole body begins to quake and a low rumble from her stomach emerges into a scream as our joint efforts bring her to a glorious orgasm. She sways violently now in her restraints, her body racked with the sweet pain of release. I rise from my crouched position and pull the flogger clear of her anus. The other three back off a little so I have room and I take off the blindfold. Martha blinks a few times before her eyes get accustomed to the light once more.

"So, my child, here endeth the lesson."

"Thank you, Teacher." She answers in a ragged breath, kissing the handle of the flogger as I run it along the length of her lips.

I turn around to see that every person in the room is transfixed on what has just happened. No one more than Magdalene, whose eyes never leave my own. Now that I have partially revealed my true colours, will their opinions of me change? From the looks that I am receiving, I think not. I have chosen well when gathering my disciples together. An impressionable and weak-willed group that I can mould into my own image. My version of the scriptures and outlook on the world around us, a fresh new beginning for us all.

CHAPTER SIXTEEN - PETER

Even though I am almost eight months into my first undercover operation, I am still questioning my suitability for it. Working as an undercover agent probably ranks as one of the most terrifying and dangerous things you could choose to do with your life. I have chosen to do this with the additional pressure of having a young family to support. If things were to go wrong, how would they survive? Have I been selfish by allowing myself to be thrown in at the deep end? Just so that I can infiltrate a low-level individual or group, who may or may not be a danger to national security. Daily, I face immense pressure to try and extract any intelligence I can, that might be meaningful to my handlers. So far, I have drawn a blank and think it is maybe time I was pulled out.

There's also the murky ethical ground I'm constantly treading. That fine line between enticing criminals to reveal their most sordid plans, and entrapment. It is a tightrope and one that I don't wish to fall from if I can help it. I have learned that as an undercover agent, you have to see the grey, you have to find some goodness in a person in order to be attracted to them. Criminals can smell fear, they can smell hatred, and they know when you aren't accepting of their lifestyle. You've got to understand them in some way, be it the child molester, drug dealer, or religious fanatic.

I have managed to divorce myself from my true persona. With no form of identification to say who I really am, that person is banished to the past. I have immersed myself in Draven's past, consumed his life from the pages of my legend. The location of California was ideal for my cover, as there was a very limited chance that I would run across anyone from my real past. I could only imagine the look of recrimination, if one of my old school friends recognised me in a bar and asked how I was, using my real name. This could happen anywhere, of course, but the closer you are to home, the more likely it is to happen to you.

Up until this point, I have met up with my handler infrequently. To be fair, I have not really obtained any information noteworthy of reporting up the chain. I suppose the only real event was giving warning of the break in at Milton's place. This fine line I tread of not breaking the law, is getting more precarious as the mission goes on. The briefing by the

Director of the Academy still rings in my ears when it comes to crossing the line. If at any time I anticipate taking part in a crime, it should be approved in advance. On normal operations, the taking of narcotics was to be strictly avoided. This was wavered by the Director, due to the nature of this particular assignment. Even though I have taken part in the lifestyle to provide my cover with the legitimacy it needs, I have been able to not get myself addicted or incapable of carrying out my duties.

The one thing that the Director pointed out during my selection process, was the remarks made by my instructors. They noticed that due to my amiable character, I was able to make friends very easily. This trait was essential for any good undercover officer. You can only fake that so much. I assessed that the key to making this task a success, was to get to know the people I would be investigating. I invested a great deal of my time with the group so that they began to like and trust me. I would do the things that they did and agree with their ideals. When Curtis came on the scene, it took me a while to gain his trust. He seemed to be more wary of me than the others. I even began to have an affection for everyone, although some of the concepts they believed in went against my moral principles.

One of the most difficult things for me was the sexual side to it. I'm a huge romantic, yet my relationships are private. By their nature, that's what they are, intimate. To me, that is the normal way to live in a relationship, keeping yourself true to that one special person. The downside to this, is when we think this way we create a stigma for those who choose a different path. The idea of free love and sharing one another without boundaries or petty jealousy, is an interesting theory. That is, unless you are devoutly religious and a faithful person as I am. In all of the sexual encounters I have taken part in, I have struggled with my conscience. Images of Emily and Liam a constant barrier to letting myself go completely.

Yet, I have still passed the scrutiny of the ever-watchful Curtis. These types of operations usually last a few months. At least, that is what I was told. It has taken me until now for Curtis to reveal a little more about himself and a chance for me to assess if he was a genuine threat or not. Although I feel that I am not under any undue pressure, over time the cracks will begin to show. I will need some form of psychological counselling to deal with the experience and for me to readjust back to family life. This will be tested over the next thirty-six hours.

Things have begun to get a little more extreme in Curtis' daily teachings. His support for the African-American struggle against white oppression, while admirable, is also bordering on fanatical. Also, an unhealthy interest in the Nation of Islam, an African-American political and religious movement, founded in Detroit, Michigan. Its aims were to improve the spiritual, mental, social, and economic condition of African-Americans in the United States and all of humanity. That all sounded very well on paper, but there was something sinister about the movement and I know, during my training, that they have been watched by the FBI for a number of years.

When Curtis called myself, Lydia, Bethany and Magdalene to him three nights ago, it was all a bit mysterious. It quickly turned to shock when he revealed what he wanted us to do. On his many excursions into the nearby town of Sebastopol, he identified a wealthy family in a white residential area. His views on the race war issue, happening in the country at that time, was fuelling his thoughts. Like many reactionaries, he saw race in America in apocalyptic terms. He believed that African-Americans would soon rise up and begin to murder white people. Because of his and the Seekers of the Way's support for the black struggle, they would be spared. When it was all over, they would emerge from the temple they had built and rule over the black population.

His ideas were radical to say the least and for the first time since my inception, I felt that I needed to pass this on to my handler. It was time for us to "accelerate this race war to hasten the end of days", he told us. My heart began to race at the thought of what his plans were. When he spoke, it was as if someone sucked the air out of my lungs. I literally could not breathe as my mind tried to make sense of what he said on that night.

"Can you say that again, Teacher? I'm not quite sure I heard you properly." I look from Curtis to the other members assembled in his dormitory.

"I thought I was quite clear, but of course I will repeat it for clarification. I want you to break into this address and kill the people who live there. I want you to write a message in their blood, so that it appears the killings were done by the Nation of Islam." I shake my head at the enormity of what I heard.

"Yes, Teacher." The other three answer like the mindless zombies they have become. They will do anything for this lunatic.

"Do you have a problem with that, Peter?" My mind is still trying to process the information he has just delivered and I am stuck for words.

"No, I don't have a problem with it. I just wanted to be clear on your instructions." My answer does not sound in the least bit convincing.

"Good, I will leave you to plan the arrangements. You can leave me now. Magdalene, can you stay behind?" It was not a request, it was an order, and the rest of us leave them to it.

That was just a mere three days ago and I have racked my brains of a way out of this one without blowing my cover. The alternative to murder, would mean the involvement of the FBI, which I hope will bring this to a swift conclusion. I definitely need to speak to my handler before I proceed with what I have in mind, so I leave my dormitory and descend the stairs to the hallway. We have already attended Lauds, Prime and Terce prayer meetings and it is fast approaching 10am. If I am to get to town for my meeting and back in time for Sext, or Midday prayer, I need to leave now. I pick up the keys for my truck from the bowl on the table. As I open the door, my path is barred by the figure of Curtis who is stood on the porch.

"You seem to be in a rush, brother." A beaming smile is painted across his face as I check my stride after almost colliding with him.

"I want to get into town and take a look at the house in daylight. It will be easier than having to adjust my plans in the dark if I can get a picture of the place in my mind." I give my cover story for leaving the confines of the temple grounds.

"Good idea, brother. That is one of the reasons I chose you for this historic task. You and your sisters are the most devout of my followers." I felt like a little boy being patted on the head for being good.

"Thank you, Teacher. We won't let you down." I submit to his flattery and give his ego another little boost.

"I am sure you won't." There was a hint of sarcasm in his voice and a derisory look as I pass him and climb into the truck.

I turn the ignition and the engine bursts into life with a throaty roar. I press my foot to the metal and the wheels spin on the dry, parched ground of the compound, throwing up a cloud of dust. I look in my rear-view mirror, to see Curtis still stood on the porch watching my departure, until I disappear over the hill and join the interstate in the direction of Sebastopol.

The California sun beats down on me as I drive the twenty minutes into the town of Sebastopol. In the time that we have set up the community, I have only been here on a couple of occasions. They were always under directions of Curtis. Myself and the others were not allowed to make excursions on our own without a good reason. The rest of the followers did not seem to mind it, not even giving it a second thought that they were actually willing prisoners of this control freak. I went along with it, but it was becoming more and more difficult to keep my feelings in check.

I turn off Main Street and into a quiet, leafy suburb of town. The houses are those ones rich people buy when they get paranoid about having too much money. I look at the piece of paper I have taken from my pocket. Turning my head from one side of the street to the other, I locate the building I am looking for. It's like a fortress, tall gates with more security gadgets than a military compound. Perhaps behind those yellow bricks they feel safe from harm, but I can't help thinking they've only built themselves a beautiful prison. Either way, though, it's none of my concern. I'm just here to make sure my plan goes ahead without any hitches.

I drive the full length of the property, observing and taking mental notes of any flaws in the security. There are places where the camera views will be hidden, so that is where we will make our entry. I am satisfied with my assessment but think to myself, if someone is going to pay that much money for a house, they should invest the same in getting a proper security assessment. I drive on by and head back into town and my pre-arranged meeting point and time. My handler would be in the designated place every day at 11am, which will not give me much time to deliver my message and get back in time for midday prayers.

The building before me is beautiful, old stone and stained glass, but to me it is more than just a building. It is the home of God. Before I enter the church, I can hear the organ music. As I pass over the threshold, I can smell the fresh flowers brought by the fussy old ladies that dust, even when there is none. I feel Him here, I thought He would be gone, that these walls would be deserted. His presence is overwhelming and fills my heart with joy. I say a silent prayer as I make my way to the confessional. The church is empty and I do not have to wait in line for my turn. I open the door of the booth made from burnished maple. I settle down on the wooden bench and place my face against the wooden lattice grill to my right.

"Forgive me father, for I have sinned. It has been four weeks since my last confession. I have had murderous thoughts." I quickly calculate the last time I met with my handler.

"May the Lord be in your heart and help you to confess your sins with true sorrow." The gravelly voice from the next booth conveys the passphrase to me, so I know that it is my handler.

"Okay, I haven't got much time. The preacher has asked us to commit a murder on the family living at this address." I slip the piece of paper through the lattice work between the two booths.

"Wow, that has escalated quickly. Do you want me to pass it on to the local Police Department?" My handler is caught by surprise by my revelation which is understandable.

"No, I want to see if we can get more on this guy. I will intervene and kidnap the couple and take them back to the Temple. That way I can keep an eye on them if I feel it necessary for us to intervene and arrest him and some of his crazy followers." I outline my intentions and there is a moment of silence while my handler thinks about it.

"That sounds like a plan, but I will have to get it cleared from up top. If it is a go, I will leave a message in the woods at the usual place. When is it to happen?"

"Tomorrow night. I was thinking if we give him time, he might provide us with other crimes to give him a heavier sentence. I also would like you to get me a couple of items and leave them with confirmation if it is a go or not." I give the reasons behind my way of thinking and slide another piece of paper between the grill.

"The abduction and intention to plan a murder will be enough, but if he does not actually take part in it, then it will be difficult to prove in a court of law. I better find out if it is a go and get back to you. If it is, I will drop off the items as well at the same time." The wood grill is pulled shut and I hear the door open from the other booth.

I give it a moment before rising and exiting my confessional. An elderly couple are kneeling in the second row of the church. A middle-aged priest busies himself by the Altar. I pick up a service leaflet and scan through it for times of the various services. I have missed my weekly devotion and long for the time when this will all be over. As I scan through the leaflet, I notice that the priest is of Irish descent, as are many who take up that vocation. Father Sean Murphy is one of the younger breed of those who enter the seminary, to devote their lives in the service of God. He looks up from what he is doing and our eyes meet and a warm, welcoming smile greets me. He raises a hand and I return the action before setting off out of the church to head back to the community.

I feel the soothing breeze and become absorbed in the music that is playing on the radio of my pickup. The three girls are all dressed in dark clothing, as I instructed them. All signs of skin have been covered up and would be hidden from view, once we put on the balaclavas we have brought with us. If this is to be a crime committed by the Nation of Islam, we don't want someone spotting a group of white people entering the house. If I carried out my reconnaissance correctly, we should be able to approach the rear of the house unseen by any onlookers.

There is a nervous excitement emanating from the girls. Lydia and Bethany are playing with the rather vicious-looking hunting knives they have brought with them. I appreciate that they were brought up on the streets and living as prostitutes is a hard life. They were an obvious choice for Curtis to assign this crime to. Magdalene is another story. From what I have gathered, she comes from a wealthy family and will not have been exposed to the same experiences of her sisters. The inside of the truck smells like a cannabis plantation, as they take the sweet, pungent smoke deep into their lungs. We took a cocktail of mind-bending drugs, along with the rest of the group, before leaving for tonight's mission.

Curtis declared it as the first step on the path to a brave new world. He appeared even more crazy than usual. His behaviour was becoming a little more erratic and unpredictable. His teachings seem to have taken on a more political, rather than religious, nature. But, there was always a reference to the Scriptures when justifying anything that he did or said. It is only now that I have realised the hold that he has over the community. He has managed to bend them to his will through his manipulative nature. He has become really friendly towards me, but I sense that he is still a little wary about my reasons for being there. When I retrieved the message about tonight's operation and found the items I asked for, I could have sworn that I felt as if I was being watched. It was all probably just my imagination and I dismissed it as quickly as it entered my head. What we were about to do would make anyone nervous. The others have no idea that things are going to change from Curtis' original instructions.

The sun sinks lower in the sky. Light of day draining away, giving way to the velvety dark of night, crickets chirping, dusky colours subdued in the fading light. We drive into the suburbs and street lights click on, the day coming to an end. The first stars appear in the night sky. The sharp shadows of the lampposts fade into the darkness of the sidewalk. Only the faintest of light shines through the leaves of the trees. I release my foot from the gas and we coast slowly to a silent halt and I turn off the engine.

The stillness of the night is almost deafening. I can hear the beat of my heart as I contemplate what we are about to do. I scour the street to see if anyone has observed us or taken an interest in a strange vehicle in the neighbourhood. All seems quiet and the streets are deserted.

"There's been a change of plan." I turn to my partners in crime who are, by now, well and truly under the influence of the narcotics. Their eyes are wide and have difficulty focusing on me.

"What has changed?" Lydia slurs her words, holding onto Bethany for support.

"Curtis has decided that we kidnap the couple, rather than kill them. The money a ransom would make, could set us up for the next few years.

"Yeah, man. That sounds cool." Bethany answers this time and does not even question my lie. There is a definite sign of relief on the face of Magdalene. I guess she only was going to go through with it because Curtis had asked. There was a special kind of bond between those two. Others have noticed it as well.

"Okay, let's get on with it. Follow me." I whisper to the other three and throw the rucksack I have brought over my shoulder.

We make our way around the back of the house, keeping in the shadow of the brick wall that surrounds the property. When we reach the rear of the house, where I know the cameras will be blind, I place the rucksack down on the ground. I turn my back so that it is against the brickwork and bend my knees slightly, interlacing my fingers and cupping my hands.

"Okay Lydia, take a short run up and put your foot on my hand. I will lift you and I want you to pull yourself up onto the top of the wall. Do you think you can do that?"

"Yeah, I can do that." Lydia nods her head before answering.

I brace myself ready as she approaches, and as if she had done this many times before, places her foot in my hand. I pull up and easily assist her to the top of the wall. She pulls herself over the wall and leans over it, ready to help the next one up.

"Okay Magdalene, are you ready?" I have no reason to ask as she is already lined up and striding towards me.

Once more, her foot is placed perfectly on my waiting hand and I push her up to the waiting hands of Lydia, who helps her over the wall. The last one to go over is Bethany and being a little older and heavier, she is a little more difficult, but with a bit of pushing and pulling she manages to get her legs over the other side. I push myself away from the wall and take about six strides before turning back to face it. I pick up the rucksack and place my arms through the straps securing it to my back.

"You will have to catch me and pull me up; are you ready?" I whisper from out of the shadows.

"Yeah, we're ready." Bethany has joined her sisters and is hanging over the wall with hands outstretched.

I run towards the wall and leap so that I catch hold of the nearest pair of hands. They belong to Bethany, and being the more powerfully built of the three, she manages to keep a firm grip on me while both Magdalene and Lydia assist her to haul me up the wall. I swing my leg over the top and jump down onto the other side. I watch as, one by one, the girls lower themselves a little more elegantly from the top. As soon as all of us have negotiated the obstacle safely, I lead them to the rear of the house.

It was my intention to pick the lock of the door at the rear of the house. Just as we arrive at the steps to the porch, I notice a pair of wooden doors which have a padlock through a hasp. The doors must lead down to a basement area and I decide that would be a better point of entry. I fumble in my pocket and take out a lockpick. It takes me seconds to unfasten the rather antiquated piece of metal and we are descending the stairs in no time at all. I search around in the darkness for a light switch and manage to locate it at the foot of the stairs. We all blink and take a few minutes to allow our eyes to get accustomed to the light. We take the stairs step-by-step, one behind the other. I lead the way and we depart the bowels of the house into the main living area.

I tread warily through the living room, hoping against hope that the family do not own any pets. The last thing we need is to come face to face with some vicious canine. I want this to go off with as little commotion as possible. If it goes to plan, the couple will not even know we were there until they wake up. I locate the staircase that leads to the upper floor and motion for the girls to follow on behind me. There is enough light from outside to illuminate our way and for them to see my hand gestures. As we reach the summit of the stairs, I slip the rucksack from my shoulders. I rummage deep down inside and find the items I am looking for. I hand over a piece of cloth to Bethany and take one myself. I unscrew the cap of the chloroform and douse the cloth with it. I then hand over the bottle to Bethany.

"Be sure to get it good and wet." I whisper to her and she nods that she understands.

At the same time, Magdalene creeps along the corridor looking for the couple's bedroom. She stops about halfway down and turns in our direction. She uses her finger to point to the room indicating that she has found them. I give her the thumbs-up and we join her at the door. I peer into the gloom and can make out two shapes in close proximity to each other. One has flowing hair and appears to be looking up at the ceiling. The other has their back to us but from the width of the shoulders, I would say it was male. The shoulders rise and fall regularly as if he is in a deep sleep.

I gently push myself past Magdalene and Bethany tags on behind me, closely followed by Lydia and finally Magdalene. I move to one side of the bed, pointing to Bethany to take the other. I thought it better that I tackle the male, just in case if he was to wake prior to me administering the chloroform. We both take up our positions and I signal for Bethany to apply her cloth first. She places the material over the nose of the woman whose eyes open immediately. She uses all of her weight and strength to hold her in position, as she applies more pressure with her hand. I take my cue from her do the same to the male. He struggles a little but within seconds he has gone limp, as has his partner.

"Well, that was painless enough!" I break the silence and return the cloths and bottle back into the rucksack.

"Now take this and these. I want you to write a message on the wall to alert the authorities to who has carried this out." I pass over the bag of pig's blood and a couple of brushes to both Magdalene and Lydia.

"What message should we write?" Magdalene sounds confused and bewildered.

"Something along the lines of. "Death to all Pigs!" Oh yeah, and sign it NOI. That's all, we'll let them make of it as they will." The use of NOI would inform the authorities that the act was carried out by the Nation of Islam. They would be unsure whether the couple had been murdered or abducted.

"Hell, yeah!" Lydia has enthusiastically ripped the seal off the tin of pig's blood I have acquired through the request to my handler. Quite ironic really, seeing as the pig is an animal that is loathed by all Muslims.

My mind begins to race as we prepare to move the couple to the truck and on again, back to the community. A more important and pressing matter, was how I was going to explain and convince Curtis that my actions made sense. Well, I will face that problem when it comes to it. The pieces have been placed on the board and the game has begun. Who knows how this will end.

CHAPTER SEVENTEEN - MAGDALENE

The sound of the door closing behind the others, is just a background noise. My eyes are fixated on his. He is beautiful from the depth of his eyes to the gentle expressions of his voice. The same voice that, at times, commands respect and it is given freely. He is gorgeous inside and out. I love the way his voice quickens and becomes enthusiastic when he sparkled with a new idea, or was so enjoying one of mine that he lost himself for a moment and quite forgot the mask he wore for others.

His eyes bore into mine as if they are searching for signs of my emotions. From them comes an intensity, an honesty, a gentleness. Perhaps this is what is meant by a gentleman, not one of weakness or trite politeness, but one of great vision and noble ways. He encapsulates all of these things. To me he is the perfect man, but I have become biased over time. From the moment I first laid eyes on him with his confidence, drive and ambition, masculinity, and emotional strength, feelings of sexual desire were triggered. They say that attraction comes first and then everything else will follow quite naturally. I cannot disagree with that and he has made it so effortless.

Many men go through life believing that the reason they can't get a woman to fall in love with them, is because they don't fit into some ideal package of physical attraction. If they only knew that all we want is confidence, masculinity and the ability to make a woman feel safe and secure. His looks are secondary, if he possesses the ability, for example, to make her laugh, make her feel girly and feminine in his presence. At the same time valuing her opinion, while not losing that dominant alpha male characteristic that I have always been drawn to.

I didn't know until now, how much I love being submissive to a man. Not just any man, but this one in particular has that magical quality about him that makes me want to do everything he asks of me, without hesitation. To please him in every way possible. To carry out every instruction and whim, the only reward in return is to be needed, loved and protected. Yes, if he wishes that I share him with others, I am willing to do so. It was not so difficult in the beginning, but as my feelings grow for him, it is becoming more of a struggle.

He never made the classic mistake that a lot of guys do and use the friendship thing hoping that it would develop into more. Hoping that by being really nice around a woman, and by not showing his sexual attraction for her, she will see him as being different from all the other guys that hit on her. She will fall in love with him because he is not being disrespectful and has "good" intentions towards her. It amuses me when men think this way. There is a big difference between a woman really liking a guy as a friend and her really wanting to have sex with him.

On one hand, I may like a guy as a friend for different reasons like he is sweet, reliable, and someone I like to talk to and hang out with, without the pressure of having to dress in a sexy dress, or wear makeup, because in my mind I don't have to impress him. The flip side of the coin, is when I am around a man I want to have cunt-tingling sex with, or in a loving, committed relationship with, I will do whatever it takes to be more attractive to him, because he is actively triggering my feelings of sexual attraction. I am sure this is the case for most women.

"Does my request alarm you?" His voice pulls me back from my daydreaming.

"It does not alarm me, Teacher. I know that you give great thought to everything you ask us to do." I do not hesitate with my answer, after all it is the truth. I would do anything for this man, as would the others.

"What did you think of Martha's punishment for missing Vespers?" He changes direction without warning and I have to pause before answering.

"I thought it was necessary to reinforce the rules that you set out for the community. Without order, there is only chaos." My voice sounds as if it belongs to another. Have I become so obsessed with this man that I will say anything I believe will please him?

"Yes, we must discipline and control the mind and body. It is central in everything that we do. With this, we will experience a higher level of consciousness, openness and general well-being." His tone has become hypotonic and I hang on every word. It is so soothing and I could drink it in for hours.

"You are one of my keenest disciples and I sense that you want to push your limits. Would I be correct with that assumption, my child?" I wish he would not call me his child. It sounds so wrong. But what he says is the truth. I want to experience so much more.

"Yes, Teacher. I want to test my boundaries. I want to be found worthy of your trust and esteem. Tell me what to do and I will do it!" I blurt out my reply, almost too eager that I sound like an infatuated schoolgirl.

"That is good to hear. If at any time you want me to stop, then you must use a word of your choosing. What word would you like to use?" Now my mind goes into overdrive. I rack my brains for a word I could use. It comes to me out of the blue.

"Passion, I will use the word Passion if I want you to stop." It seemed apt as the term passion originates from Latin where it means suffering and pain.

"Well chosen." He smiles outwardly at me, which makes me feel warm inside. I am sure that he knows the meaning behind the word.

"Now, undress and kneel with your palms facing down on your thighs, back straight and look directly to your front!" He does not give me time to bathe in his smile, but commands me to obey him.

"Yes, Teacher." I fumble with the material of the robe at my shoulders and slip it over and it cascades to the floor.

The sensation of liberation as the cool evening air circulates around my areola, is stimulating. It is only heightened as Curtis reaches out and he cups my left breast, bringing it up slightly so that his lips encircle the bud. His tongue flickers over the surface and he applies a gentle pressure to the, now swelling, peak. His teeth bite softly down on it, teasing me even more and I squirm under his touch.

"Now kneel." His lips part from my skin and he stares directly in my eyes. The kindness is replaced by a wild, almost manic, look.

"Yes, Teacher." I obey him and lower myself to my haunches, then rest my knees on the floor before lowering my buttocks down so they rest on my heels. I look directly ahead and Curtis disappears from my view.

I can hear sounds behind me and my mind races to try and calculate what is going on. There is a creaking sound and then silence. The sound of his approaching feet is soft, but discernible. The light is extinguished as he ties a piece of material around my face. Just as in the recreational vehicle, my sight is taken from me. I am instantly aware of his body, scent and heat. His skin touches my bare shoulders and I shudder slightly. Fingers run through my hair massaging my scalp and I murmur softly. His hands move from my head, down to my neck and along my shoulders. The tips of his fingers tracing a line, barely touching the flesh, but enough to excite me and squeeze my legs together.

I feel him move around me with a graceful, silent stealth. My head jerks backward as something touches my upper lip. It is warm and sticky on the skin and covers my lip and septum with a silky coating. I instinctively push my tongue from between my lips and search out the source of the invasion. Just as it makes contact, a hand grasps tightly on my hair, pulling my head back.

"Do not taste me unless I say so. Is that clear?" Curtis warm breath ripples over my neck and he whispers rather forcefully in my ear.

"Yes, Teacher! I understand." He releases the grip on my hair and I bring my head back to its former position.

From my right-hand side, I hear a crack and a movement as I imagine him kneeling down in front of me. This is confirmed as his hands first rest on my shoulders and I feel him sway for a second or two before he gains his balance. His hands descend from my shoulders and in unison, cup each breast massaging them vigorously, with his thumbs circling the nipples. Then he pinches each one between his thumb and forefinger, causing me to wince. Fuck that feels so good! Once more, I press my legs together to attempt to quell the surging stream that is beginning to form, deep down between my thighs.

His hands descend once more and rest on my knees. With direct pressure, he pulls open my legs so that they are almost a shoulder-width apart. I relax my muscles and allow him to adjust me into the position he wants. I do not speak, nor does he. I take a deep breath and control my breathing, which is now becoming deep and slow. I bite down on my lip to give myself something to concentrate on. Then something touches my soaked pussy lips. It is only brief and from the sensation, I would say it is not human. It is soft and pliable and I feel it being drawn along the length of my opening. Not for long, but long enough for me to murmur out loud.

"Fuck yes!" I cannot help my outburst. The situation is so sexual, I think I will explode.

"You will speak when I say so, my child, and not before." He grips my jaw with one hand and his lips press hard against mine, sucking the air from my body. I capitulate and allow him to kiss me deeply.

His tongue probes my mouth and we perform a mutual dance, tasting one another. He breathes deeply through his nostrils and I do the same. The pounding of my heart is transferred to his chest as our bodies are pushed against one another. Just as I think I will collapse from lack of oxygen, he breaks the kiss. A finger strokes my cheek and I open my mouth. As if it is an invitation, I feel the bulbous head of his cock forcing itself between my lips. I open my mouth wider to allow it to pass. The shaft glides over my saliva-covered lips until the tip hits the back of my throat. He holds himself there for a second or two. Then pulls himself clear and my head drops with my chin resting on my breastbone. I cannot hide the disappointment.

"Stand up!" His voice has risen noticeably, as I can sense a change in mood.

"Yes, Teacher." I meekly reply and lean forward to use my hands to push myself up. The blood rushes from my upper to lower limbs causing the soles of my feet to tingle.

Curtis places his hands firmly on my shoulders once more. I stand there for a moment, trying to fight off the wave of complete disorientation. His thumbs have landed exactly where he intended, upon my upper-most trigger points where my neck meets my shoulders. He presses down and my shoulders fold backwards. He again presses harder, and my legs somewhat collapse under me. He does not allow me to fall, but catches me. With strength and ease, he manipulates my body so that I am rotated. Then holding my wrists together, he pushes me forward. I can feel his erect penis between the cheeks of my ass and I long to push back against him.

"Lean forward with your arms outstretched, palms flat against the wall." After a few paces, he halts my movements and issues his next command.

I do not answer. As he lets go of my wrist and my hands drop to my side, I raise them and shuffle forward until my palms make contact with the smooth surface of the wooden wall. I spread my legs shoulder-width apart and bend from the waist as the wall takes my weight. It is then that I feel something soft against my cheeks. My mouth is forced open and I can taste the leather of the strap which forces my lips open. The strap or belt is pulled tight and secured at the back of my neck. I groan lightly over the gag and I small amount of saliva builds up at the corners of my mouth.

His hands are upon me once more. Fingernails digging into my flesh and raking down either side of my spine. I shiver and the outer flesh is raised in goose bumps from the thrill. He continues to move down my back, thumbs pressing in hard followed by raking nails. Each time, I moan over the gag, and bend further forward, pushing my ass up and back. My spine arches at the same time, exposing and making taut the flesh of my back. I am fully attentive with pain awareness since he has deprived me the sense of sight. His hands sink, and he grabs onto my ass hard, with fingers and nails digging in. The breath is forced out of my body from between clenched teeth, as I succumb to the pleasure of the action.

"This flesh is full of sin!" He admonishes me, while at the same time massaging my buttocks with both hands.

He leans forward, his dick again forcing itself against me and I feel his chest pushing against my back. I feel his teeth dig into my right shoulder, hard! I scream softly over the gag. An arm encircles my waist, then moving up to my collarbone and working downward across the top of my left breast, his teeth dig in again. My legs weaken, and I feel his steadying hand grip me tighter. All I have now is my heartbeat, rushing blood and tingling flesh.

I suck in an abrupt breath when I feel the cool leather of the crop rest softly upon my shoulder. Yes! It has taken me until now to work out what the implement was that touched me down there. Curtis lets it slide, languorously down my back, over my ass and down my left thigh. Then as quickly as it appears, the sensation is gone. Not for long. It returns four times in rapid succession, two times on each of my ass cheeks. I try and scream through the leather belt but it comes out as a muffled moan. I struggle slightly against his body, mostly from surprise. He pushes me firmly against the wall.

Before the sting of the first has subsided, more fall upon my upper back and my thighs. He takes careful aim in-between my legs, smacking at my inner thighs. I am shuddering ever so slightly, caught between the sensation of escaping the pain and falling into it. Suddenly it is his nails I am feeling again, clawing at the inside of my outstretched arms raking downward to my ribs and my hips and deep into my thighs. The roughness of his finger, rubbing against the swollen bud of my clit, causes me to convulse against him. I cannot fold. I cannot curl up. I will myself to hold back the tide that threatens to unleash between my legs.

"That's a good girl. Hold it there. It will be so much sweeter in the end." His cheek presses against mine as his fingers manipulate my throbbing bud. His hot breath against me.

I am almost bereft of oxygen, my heart ready to burst from my chest. I can feel, almost smell, a light amusement about him, as if he is enjoying every second of his temptation.

The crop returns between my legs, and he brings it in rapid, accurate, stunning delivery against my opening. I am so close now and I begin to hyperventilate. Unexpectedly, his hands are gone, and I am left wondering and waiting again. They return with a vengeance, roughly grabbing my right breast and pulling out the flesh of the nipple, extending it. Once more, I bite down on my lip to take my mind off the orgasm that is fast approaching. I feel my body sag and quiver as his other hand rubs my clit with even more fervour.

"Now my child, cum for me!" At last! Those words are like music to my ears.

The burning between my legs does not fade, merely intensifies and cannot be blocked. I feel a stinging against my ass as the crop rains down on my flesh. His fingers still work on my clit and I see stars before my eyes. I have never felt this before. I can feel my flesh become hot through the pain, which is building more and more with every strike. Only to be matched by the fire that is building in my cunt! By this time, I cannot control the tears that have been welling and seeping out from under the blindfold. My body begins to shake with sobs. They are sobs of pleasure as he presses his body against me and brings me over the edge.

The warmth and sheer presence of his body is beyond soothing to me. The left arm wraps around my waist, as my tears subside, and I am anticipating a full embrace. I am not disappointed and he draws me to him and I rest my head on his shoulder, the stiffness of his erection against the delicate skin of my inner thigh. I am panting rapidly from the exertion of my climax. Curtis softly strokes my hair and unties the blindfold. Our eyes meet in the most touching of moments. There is no need for words, but he speaks anyway.

"Well done, my child. You are the best of my pupils. I see a long future for us together." That was all I wanted to hear. To know that I have pleased him.

He begins to unbuckle the belt that was preventing me from speaking and drops it to the floor. His head descends again to my shoulder and I feel the exquisite bite of his teeth. The aftershock of my orgasm ripples through me. I sigh, now that I am able and tilt my head to one side to allow him better access. I am trembling uncontrollably now. With both hands upon my shoulders, he releases his grip with his teeth and steps back. He pushes me down so that my eyes pass his chest, lips only inches away from that well-chiselled, tattooed body.

"Now it is my turn, to receive atonement of my sins." His hands force my head down, until my mouth greets his swollen cock.

I let his shaft run through my fingers, as I gently masturbate the veiny rod. The blood surging through it makes it come alive under my touch. I take him deep in my mouth, cupping his heavy balls in one hand, massaging them as my head bobs up and down on his meat. I would commit murder a thousand times for this man, just to feel like I do now.

CHAPTER EIGHTEEN - CURTIS

The footpath flows through the forest, my footfall covered by the sound of evening birdsong. The path was broken; at times, with twisted tree roots as it meanders its course deep into the darkness. Mighty trees arch over me, forming a protective guard. It is as if they are welcoming me into their secret world. There were hoofprints and footprints embedded in the path from the many tourists who use the trails up here in the hills. Each print a memory of their passing. I am not interested in their story. It is the lone, hunched figure that navigates the path some fifty-feet in front of me. I step off the path into the shadows of the trees, as it turns now and again, checking that it is not being followed.

Somewhere along this path are the answers I need. I have suspected, for some time now, that Peter is not all that he appears. I run my hands along the cooling bark and gentle foliage as I pass along the edge of the path, keeping myself concealed from sight. Peter continues on, happy that he is not being followed. The utter blackness of night-time in the woods is a childhood memory. A nightmare that would visit me from time to time. The black trunks against a bluish charcoal sky, the path a deepest brown and the moonlight would bleach the stones within it. The moonlight's silvery rays do not penetrate the thick canopy of this place. I follow on behind, deeper into the darkness.

All of sudden Peter stops, he turns around once more, his gaze penetrating the dark shadows. I crouch down behind the nearest tree, but from that distance he would not be able to see me. He listens intently, to the forest attempting to discern any sound that is alien. I can feel the beating of my heart in my chest growing louder. It is not anxiety that has caused this, but an anger that is formed from betrayal.

Rage was never really a choice for me. Not something I could easily control. I'm afraid if I ever let go and just really feel it, I'll blow up the whole world! I have feared the enormity of the repressed emotions caged up inside of me, for what seems like most of my life. I have always feared what might happen if I were to just let the dam burst and let the rage flow from me. I learned, over time, to train my mind to count to ten and walk away. But anger, at all levels, is more than just behaviour. I would equate anger with hitting out at someone or something. When I didn't do this, then it was a small victory.

Peter drops to his knees and begins to fumble around at the root of a tree. I creep forward silently, careful not to disturb any foliage or give warning of my presence. Peter is oblivious to me as he retrieves something from the base of the tree. I cannot make it out from my position, but it appears to be a small box. He opens the lid and takes out a number of items and places them in the rucksack he has brought with him. Then he unfurls a piece of white paper and his head scans back and forth briefly before returning the note to the box and placing it back in its concealed position. I fucking knew there was something not right about this piece of shit!

I believe that it is sometimes fear that brings rage. A hot, searing anger that seeks to harm. When we feel threatened or are frightened by something, then it is a primitive reaction for the brain to produce aggression. So, my whole life, my brain has continually been triggered into acting this way. The rage that built up inside me destroying any sense of belonging or community, leaving only suspicion and fear. I have been let down all my days, from my mother to the lecherous monks at the Abbey. Is it not surprising that, from time to time, I need the real me to take over, find a calm space in this crazy life and breathe until I feel love again? I fight against that overwhelming urge right now. Tonight is not the time and this is not the place. I retreat further back into the shadows and observe as Peter makes his way back towards the temple and the community.

As he passes by my concealed body, I feel a deep sense of betrayal and loathing. To me, there are two types of betrayal. That of romantic betrayal is probably the worse, but for someone like me, it is the betrayal of a friend that cuts deepest. Someone who you have given your trust to, have opened yourself up to and allowed to get close. We have grown as a close community and shared everything about ourselves. Not only sexually, but physically and emotionally. To invest time and effort into building something like this makes the duality of this piece of shit's actions even more cutting. I had elevated him to the position of my right hand man and thought that we were both on the same wavelength. It was only lately, since our move to our new home, did I notice a change in him that I couldn't quite explain. He seemed to have distanced himself from my teachings and was not as involved in our mutual lovemaking and sharing of ourselves. His faith I have never been in question of, having found him ardently reading the scriptures in his spare time. That would be the perfect cover for someone sent to observe a person like me. Who the fuck is this guy? I am going to find out and he will suffer for trying to intercede in my grand design and plan.

I allow Peter to make his way back the way he came. He is out of sight by the time I emerge from the undergrowth. I am still trying to process how he could betray me in this way. What is it about me that attracts his kind of poisonous wretch? All I wanted was to be adored and followed. The scriptures were the perfect vehicle to gather together young people with the same impressionable outlook on life. Until now, my plan seemed to have been faultless. Yes, I do believe in a supreme being. A great architect that designed this universe which we now inhabit. The acts of the creatures that he placed on its surface surely were not in his image. How such a magnificent creation could be tainted with such aberrations. This divine being sat back and watched as his creations abused the young and weak. If he was not willing to intervene, then I most certainly will.

I glance at the luminous dial of my wristwatch and increase the length of my stride. It will be time for the last prayers of the day in less than half an hour and I cannot break my own rules. The darkness conceals me as I depart the woods and move in the shadows to the rear of the house. I slip off my shoes, which are covered in dirt, and leave them on the porch. As I enter the house, the sounds of voices carry as Tabitha and Magdalene pass by the kitchen on their way to prayer. I step from the kitchen into the hallway and am met face-to-face with Peter. His face does not show any evidence of guilt. He is the perfect actor, but this particular film set is not one he would have chosen if he knew what I have in store.

"Good evening, brother. It is a beautiful night for a late, relaxing stroll." My greeting, which is meant to sow a seed of doubt, is met with a nod of his head and a wry smile.

"It is indeed, Teacher. Perhaps I will take some air after prayers." The lies drip effortlessly from those silken lips and I take a deep breath to control my anger.

"When are you leaving to carry out my instructions?" His look is guarded and he appears a little nervous as he prepares to answer.

"Everything is ready. I have asked the others to meet at my truck around an hour after prayers." The uncertainty from moments earlier has gone and is replaced by his usual confidence.

"Good, good. Now let us go and beseech the Lord for strength in carrying out his will." I place my arm around Peter's shoulder and we walk side-by-side into the chapel.

The last murmur of Amen rings around the room and I look about the joyous faces of my flock. It surprises me how easily they have bent to my will. How simple it has been to manipulate them to do my bidding. That imbalance of power where they serve my agenda. My dominance of them is not only sexually stimulating, but makes me almost understand why the priests did what they did. So much has happened since I left the Abbey. I have grown as a person. This has not just been intellectually, but emotionally as well. With Magdalene, I've been tempted to enter into a relationship that would be more than one-sided. A relationship that could be built into something beautiful. All I needed was time. That is the crux of the problem, as I fear that time is running short for me.

I look directly at Peter, who returns my gaze with a smile that would be befitting Judas Iscariot. Yes, Peter or whatever is your real name. You would kiss me on one cheek with those lips and betray me as quick with the same. I have become an excellent reader of people and this fucker is oblivious to my suspicions. I make the sign of the cross and give the customary blessing.

"May God go with you, my children, and I will see you at morning prayers. Peter, I will bid you goodbye before you leave." I remind Peter and the others of tonight's operation. This will be the final test of obedience. The complete community have carried out all manner of things, but never something like this.

"Yes, Teacher." Peter bows his head in recognition.

One by one the group disperse and leave the chapel. There seems to be an excited buzz about the community. The main centre of attraction being the small group that were preparing to carry out my instructions. Some of the group were a little disappointed that they were not chosen for this task. It just goes to show how I have influenced them in our short time together. I could have built something great here, and as I look at each of them in turn, I feel a pang of regret.

For the next hour, I busy myself in my cell. I read through the newspaper cuttings I have arranged in a large open leaf ledger. I can't help the great sense of satisfaction as I read each one. If my flock were to know the real person who was leading their church, would they be so eager to follow me? If they were to read through my litany of past acts committed in the name of retribution, how many would agree with me? That is immaterial as I entered down that path and I have almost reached my journey's end.

I close the scrapbook and put it back in its hiding place, in the hidden compartment in my wooden chest. I place the heavy metal padlock back in place and turn the key one full turn clockwise before returning the key around my neck. The sound of voices outside causes me to make my way quickly from my room to join the small group waiting to depart. Tonight we will rewrite humanity on my terms.

Magdalene is sharing a joint with the others who already seem to be quite high. I just hope they've got their shit together for this! Of course, Captain Sensible Peter is as cool as a cucumber, as if he was about to embark on a normal night out with some friends. I need to know what makes this guy tick and who the fuck he actually is. I should have enough time before they return to have a look around his cell and belongings.

"Good luck for tonight, brothers and sisters! May God be with you." I go to each in turn and kiss them on both cheeks. I linger with Magdalene, kissing her on the lips as well.

"Thank you, Teacher. We must be off now." Peter rebuffs me slightly and climbs into the truck. The others follow his example. He most definitely has a leadership quality about him, which annoys the fuck out of me.

The vehicle's engine roars into life and with a screeching of tyres on the dried ground, Peter steers the truck out of the compound. I stand and watch as it gradually disappears into the night in a cloud of dust, before returning to the house and the direction of Peter's private cell.

I peer into his communal living space which, by luck, is empty of his roommates. I take the chance and quickly search through his belongings. It does not take me long as none of us has many possessions, as I stipulated in the beginning. What we have, we share. After checking his locker, I turn my attention to his bedside table. A picture of the Virgin Mary and child looks up at me from the table next to the bed. The rosary beads and crucifix hanging across it. There is nothing out of the ordinary that would give me any clue as to Peter's real identity. That in itself is strange, as most of the Seekers of the Way have little reminders of their former lives. This only drives me on to find something.

I make my way from the room, just as Thomas returns from his evening walk. He bids me goodnight, but does not ask what I was doing. I am disappointed, but not at all surprised, that I did not find anything among Peter's possessions. One thing that I did observe was the lack of anything that reminded him of his life before the commune. Not one single memory of family or friends. I will have to check his vehicle later after his return.

First, I need to find out if he has anything hidden in his private cell in the basement. I pause at the top of the stairs and peer down into the gloom below. It is time for my eyes to adjust to the difference in light. I have illuminated the space, but only just enough so that you can safely descend the stairs.

The sound of my sandals shuffling against the cold concrete steps is magnified by the enclosed space. The air is cool and I wrap my robe tighter around my body. On reaching the foot of the staircase, I locate the ladder that assists on gaining access to the level that is dug out of the rock, just ten to twelve feet above the main catacombs. There is a basic cell for each of my disciples carved into the hillside. I pass by three until I come to Peter's. Each cell is identical with a single wooden bed and mattress and a hook with a cilice and flagellation implement hanging from it. It is designed to replicate the cells of the priests in the Abbey.

My eyes move from right to left, piercing into the darkness but, as I suspected, there is nothing here that would indicate Peter is anything other than a devout follower. I didn't know what I thought I would find and perhaps I was making more out of it than I should. I think I might just broach the subject when he returns. Get things out in the open, as I could, of course, be mistaken. I turn to leave when my attention is drawn to the bible resting at the top of the bed. Something inside me compels me to pick it up. I flick through the pages until I find myself staring at something from within the well-thumbed tome.

Two faces stare back at me. One is a pretty young female who appears to be in her mid-twenties. The other is an infant being held in the arms of the woman. It is such a happy, joyful looking image. Is it Peter with his mother? The photograph is almost pristine so I discount that theory. That only leaves one other choice. The image I am looking at is the wife and child of this traitor in our midst. Even though I suspected there was more to him than he let on, it was still a shock to have it confirmed.

I return the picture to the bible and flick through the remaining pages. Not expecting to find anything, my eyes widen as a few pages from the back, a bright white piece of paper is contrasted against the cream, worn pages of the scriptures. My hands are shaking as I unfold it and begin to read through the handwritten notes that are embossed on its pages. Names dates of everyone in the community, from our first meetings in the bar, where I began as a singer, through to this last few days. My name features heavily in this makeshift diary. Just simple words beginning with things like, likeable, charismatic, religious, devout, non-threatening. Then over the past few months the wording has become a little more sinister as Peters opinion of me changes. The last sentences I read have me reeling. *"Informed handler of targets intentions and waiting for authorisation to carry out my plan."*

I fucking knew it! The bile rises up from my stomach and I fight to control the urge to empty my stomach on the cell floor. The act of betrayal has that kind of effect on me and on anyone, I imagine. If I could get my hands on Peter right now, I would not be responsible for my actions. I sink down onto the bed and gather my thoughts.

Human beings are just programmes that destroy everything. I want to change that. I will create through destruction. I realise that I might be playing God and that we might be flawed for a reason, but I just want to fix people. Some might call it revenge for wrongs done in the past. Perhaps someone who thinks they know the answer to life is full of shit. I don't sign up to that way of thinking. It has been a while since I heard his voice, but it returns with a vengeance.

"Here I am, my friend, your own personal conduit to the Lord." Tom grins at me inanely, just like he always does.

"Do not take his name in vain!" I'm not in the mood for his smug ways.

"It is you that is the problem, not humankind, man. I thought ending the others would put a stop to all of this." That is not what I want to hear at this moment in time.

"I don't know how I became real, but if this is what being broken feels like, fuck!"

"Curtis, you can make any choice that you want. We could stop all this crazy shit and just live our fucking lives." What the fuck? He was the one who set me off down this path.

"I don't understand."

"I've been thinking. None of this matters. None of it is worth it. You know, like people aren't worth it."

"What are you saying?"

"There is more to life. So much more to life. Enjoy yourself. Fuck saving everyone. You and your noble "one man crusade" for the young and innocent."

"I did it for us. You know that I did it for us and all who suffered at the hands of the fucking black-robed monsters! I need to fix this. I need to fix us."

"That's what this has been all along. You don't want to save the world. You just want to fix your crazy, broken mind. No amount of extinguishing lives of paedophiles, can put back together what has been taken from you, and those you purport to represent, in your vengeance." His words hit home like an arrow to the heart. I know he is right. I have known for some time.

"There is just one more and this will all be over. You know I have to do it." My conscience stares back at me and he shrugs his shoulders.

I take a joint from my top pocket and light it up. The sweet taste of the cannabis fills my mouth. I feel my cheeks pinch on the first inhalation, but this is replaced by a mellow sensation. After each toke, my body begins to relax, but my mind is still racing over my recent discovery. The face of my conscience begins to fade, as the effects of the pot and the other pills I took earlier causes me to drift off.

The sound of voices from up above me startle me out of my stupor. I shake my head and run my fingers through my hair. I rise from the bed of the cell and rub my eyes in an attempt to become a little more lucid. I really need to get on top of this habit as it is becoming almost uncontrollable. It seems that I am under its influence more than I am not and that is not good. I make my way from the cell and ascend the steps out of the catacomb.

On opening the door and stepping into the hallway, I can't believe what my eyes see. Gathered in a close group are my killing party. Two of the girls have a figure draped between them. A muffled sound comes from the hood that has been fastened around the head. Peter has a larger body thrown motionless over his shoulder. I do not even try and process the scene. All I know is, this is not what I ordered.

"What the fuck is going on here?" The sound of my voice alerts the group to my presence and they freeze in their tracks.

They all, as one, look in the direction of Peter who is carrying his body, as if it was nothing. If it had been anyone else, I would have expected a look of fear in their eyes for disobeying my orders. Not with Peter, or whoever he is fucking called. He just returns my gaze with a steely one of his own and speaks confidently.

"I thought we could use them for ransom to further our cause." The group turn from him to me, waiting to see what my reaction will be. I let a minute or so pass, keeping them guessing while holding a straight poker face.

"Now that is not a bad idea." There is a huge sense of relief on the faces of all at my reply. I should have received an Oscar for that, I think to myself. That devious fucker will get what is coming to him!

CHAPTER NINETEEN - MAGDALENE

Everything that Curtis has taught us, I have gone along with. The one thing that is most difficult for me, is sharing him with the others. When I see him, all I can think is there he is, he is all mine. His rugged good looks with strong jaw and perfect body. Not the clean-shaven all-American, Ivy League guy that my parents planned for me to marry. That hint of danger, charisma and mystique, but above all, the dominant way he commanded your attention without even trying. It was this confidence, intelligence and kindness that he exuded that drew me to him. He is the kind of guy that makes you feel safe, special and protected in his company.

Before we met, I was never one to be told what to do. I was quite a rebel; some might call me a brat. It wasn't long before that was all eroded under his tutelage. He introduced me to a subspace with its own set of rules and physical properties, but with boundaries. I never thought that I would submit to this, but I actually miss and crave it when it is denied me. He makes it so easy for us to leave our normal emotional state and everyday worries and enter a reality where we can truly be ourselves.

He put so much thought into creating a physical space, where the altered state of reality is not just in the mind, but in the surroundings too. The catacombs were the perfect place and the intentionally designed settings make it easier to get into the mood of an interaction. To enter a psychological state where all the worries, cares, underlying thoughts, and emotions are stripped away, and our deepest, darkest fantasies can become reality. I feel completely safe in his presence. Nothing existed except him, and the experience of this Dominant/submissive relationship. It is not the kind of relationship I saw for us at the start, but I am growing to understand how the pain, obedience and devotion can free and sharpen the mind.

In the beginning, I was fascinated on his fervour and unique thoughts on the Bible. His ideas of building a new community and living in harmony without outside influences were spellbinding. Of course, I was not the only one. Every person in the community believed that there was something special about him and his vision. It appears recently, though, that his preaching has turned more from the Bible to the political and socioeconomic state of the country. He still uses the scriptures to reinforce some of his rules and highlight any similarities from today and the times of Jesus and his followers. The tasks that we were given, from time to time, seemed also to have grown in frequency and daring.

They began with us wandering the local forests like wraiths, quiet and stealthy. We would watch tourists who would use the area for camping and hunting trips. Oblivious to our presence, Curtis would command us to steal items of value, which we could sell to provide some kind of income to supplement that of the produce we sold at the local market in Sebastopol. I remember approaching him and offering to provide a much needed injection of cash. With the money my parents put in trust for me now available, I was only willing to hand it over, if it would please Curtis. His reaction was something I was not prepared for.

It's a mystery that we humans have certain positive and negative emotions and feelings. Without these emotions our lives would be so drab and dull. So psychologically, anger is a fact of life, but the level of it differs from person to person. From being infants, we struggle with anger and frustration. This is only magnified as we grow and the primitive fantasies of aggression and guilt become more noticeable. We grow up with anger from the beginning of our lives. It is a common part of our lives, but it is how we deal with it that differs from person to person.

I have never really seen this in Curtis, until now. Yes, I have seen him mildly irritated by things that have been said or done by other members of the group. However, I have not experienced him dealing with criticism, or simply not getting his own way. My offer was a genuine one and not meant to go against his plan or belittle him in anyway. As a community, we have made a good start and all I wanted was to give us a bit of financial security to build on what we already have created.

"Are you the devil incarnate? Are you trying to tempt me from my holy path?" His eyes burn with anger so bright, they sear into my very soul.

"No, Teacher, I did not mean to tempt you. Forgive me." I lower my head in supplication.

"I will not yield to the forces of evil and you must be shown how to guard yourself from such incursions from the dark one. Your mind must be strong against his will. Go to my cell in the catacomb! You will undress and cleanse your flesh with the lash. You will then wait for my arrival. Is that understood?"

"Yes, Teacher." I raise my head to look at him and the glare in his eyes still remains. It is matched by the burning of his lips, as he kisses mine passionately.

"Then go!" He releases my chin and I turn and run back towards the house.

Curtis' cell was larger than the rest, with a full length mirror at one end. It contained a leather bench that was at waist height and a pair of medieval looking stocks stood against the right hand wall. I observe the flogger hanging from its hook next to the mirror and undress as I walk towards it. I throw my robe onto the wooden bed and retrieve the leather flogger from the rack. I turn and face my reflection in the mirror, admiring how my flesh is illuminated in the meagre light of the space. Curtis had not said how many lashes I was to give myself, so I decide on a minimum of ten. If he requires me to do more, he will order it.

As the final strike tears at my skin, I sense someone watching me. I peer into the mirror and behind my reflection, framed in the door stands Priscilla. She is wearing a pair of red lace up boots which are laced tight up her slender legs. My eyes are drawn to her wasp-like waist and generous hips. The dark crimson material of the boots contrasts with her pale but unblemished skin. Her dark pubic mound is visible, as she is not wearing any panties. Around her torso and hips she wears a twisted garment made of black leather strips, criss-crossing her flesh, leaving her breasts and sex bare. Curtis has begun to buy clothing, such as she is wearing, for special nights of punishment and instruction. I feel a pang of jealousy that Priscilla has been chosen to wear one this evening. That being said, from the throbbing in my clit, she is fucking hot!!

Her nipples are thick, tight, proud already and of similar colouring to her boots. The leather straps are pulling her small breasts into hard peaks. Her mane of dark, long hair falls in a twist over her left shoulder. Seductively, she runs her finger down the edge of the door frame. Her other hand meanders over her flat stomach before descending down between her legs. She pauses there for a second before reaching across to her left. The sinews of her arm tighten as she pulls something towards her. The hooded figure of Curtis appears at her side. His bright blue eyes piercing the darkness of the shroud of his robe. His pearly-white, even teeth, breaking the darkness as he smiles in a salacious manner. In a theatrical way he steps forward, pulling the willing Priscilla to him. Step by step they advance into the room towards me. If there were an audience, I would imagine you would be able to hear a pin drop at this point.

They both halt only two paces from me. I can't help admiring the perfect symmetry of Pricilla's body. The tightly placed straps pull her flesh into a provocative pose and I involuntarily lick my lips. This does not go unnoticed by Curtis, who leers at me as if it was the reaction he wanted.

"You like what you see, don't you, my child?" His husky voice breaks the drama and silence.

"I do, yes, Teacher!" My reply is almost a breathless whisper, as my temperature and heartbeat rise at the sight of my beautiful sister.

"Then that is perfect. Now it is my turn to play the part of Satan and you will fight your carnal urges, unless I say otherwise. Is that completely understood?" His voice has turned harsh and his eyes burn even brighter, if that was possible.

"I understand, Teacher." I lower my gaze to the floor in submission to his will.

Pricilla was scouring the cell, checking out the devices that inhabited the space. Her eyes fell on the medieval stocks to her right. She let go of Curtis' hand and wanders over to give it a closer inspection. Her hands run along the smooth, black surface of the device, her fingers trailing over the metal hinges and clasps.

"This is the first time I have seen this. Did you build it yourself, Teacher?" Her voice sounds as if she is in a dream. That is probably from the pot she has consumed during the day.

"Yes, it is a replica of something from my past. I thought it would be a fitting addition for my room of contemplation." He turns to look at Priscilla, before returning his attention to me.

"It is gorgeous. A true thing of beauty." Priscilla lifts the wooden structure, which is separated by a hinge at one end. It has a hole in the centre with two smaller ones approximately four inches from each end.

Priscilla glances back at Curtis, who is examining my reaction to the device closely. I cannot hide the thrill that is running through my body. I can't wait to try out this contraption and let him do what he wants. What happens next, I was not expecting.

"I am so pleased you like it, my child. You will be the first to feel its touch." He addresses Priscilla, but his eyes do not

leave mine, wanting to see the hurt in my eyes. He is not disappointed.

"May I, Teacher?" There is an excited tone to Priscilla's voice as she indicates the stocks.

"Of course, my child. Come. Magdalene, kneel and place your palms downwards on your thighs." I do not question the instruction and lower myself immediately to my knees and settle myself into a comfortable position.

Curtis takes Priscilla by the hand, leading her towards the device. Once he has escorted her to the device, he makes his way around it and faces her. He takes her by both hands and rests her wrists in the cutaways. Then he cups her chin in his hand and with the other, applies pressure so that her head is lowered on the half-moon at the bottom. Satisfied that she is comfortable, he lowers the top half of the stocks and secures them shut with a sliding bolt on the left hand side. In three strides, he steps to just behind her and crouches. I never noticed before, but there are leather shackles at the foot of each of the uprights. He fastens her in place so that her legs are spread wide apart. Her sex is bulging and glistening wet with arousal. Curtis uses two fingers of one hand to part her lips so that I get a better view. He looks directly at me as his finger slips effortlessly inside her. She murmurs out loud and I close my eyes for a moment and press my thighs together.

"You will not avert your gaze! Stand up and come here!" Curtis commands me in that way only he can, that demands complete adherence.

"Yes, Teacher, at once." I take my weight on the palms of my hands and leaning forward, I aid myself to stand.

Curtis watches me carefully, his finger sliding in and out of Priscilla, in time to each step I take closer to him. It is like he is keeping time to a sexual ballet, and only stops when I am two paces from him.

"Kneel there." He points just to the left of the stocks, but his voice has taken on a more compassionate tone. I silently carry out his instruction and he waits until I have shuffled into position.

I gaze intently at Curtis as he withdraws his finger, covered in Priscilla's silky juices. He sensually parts his lips just enough so that his finger can pass between them. He licks his finger, slowly tasting her and delighting in the effect it is having on me. He pulls his finger from his mouth and runs it around my lips. I can smell that sweet, sticky potion and have an urge to flicker my tongue out and taste it for myself. That is the test, I know. He lingers there before moving his hand down my neck applying a little pressure around my neck, feeling the pulse of my carotid artery as the excitement in me pumps the blood faster around my body. He lowers himself and his robe falls open and my eyes are in line with his erect cock. He pays it no attention, but rests his hand on my knee, then runs it along the inside of my thigh. There is no finesse as he roughly probes my cunt to see how aroused I have become.

"Good girl! I see that the temptation is having its desired effect. Be strong, my child; rewards await those who hold firm." His warm breath washes over the skin of my breasts, as he flickers his tongue over the nipple and I have to suppress the murmur of satisfaction.

I move my body so that my breast is forced against him, but he releases the nipple and stands once more. He can be such a bastard and knows exactly how to press my buttons.

"Magdalene is horny as fuck, my child. Have you ever seen such a look of wanton desire? Shall we make her beg for release, my child?" Curtis yanks on Priscilla's long hair, forcing her head around to look towards me.

"Oh yes, Teacher!" She purrs like a feline and wiggles her ass.

From my kneeling position, I am in the ultimate place to see every little movement from both Curtis and Priscilla. This is going to be torture, I just know it.

"Maybe being degraded will teach Magdalene her place, and not to try and tempt me with materialistic things." There is a definite hint of sarcasm in his reply, at my fortunate family upbringing.

"Why don't you give her that stool so she can look me in the eyes as you give me everything she is to be denied?" That was a rather vicious blow and not one I expected from a sister and a seeker of the way. I guess we are all changing, and some not for the best.

"An excellent idea!" Curtis exclaims and leaps to his feet and retrieves the small stool from the corner of the room.

"Sit here. Legs open and hands on thighs. I want to see that wet cunt of yours." He manhandles me onto the wooden stool, and I am only about ten to twelve inches away and in line with Priscilla's head.

Curtis steps back and pulls back the cowl of his hood. It reveals that set of strong, thick, dark hair. Since coming to this place, he has it cut a lot shorter than the fashion of these times, but it frames his handsome features elegantly. He slowly slips the robe down over his broad shoulders and allows it to fall to the floor. His testicles are round and full and his hand fondles them gently. I feel my breath hitch and I bite down on my lips. I would love to have those fleshy orbs in my mouth, sucking on that sensitive skin.

"You have the perfect view there, my child. Does it excite you as I do this?" He leans forward so that I imagine his shaft resting between Priscilla's buttocks. His hands grasp both of her breasts and massages them roughly, tweaking the already taught nipples between fingers and thumbs.

"Fuck yes, teacher!" Priscilla's outburst interrupts my own answer, which is a split second after.

"Yes, Teacher! It really does excite me." The sound of desperation in me is difficult to conceal, even more so as he begins to spank her ass cheeks in turn. I would give anything to exchange places right now.

Things are pushed to a higher erotic state as Curtis runs his fingers through her long hair. Then he grasps hold of it and like a cowboy riding a bronco he pulls back on her head. Due to the stocks, her movement is restricted but her head is lifted and she stares me straight in the eyes. A faint grin paints her face as the slapping sound of hand on flesh grows ever louder. My breathing is almost ragged now, as my arousal grows and I feel my juices dribbling down and pooling on the wooden seat. I fight not to move my hands to my opening and pleasure myself at the scene being played out before me.

Curtis grabs hold of her right hip, and with his other, furls his hand around his throbbing piece of meat. The veins are standing high, like rivers on a three dimensional map. A bead of perspiration has appeared on his brow. I settle back a little to watch, concentrating my mind on not cumming. This will be a tough task, as with a loud grunt and explosive thrust, he pushes himself deep inside her.

"Fuck yeah, baby!! That is what I need. Fuck that pussy like you hate it!" Priscilla has become possessed as Curtis pounds in and out of her. With every forward movement, the stocks shake a little from the force. The sound of flesh on flesh is

intoxicating and even if I look away, I have the image planted firmly in my mind.

"Kiss your sister and suck on those titties!" Curtis once more commands me and as usual, I obey without reservation.

Her lips taste so sweet and I feast hungrily on each of her breasts. He is the devil incarnate, delighting in my frustration at not receiving his attentions. I am beginning to learn that maybe he does not have the same feelings towards me, as I do to him. There is a maliciousness to some of his decisions that border on the sadistic.

"Now come here and watch as I defile that sweet, tight ass!" He screams at me and I let Priscilla's nipple fall from my mouth.

"Yes, Teacher." I begrudgingly rise from the stool and navigate my way around the contraption. I stand to the right of Curtis, so that I can see him pull his dick free from my sister's dripping cunt.

"I want you to lick her clit, while I pound her ass. Now get down there and show me how much you want me to fuck her!" He is becoming slightly disconnected from what the original punishment was supposed to correct.

While my whole body is tingling with slow expectation, a stillness drops over the room as I settle down between Priscilla's legs. I am facing, at eye level, Curtis' cock, which is still shimmering with her juices. His testicles hang heavy and I resist reaching out and cupping them in my palm. I shuffle forward and the tip of my nose makes contact with my sister's folds. The sweet aroma of her sex is pervasive and I flicker my tongue over her clit, which is swollen and full. She sighs out loud as I lick around the bud with slow, languid strokes in a circular motion.

"Good girl. Now taste this, my child." A pressure against my chin and a sticky sensation causes me to halt my attention.

I pull away from her opening and the tip of Curtis' penis is resting at the corner of my mouth. He holds it by the shaft and runs the smooth, bulbous head around my lips. My tongue tastes the silky secretions before allowing it to enter my mouth. I glide my head forward, taking him fully inside and with an applied use of suction, pull my head rearward. After only two or three of these movements, he seems frustrated and forcefully pulls back.

"That is enough! You have not earned my seed just yet. Although I feel that your sister would like that. Am I right, my child?" He directs his question to Priscilla, who is quivering in anticipation.

"Yes, Teacher." It is more of a whisper now and I wish I was in her place.

Without another word, I observe as Curtis moves the tip of his dick between her ass cheeks before once more grasping hold of both hips. In one fluid, aggressive thrust of his own hips, he pushes himself deep inside her. He wriggles for a moment, seating himself fully to the hilt before slowly building up a forward and rearward rhythm. His balls are hypnotising as they swing more violently, as his tempo increases. Still watching as commanded, I lick tentatively at Priscilla's pussy, probing my tongue deep inside her. I am disturbed as his balls make contact with my cheek as he rides her faster and faster.

The frame of the stock begins to creak louder as he nears his climax. I, myself, feel as if I will explode at any moment, but I manage to stop from touching myself down there. I don't want to fail his test. Mercifully, before I know it, his whole body begins to stiffen and Priscilla's wails reverberate throughout the whole catacomb. I am sure that her cries of pleasure will be heard from above.

"Yes, Yes!!" Curtis' fingers grip her hips even tighter, her flesh discoloured from the force.

"Oh my fucking God! Give me that sweet cum!" She has lost herself as the combined efforts of my tongue and Curtis' cock, brings her to climax.

"Receive the Lord's bountiful harvest, my child!" Curtis pounds into her and throws his head back, as his thighs lock and spurts his semen deep inside her ass.

The sounds of sex and pleasure slowly subside and the place returns, once more, to silence. All I can hear is the laboured breathing of both of them. My face is covered with Priscilla's cum and I watch as Curtis' seminal fluid runs from her ass into her vagina, mixing in a sexual, carnal soup. At that moment in time, I feel a profound sense of disappointment and deep regret. I don't know why, but for the first time since meeting Curtis, I have doubts about him. I watch in a resigned silence, as he unfetters her from the contraption and puts on his robe once more.

"Leave us, my child." He kisses Priscilla on the cheek and she returns it before leaving us alone.

I watch her as she leaves and the feelings I just experienced towards Curtis, are coupled with ones of fear and apprehension. There is a definite sense of evil and foreboding that fills the space. It is almost something you can taste. I shiver as I raise my head to look into Curtis' eyes, and he extends his hand and speaks.

"Rise, my child. Come, you shall sleep with me this evening." Those eyes reveal something that I have dismissed all of this time. It is almost satanic and I shiver as I take his hand and rise.

CHAPTER TWENTY - CURTIS

I don't know what makes people want to be friends. I don't know what makes people attractive to one another. I don't know why people want to socially interact. I was never a person who knew how to deal with empathy. In fact, I don't believe I have an empathetic bone in my body. I have tried my hardest to portray myself as this kind of person. It was key to me making my story believable. A vision of a future where everyone lived together in peace, love and harmony, for the good and benefit of mankind, was an honourable one. A utopian society of free love and empathy. All of this was, of course, bullshit! I don't give a damn about anyone except myself. I have always been a self-centred individual. My mother and foster carers made sure of that.

I think the cracks are beginning to show and I have noticed a change in some of the others recently. In particular, Magdalene does not seem as completely besotted with me as she was. Yes, they all seem attentive and follow my instructions without question. I have persuaded them to commit acts that go against their normal characters, but they did them all because of their devotion to me. This, of course, was what I craved. The adoration and love that I have been missing all of my life. A little bit of history repeated itself, as on a few occasions, the females of the group lured unsuspecting men back to motel rooms where they were relieved of their hard-earned cash. The memories of my mother come flooding back and I find it almost ironic.

With regards to Magdalene, what started out to be a romantic journey for both of us, slowly turned into a one-sided affair. Thoughts and experiences from my past lingering there in the shadows, always waiting to emerge. Her willingness to participate most fervently in all things which involved submission and pain, was something I could not resist. Maybe this would be the first time that I could commit to a relationship. But, that fear of commitment and taking on responsibility vanquished any idealised notions like that. A relationship to me is a series of cost and benefits when you look at it critically. Unfortunately, the benefits were not enough for me to go against the type of selfish person I am.

Everything that I planned, and the diversions and distractions that were to be put into motion, have not come to fruition. The main reason for this was the thorn in my side, Peter. In the beginning I thought of him as a kindred spirit, even giving him an elevated position of my right-hand man. I respected that piece of shit and he betrays me. My teeth almost break my skin as I bite down on my finger. The reason for my pain and anguish leaves his vehicle outside of the church in town. I have only been sat here for five minutes and was gathering my thoughts, when the truck came into view. I left the community directly after morning prayers and he must have left around the same time.

With the ransom deadline for the couple trussed up in the catacombs only thirty-six hours away, time is of the essence. It has forced my hand and I need to bring forward the timing of my original plan. If that fucker could only have carried out my simple instructions, we would not be in this predicament. I should have put an end to it there and then. It is not as though I have not taken a life before, is it? There is only one more to extinguish and the loathsome creature resides behind those grey stone walls. But, my vengeance will have to wait just a short-while.

I wait until Peter is halfway up the path towards the entrance to the church before I open the door to my car. I know that he is deeply religious, but why on earth would he need to visit a church directly after prayers? Something just didn't seem right. Perhaps I will uncover a little more about the real man behind the façade. He disappears inside and I quicken and lengthen my stride, so that I enter the church a short time after him.

As I suspected, the church, at that time of day, was devoid of worshippers. The morning mass already dispensed and the congregation dispersed to their own devices. Each of them filled with the word of the Lord and his son, Jesus Christ, the perfect breakfast for any devout Catholic. My skin crawls at the mere thought of the hypocrisy of it all. Peter is being cautious as he walks between the rows of chairs, looking back over his shoulder to make sure that he is alone. I conceal myself deeper in the shadows, behind a pillar and obscured from his view, but enough that I can observe his movements. He is heading to the far side of the building, in the direction of the confessional. With one last glance over his shoulder, he opens the door of the booth on the left-hand side, and closes it behind him. It looks like the kidnapping of the couple was weighing heavy on his mind and he needed to unload his burden to a higher power.

As I wait in the relative concealment of the shadows, I glance around the church. It is an old building with all the charm of the Gothic period which was so popular in Europe. The kind of place that was familiar in all of those horror movies which contained some religious connection or demonic possession storyline. The fight of good against evil was always a money spinner and I chuckle to myself at how ludicrous that was. The man I have come to confront is nowhere to be seen and my heart sinks. Have I timed my visit wrong? Has he decided that he chooses today to not show his face? Whatever the answer, I am distracted by the sound of a door opening to my left.

I whip my head around to see the figure of a giant of a man stepping from the right-hand confessional booth. He is powerfully built with a shaven head and a rather expensive-looking suit. He is the first priest I have seen take confession not wearing a cassock! Of course he is not wearing holy vestments, because this man is not an ordained priest. He is something else completely! His stride and gait have purpose and his face is serious as he rushes from the church. The other booth is opened only a minute later, and the now worried-looking Peter exits as if he had been scalded by boiling oil. With my suspicions confirmed that he was not who he portrayed to be, I watch as he rushes to the entrance of the building.

As I linger, in the semi-darkness at the outer edge of the main hall of the church, a movement catches my attention. A black shock of wavy, well-groomed hair beneath which is an almost angelic face. This particular cherub has inflicted more pain and suffering on young innocents than I like to remember. Dressed in the long, flowing cassock and adorned with a large bejewelled crucifix as worn by all members of the catholic clergy, this particular cleric, with his highly polished, patent leather shoes, made my life and others lives miserable in our time at Upton Abbey. Many times, had those long, sturdy fingers probed and explored the nubile bodies of the people in his charge. I feel the anger in me rise as I observe him from my hidden position.

I fumble in my pockets to check that I have not forgotten the items I put there earlier when I awoke. I have planned this moment for a while, just never thought I would have to carry it out as quickly. I fear my time has almost come to an end and my past and future intentions will be discovered. Peter's presence there and the powerfully built stranger, only strengthen that opinion. My fingers curl around the glass cylinder in my pocket and I begin to calm down. Father Murphy makes his way to the far side of the church and walk towards the confessionals. His shoes are barely visible at the hem of his robes and it appears as if he is gliding over the floor. It is only the sound of the leather heels on the concrete floor that dispels that notion. He reaches the booth that the stranger vacated only a few minutes ago and he disappears inside.

I let the echo of the wooden door subside from the open space before stepping from my concealment and scurrying across to the left-hand confessional. I check around me that we are still the only people to occupy the church and thankfully we are. I just hope that my luck lasts for the next ten minutes or so. I might have to rethink my original plan, if we are joined by any other parishioners. Opening the door, I slip inside and take a seat facing the wooden grill. I compose myself, going through the words I have rehearsed for so long. Then as the wooden grill is drawn back, I take a deep breath and begin my confession.

"Forgive me Father, for I have sinned. It has been eight months since my last confession." The words fall effortlessly from my mouth. Words that I have spoken time and time again through my young, tortured life.

There is an uncomfortable silence as the priest waits for me to confess the things that are weighing heavy on my mind. That is the beauty of the Catholic faith, you can admit your wrong doing and a priest, as God's servant on earth, can absolve you of them. Also, what you reveal is between you and God and cannot be passed onto anyone else.

"I have committed murder six times against God's holy commandments." The silence that preceded this one is nothing compared to now. It is as if we were in our own little microcosm of a world. My revelation so shocking, I can only imagine what is going through the rapist's mind.

"My son, this is not something that I can give you absolution for off-hand, without knowing what drove you to break God's holy laws in such a way." There is a definite quake and uncertainty to the priest's voice. I'm not surprised, as it's not everyday someone confesses multiple murders to you.

"They were abusers of young children and innocents. Most of them were servants of the Lord, just like you, Father Murphy." I lean forward and whisper his name through the grill.

Through the wooden latticework, I see the figure recoil. I cannot make out his features clearly, but see the colour drain from them. After the initial shock has worn off, he moves nervously on the wooden seat before shuffling forward, his voice lowered so not to project it outside of the wooden box.

""Do we know each other, my son?" There is fear in his tone now. That is exactly what I have dreamed of. It is his turn to feel what it is like to be vulnerable. I slip out silently from the booth.

I thrust my hand into my pocket and pull out the glass cylinder and piece of gauze. Once more, I look around to see if we are still alone. This town must be sin-free as they are not lining up to confess their misdeeds. I unscrew the cap off the bottle and place the gauze over the opening. Turning it over, I feel some of the liquid soak through the material onto my fingers. I return the cap to the bottle before putting it back into my pocket and with my free hand, I open the door to the priest's confessional booth. As our eyes meet, for that brief moment, there is recognition and fear all rolled into one. Fucking perfect!

"Hello again, Father. Are you ready for your punishment?" My arm holding the gauze shoots out while the other holds his head against the back of the booth. The liquid on the material quickly does its work and Father Murphy sags against me.

I hoist him over my shoulder and struggle out of the confessional and into the church. With no one to ask any awkward questions, but not wanting to walk out by the front entrance, I carry his body to the rear of the church. I know from past visits that there is an entrance which I can use to make my way, unobserved, from the building and back to my vehicle. It couldn't have gone any better and I grin to myself, as we leave the confines of the church while I carry the hapless paedophile back to my car. My journey is almost complete. Just one last celebration, to thank my flock for their love and support, and to disclose how much evil and betrayal wanders this world.

The room is full of joyous laughter and I sweep my head along the table and regard the people who have come as close to friends as I have ever had. Should I not then feel a pang of regret that I have used them for my own ends? Of course I shouldn't. I have not changed that much that I should feel any emotional attachment to these fuckers!! I am not sure if it has been noticed that the meal we are having this evening closely reflects that of the last supper. That particular meal was taken on the first day of Passover by Jesus and his disciples. It was a remembrance of Israel being freed of slavery from Egypt, and specifically when the angel of death passed over the homes of the Israelites that had lambs blood over the doors. There were no such things here, but it was still a little bit of theatre where I could reveal how we have been betrayed.

I let the conversation flow and everyone to get high, including myself. However, I did hold myself back as I needed to have some clarity of thought and action for later. I was not surprised to see that Peter was not the life and soul of the party this evening. Whatever the mysterious stranger conveyed to him, had clearly shaken him. His stoic reserve is replaced with a nervous and furtive withdrawn character that seems to have retreated inside his shell. His eyes are alert and dance around the room. He seems to be making an assessment of each member of the family. It makes sense now that he is a member of some law enforcement agency. I should have worked this out earlier, and that enrages me. Well, it is time for him to learn that no one gets in my way! Tonight it ends, however that may be, only God can say.

"Brothers and sisters. Tonight we celebrate all that we have achieved since we began on our journey together." The sounds of conversation die down until the room is silent. Every face is turned towards me.

"The road we have travelled together has been hard at times. You have all proved your commitment and passion for this dream of ours. It is with a sad heart that I must tell you, one of our number will betray not only me, but our entire family and new way of life." The quiet that descended on the room, as I called for silence, is magnified. Mouths are agape as the enormity of my statement sinks in.

"Never, Teacher! That would never happen!" Tabitha jumps to her feet and glares at me, then to each person in the room. Some nod their heads in agreement with her, while others are sat motionless and stunned.

"Unfortunately, what I speak of is the truth. Let that person examine their heart, and know that I do not bear them any ill will." I have to put on the performance of my life, as I utter the final part of my revelation.

"Do you know who this Judas is?" Magdalene now addresses me. There is a worried look on her face, as if I was suspecting her. Has she something to hide? Was she in league with this piece of shit? How could my fixation with this whore blind me to such a level? Now I can see why I have never become involved in a trusting relationship!

"Yes, my child, I do know, but it is as I have said. It is up to that person to look at himself and to see what they are attempting to destroy." The hint of sarcasm in my reply and the brief look at Peter does not go unnoticed, I fear, by Magdalene. It is of no consequence, it will soon all be over.

"Let us not dwell on things we cannot influence. Come, break bread with me." I take the freshly made loaf of bread, still warm to the touch, from the centre of the table.

"Eat this bread, for this is my body." I tear off a chunk of the bread and offer it to Thomas, who is sitting to my left. He takes it gratefully.

"Drink this wine, for it is my blood." I slide my wine glass towards him and he takes a sip before returning it to me.

One by one, I call each of my flock to me. They leave their seats and traverse the table so that they are facing me on the other side. They kneel before me and I offer each of them a piece of bread which represents the body of Christ. This is followed by a sip of wine to represent his blood and the sacrifice he gave for the world. It is a ritual that is carried out every day in churches all over the planet, but nothing seems as significant as this particular ceremony. I cannot explain it, but there seems a genuine air of solemnity around the room.

Priscilla was the penultimate disciple to partake of the bread and wine. I have engineered it so that she finishes the remnants of wine in the glass. As she stands and returns to her seat, I fill the glass once more from the bottle that I have emptied into a glass decanter. The other glasses were filled from a regular bottle. I have saved this particular glass for Peter. He makes his way towards me and placing his hands together in prayer, kneels in front of me. I pass the broken bread to him and place it on his outstretched tongue. He chews it slowly, his eyes never leaving mine. As I reach forward with the glass, he seems to recoil slightly. Surely he cannot smell the concoction of drugs that I have mixed with the dark liquid? It is only a momentary reaction, as he opens his mouth to receive his communion. He passes the liquid around his mouth and I see his eyes widen, as he suspects what has just happened. I do not conceal the wry grin that spreads across my features as he rises and leaves the room.

The piece of filth is stretched out over the spanking bench before me. His cassock is torn open at the back, so I have free reign to his putrid flesh. This man, if you can call him that, has taken many an innocent soul. They tear away that innocence and feel the evil joy, as they sink into the filth of indifference. He, the Abbot and the rest of their disgusting circle, have inflicted that torture on their victims for the last time.

I look up from his prostrate form and Peter takes centre stage of the far wall of the main space in the catacomb. I have secured his eyes open with clips, to prevent him from blinking. I want him to witness everything that is about to happen. Our male and female captives are secured on either side of him. They, as well, are fastened by their arms and feet to the wooden beams which are inset into the walls. Their blindfolds have been removed, but their mouths are covered with duct tape. My disciples are gathered to the left and right of Father Murphy, whose back is now criss-crossed with deep lacerations, from the bullwhip that is being wielded in my unpractised hands. An expert would not have inflicted as much pain and suffering that I have just done. For me, that is irrelevant. Sub-humans like this deserve nothing less than what he is about to receive.

The drugs that I slipped into Peter's wine helped me subdue him and carry his body to the catacombs from his dormitory. Then, after calling the seekers to prayer, I took them down into the catacombs. I took with me those images that I have carried with me all of my life since leaving the Abbey. The very same images that this piece of shit I have just scourged, kept of his young victims. I took them from his secret place before running away that night, all those years ago. Handing them around my disciples, I begin to speak.

"This is what this man and other so-called servants of the Lord, do in his name. I have dispensed God's justice on his vile group of perverts and child molesters. No more will their filthy habits be inflicted on the innocent. Now, I call on you to aid me in administering the same pain on him as he and his kind inflicted on others." I turn to each of my flock, and all of them look up from the images that are being passed around. As one, they nod in agreement; even Magdalene, who seems a little more withdrawn, appears willing to follow out my instructions for maybe the last time.

"Of course, Teacher. Clerics like this do not deserve to walk on God's good earth. We will do whatever you ask." It is

Thomas who has stepped forward. The look of disdain, as he stares at the now-disfigured priest, conveys his feelings for the animal.

"Use his body as you see fit. Every orifice is there for your pleasure. Do unto him as he has done unto others who could not defend themselves." I indicate the line of instruments of a sexual nature I have prepared for this occasion.

The females are first to move. They are led by the two former prostitutes, who arm themselves with nipple clamps, plastic cocks of immeasurable length and girth. and steel balls connected together in a series of link-chains. A veritable smorgasbord of pain and delight. Lydia and Bethany lead the women to the shackled Father. Lydia kneels behind his upturned buttocks. With the aid of one hand, she opens his ass cheeks and inserts the first of three steel balls into his anus. The priest wails out loud, but his cries go ignored. A shiver of pleasure runs through my whole body, as I continue to observe. Bethany has adopted a similar kneeling position but on the other side of the spanking bench, facing the priest's flaccid penis and swollen balls.

Her fingers begin at his knees and she runs them up his inner thighs, lingering a while, teasing him. I am sure he will not find this in the least bit sensual, knowing his propensity for sweeter meats of another sex. Her lips encircle his testicles, taking his plums deep into her mouth. I watch her gullet as it contracts and relaxes as she sucks on those wrinkled orbs. Her jaw tightens, just as her sister forces the final sphere into the pervert's anus.

"Fuck, please stop!" His screams are received with a resounding slap of a paddle on his hairless buttocks. It leaves an indention and immediately the skin turns a deep red.

"No, please. No!" Once, twice, three and four times. The sound of his skin being beaten by the wooden implement, the skin breaking to reveal a trickle of blood running down his ass cheeks and his upper thighs to the back of the knees. Lydia strengthens her grip on his balls with her mouth, and he fights against the restraints. I swear I think she will sever the skin with her teeth. Strangely enough, his once flaccid cock has sprung into life. Lydia releases his testicles and slips his shaft into her mouth, taking him to the hilt. Then, again she clamps down with her teeth, at the base of his penis.

"Fuck, no! Please stop!" The cleric is delirious with pain now and I chuckle out loud.

"How many have uttered those words to you?" I stride across the room and scream the words into his face. He lifts his head, the veins in his neck protruding under the effort.

"I'm sorry! I confess my sins!" He is desperate to be free of this horror. but he knows from my eyes that this is not going to end well.

"I am not worthy to hear your confession and absolve you of your sins, my son. " I leer at him, as I throw my robe off and turn my back on him.

My naked body bristles in the cool air of the cavern. With my back facing him, he gets to observe the mural that depicts the crucifixion and the suffering of Christ. The same suffering that he is about to feel. I look directly at Peter, who is shaking his head in an attempt to communicate to me to stop all of this. Not a fucking chance, my friend! At least that is what I thought you were. You are going to feel the same for betraying me, but first you must watch him receive his just rewards.

I turn back around to see Lydia pull the steel balls from the priest anus in a rough, unceremonious fashion. He screams out loud as one pain is replaced by another as a gigantic cock is forced as far as it will go, deep into his cavity. At the other end, Magdalene slides it back and forth. His eyes are forced tightly shut now as he tries to ride the pain of the sex toy. It does not take long for Thomas and Luke to get in on the act of retribution. They push Magdalene to one side and for the next ten minutes, take it in turns to empty their cum deep in the priest's ass. I look towards our captive audience, the couple have their eyes closed to the horror show being acted out before them. Peter is not afforded such a luxury but there is a resigned look on his now distraught face. Of course, there is nothing he can do about it.

I turn around and face Father Murphy, whose strength is quickly failing and whose cries are diminishing in intensity. I feared that I would not be able to carry out this act on the disgusting priest, but the whole scene has me strangely aroused. I make my way around to the rear of the bench. His buttocks and back are a bleeding mess. The semen from Thomas and Luke flows freely from his anus, mixing with the blood. I take my cock in hand and force myself deep into him, in one powerful thrust. With the leftover cum from my two disciples acting as a lubricant, I pound in and out of him. The force of it rocks the bench on its mountings. I reach forward and grasp hold of the cleric's throat and delight in the sensation of a strong pulse against my skin. With every movement of my hips, I increase the pressure on his throat. Beneath me, his body is beginning to sag and I feel my seed boiling in my balls and it begins its journey up my cock. With one final squeeze on his throat, I shoot my load hard into his filthy cavern.

A flash before my eyes as I explode is met with an acrid taste in my mouth. I look to the far wall at the figure of Peter and the two hostages, which becomes a little hazy. They appear like ghosts emerging out of the mists in a cemetery. Their faces become less recognizable. The mist appears to get thicker and the taste in my mouth even stronger and I begin to cough. Father Murphy's body has stopped moving and I prepare to push myself free.

"Armed FBI Officers! Do not move!" The smoke gets denser and figures emerge from all around me.

CHAPTER TWENTY-ONE - REVELATIONS

Religion, for me, is a difficult thing to define, as it is more than one single thing. They are a shared set of beliefs that have been passed down through word of mouth or by the written word. These religions are invariably led by people in positions of power, who embody formal aspects of the religion and who act in positions of leadership and governance, and there are certain rituals reserved for them to carry out. These beliefs lay a foundation on how we should, or should not, lead our lives.

We often ask ourselves the question of why we have been put on the planet and what our purpose is. It is religion that tries to explain this by using spiritual explanations of our place in the world. Be it a folk religion, which uses established cultural practices, or a formalized religion using formally documented doctrine. They both attempt to answer life's questions by using various tools. It is central in both, to use the worship of deities and or supernatural entities. These in folk religion may include ancestors, or the conceptions of "holy" and "sacred" activities, ideas and objects. All of these things revolve around a set of rituals, calendar events based on the changing seasons. Even when the church was formalised by the Roman Emperor Constantine in the fourth century AD, the Pagan festivals were those that were incorporated into the Christian calendar.

The religious professionals have distinct dress codes to distance them from others in society. They set them apart and elevate them to a higher place in our eyes. They are the deities' representatives here on earth. They have been given a mandate from a higher being, from a supernatural force or from the will of the Universe itself. Some Christians believe that religion is actually a relationship with Jesus. Likewise, some Muslims say "Islam is not a religion, it is a way of life."

It is the religious professionals of the priesthood who have me confused. I was taught that the Christian priest was considered a man of God. He is empowered to distribute God's Holy word, to carry out all rituals and sacraments in his most Holy name. It is their mission to proclaim, teach and guard the word of God as laid down in the scriptures. He is called to a life of service and sacrifice, not to abuse that position in pursuit of his own sexual gratification. To give up the sins of the flesh, is one of the most selfless things a priest can do. To remain celibate for the rest of their lives. I have found that this is not the case for some of the church's members.

I take the grinding, gravelly road that leads from the small market town of Upton. It has passed the witching hour, and the landscape is silent except for the occasional hoot of a lonely owl. The moonlight reflects off the thick cobblestone walls of the Abbey, which looms up before me. Four towers stand stark against the moonlit sky, giving a sense of power and control. It was a fortress of power. That power wielded in God's name by the man I have come to reckon with. It has been five years since I left these foreboding walls. An eternity since those filthy hands and fetid breath stained my skin for the first time. A compulsion in me to return and try and make right all of the wrongs that this place stood for, had driven me to that point.

As I slip through one of the side entrances that I know is left unlocked, my heart begins to quicken. The perspiration on my brow begins to trickle and runs into the corner of my eye and I have to wipe it away to see clearly. The evening is warm, but there is a cooling breeze from the mountains in the distance. Even so, my body feels like it is on fire. Of course, it is the adrenalin that is surging through my veins in anticipation of what I am about to do. This night will change my life forever and set me on a path that has only one destination. I have weighed up the consequences, but know that in my heart of hearts it is something I must do. I cannot let this abomination, and his kind, walk this earth free to do what he and others have done, to young boys and men. At least that is what I know. I would not like to imagine other crimes they may have committed in the sordid little circle.

The sound of my feet on the concrete floor of the cloisters is softened by the sneakers I have chosen to wear. I move almost silently along the well-worn open corridor and past the courtyard into the northwest part of the Abbey. The Abbot's quarters are situated at the bottom of the tower, cut off from the rest of the inhabitants. It is isolated enough for me to carry out what I need to, without being disturbed.

I listen outside the heavy wooden door of his quarters. The only sound I can hear is the trickle of the water from the fountain in the courtyard. I push down on the handle and am not surprised when I find, like most of the doors in the Abbey, it is unlocked. My entry is only betrayed by the creaking of the door, as it swings slowly open. I hold it firm so that the creaking from the hinges stops. Then, pushing it inch by inch, I wait until there is enough room for me to slip inside. I push the door gently, so that the latch reinserts itself and a muffled click tells me it is secure. I pause for a short time until my eyes grow accustomed to the dim lighting of the room. Strange shapes and silhouettes surround me. This is the main reception room, if my memory serves me right. I have been summoned here on many occasion to receive a private punishment, out of the prying eyes of the rest of the school.

I navigate my way around the furniture and step into the living room, which has more illumination from the small window on the far wall. It throws a shaft of light and falls on a door just a way to my left. That is the private bed chamber of the Abbot and I shiver as I recall stepping over that threshold more than once. With all of my courage, and fighting to quell the rage that is building inside of me, I let myself enter.

The Abbot lies on his back facing the ceiling. His large stomach rising from the bed, like a land mass erupting from Mother Earth. He is a vile, loathsome creature and to me, the epitome of evil. He and his wretched brethren and child molesters, will burn in hell for the sins they have committed in this life. Very soon, he will be welcomed by Satan himself. Delivered by my own hand and I chuckle as I creep towards him. His chest and stomach rise and fall as he sleeps, undisturbed and unaware of my presence. I take the hypodermic from my pocket and place my hand just above his mouth. In one fluid movement, I clamp my hand over his mouth and his eyes open wide. There is an almost instant look of recognition, before the sharp pain of the needle piercing his skin, turns those eyes to fear.

Most of us will never know how it feels to take another human life. That tangible sensation that comes with watching someone breathe their last breath and knowing it's because of something you've done. I feel privileged to be able to experience that with this, my first victim. As his eyes flicker and the substance mixes with his blood, I take the knife from my belt. I stuff a piece of material into his mouth to stifle his cries. Then placing the blade on the bed, I lift up the Abbot's nightgown.

His cock and balls are of average size, but big enough to cause pain and suffering for all those young boys that they have penetrated. I take hold of the flaccid shaft, moving it to one side, then gripping his balls from underneath, lifting them high. I pick

That was twenty years ago now, and the first life I took. It
would not be the last, as I hunted down every one of that
disgusting group of individuals. I can still remember the sounds
of excited voices and the taste of the smoke. I was made to
kneel down with my hands on my head, while handcuffs secured
me by the wrists. My next recollection is being charged with false
imprisonment by means of abduction and demanding a ransom.
Also, the first degree murder of Father Sean Murphy. It was
during my questioning that the FBI tied in my movements since
leaving Upton to a series of disappearances of known
paedophiles and clergy in the states where I was residing. With
the killing of Father Murphy completing the circle, they drew their
own conclusions. I was tried and sentenced to live out the
remainder of my life on death row.

I have been sentenced to die by lethal injection, I just
didn't know when that would be. Each day, a little more of me
dies inside. Lethal injection is the most common way to die for
those on death row. Other states like Mississippi, Utah, and
Oklahoma could face a firing squad. Fuck that! Give me one last
high any day. Between showering, exercise, routine checks, and
the occasional visitor, I receive an average of one hour out of my
cell per day. Unless I am in my cell, showering, or in the prison
exercise yard, I am handcuffed. Any approved visitation time is
accompanied by being cuffed for the duration. Magdalene visited
me once, more out of pity than anything else. I spoke four words
to her the entire visit. As she departed, I whispered "God, be
with you." Gone, was the look of passion, adoration and love that
she held for me back then. Whatever it was that formed between
us, that invisible link was broken. She gave me a pitiful smile
and left without saying a word.

At my trial, it came to light that my move to California was
just the final step in my quest to eliminate the final child molester
from my past. All members of my flock were present at the trial

and when I did not deny it, the room was filled with cries of disbelief. How could I have misled them in such a way? To build up their hopes and manipulate them for my own ends, was beyond contempt, according to an outraged Bethany. They carried out everything that I asked of them which led to some of them being brought to trial. This was mainly petty robbery of unsuspecting young men that the girls picked up in Sebastopol. That particular idea was spawned from my mother's past, but was just another test of how much I could manipulate them. Those involved in these crimes were handed out lenient sentences and they were probably living normal lives right now.

All of these thoughts run through my mind as I pace the exercise yard. The previous day, I was given the news that my date of execution was confirmed for the following Friday. Waiting for long periods of time for your sentence to be confirmed and carried out, can be debilitating to a prisoner's mental health. Between the appeals process and last-minute stays of execution, it's been impossible for me to know, with certainty, when I would take my last breath. Now that I have a date, I can tell my story. For years, I have been hounded by various newspapers and magazines to give an interview. Most of my life I wanted to be in the spotlight, but prison life has changed me. I am not saying I am ashamed of what I have done, far from it. If I had the chance to do it all again, I would in a heartbeat.

"Stewart, your time is up. Mr. Crane is waiting for you in the interview room." I squint my eyes against the glaring mid-day sunshine. The figure of the prison guard, waiting by the gate to escort me to my visitor, becomes a little clearer.

"Coming, boss!" I raise my hand in acknowledgment and shuffle towards him. He reaches through the grill and places the cuffs on my wrists before opening the gate for me.

He walks just one pace behind me, an arms distance away, so that he can react if he needs to. He is not close enough for me to grab hold of him and even if I did, guards were positioned along our route on firing towers to intervene, if required. I savour the sensation of the sun warming through the material of my prison uniform. How many more times will I feel that embrace, before I leave this world for the last time? It is true that we do not really appreciate life until there comes a time for us to leave it all behind? I have plenty of time to ponder on that in the days to come.

"Curtis, I'm so glad you agreed to our meeting." Gary Crane, of "Time Magazine" is one of the country's most respected journalists. It was for that reason, and the magazines distribution, I agreed to tell him my story.

I take the chair that is vacant directly opposite him. The guard stands just inside the door, but close enough to me so that he can protect the journalist, if that should be needed. Since my time on death row, I have kept my head down and not got involved in some of the politics of the place. The particular crimes that I was sentenced for, mean that in some circles, I am revered. I have done a public service eradicating the country of these vile creatures who prey on the young and defenceless. Others are not so lucky and it is not uncommon for many on death row to die before their sentence is carried out.

"So, why don't you start at the beginning and tell me a little about your life growing up?" The journalist presses the button on the tape recording device that is on the table in front of him and sits back.

"I was born in Ingleton, Virginia on August 22nd 1947. I was brought up in a religious family and it was a big part of my life. My mother tried her best for me, but never seemed to have enough time to show me right from wrong." Crane made a few notes in a notepad on his knee. From my position, I couldn't make out what they said.

"Would you say you were missing a father figure in your life? A role-model if you like?" It was from this point, I saw that he was leading me into the story that he wanted to tell. Not actually my own story!

"I would not say that at all, Mr. Crane. I am my own man and I always have been." I sneer at the fat fucker, who dabs the perspiration from his forehead with a handkerchief. My reply has him flustered.

"I didn't mean to overstep the mark or put words into your mouth, Curtis. Please, go ahead." He squirms in his seat. I can tell from the look in his eye, he thinks that he will blow his chance of a top story if he upsets me.

"That would be most kind of you." I am beginning to enjoy this feeling of power. Yet again, I am the centre of attention and I bathe in all its glory.

For the next hour, I go through my early life. From my childhood and being passed around from pillar to post. My drunken mother and wayward Uncle. The constant trouble I would be in at school, all because of other people. The first session was over before I knew it. Crane never stopped writing the whole time, and it felt good that someone was interested in my story.

The next three days, I spend each afternoon relaying my story, in graphic detail, to the journalist. At times he stopped writing, as if what I was saying sickened him to the very core. I am in my element, once more the centre of attention, even though my audience is limited to one journalist and a guard. When I leave this life, my story will be told worldwide. It will be my name that is on everyone's lips. A name that will pass down in history too, as a new Messiah who cleansed the church of its filth!

The grill of my cell door slides open and a guard passes through the glossy magazine. I take it from him and stare back at my own image looming up out of the page. It causes me to smile, knowing that people all over the world will be looking at that very same picture. The font of my name is bold enough to grab your immediate attention, but not too ostentatious. I like that. Crane promised me he would give me a copy as soon as it rolled off the press and true to his word, here it was. I am a little confused why he didn't bring it in person though. I sit down on my bed and flick through the pages until I find my article.

Curtis Stewart stares back at me emotionless, across the small table that is the only barrier between us. His hands are cuffed and his elbows rest on the wooden surface. He has all the traits of a psychopath. He is a callous, exploitive individual with blunted emotions, impulsive inclinations and an inability to feel guilt or remorse. That being said, he is an intelligent, and very charismatic man. His handsome features and softly spoken lilt, was almost hypnotic. I can understand why people followed him like they did.

The causes of psychopathy remain a mystery. We don't even have a satisfactory answer to the question of whether psychopathy is a product of Mother Nature, or a feature of upbringing. With Stewart, I think it is a little of both. The lack of a father figure in his life, caused him to seek attention at an early age. He was a rebellious youngster and habitual liar. He would lie to deflect the blame from himself onto anyone else that he saw fit. It was a way for him to justify his actions. This constant aggressive and uncontrollable behaviour, would lead him to be put into care.

His teenage years spent at Upton Abbey, were to cause something inside him to break. Not only witnessing, but being subject to horrific emotional, physical and sexual abuse by a group of priests and other paedophiles, was the catalyst that manifested his psychotic journey.

Not all psychopaths are criminals, but like Curtis Stewart, they are manipulative, aggressive and impulsive. These features, more often than not, always lead to criminal activity. In fact, during and after creating the community known as "The Seekers of the Way", Stewart distanced himself from any form of criminal activity. Little did his followers know, but their charismatic Messiah-figure had already taken a number of lives in horrific ways, of which I will now illustrate using his own words.

I continue to read the article and with each line, my anger grows ever stronger. These are not the words I spoke. He has twisted everything about my life, my purpose, everything about me! He has sensationalised and belittled what I set out to do, which was to seek retribution for the poor, innocent children who suffered at the hands of these beasts. I tear out the pages of the magazine in a rage and scatter them around the cell. As I begin to calm down, I can see that some points of the story do paint me in a good light. It was not the Boogeyman that children should fear at night, rather the opposite. It showed that to some people, crimes against the innocent will not be tolerated. Only God can judge me on that one and that time is coming very soon.

The press romanticize and sensationalize the hours and minutes leading up to an execution. It fascinated me in the past, how the taking of a human life would draw so much attention and stir the emotions of people. Does that not make them as bad as the person who is to be executed? To take such joy from what is such a barbarous act? The Bible says "an eye for an eye", but it also says "love thy neighbour as you love thyself", "to turn the other cheek" and a myriad of other quotes, that in reality do not stand up to real life. I take the last bite of my final meal of fried chicken and potato logs, with tartar sauce. It sticks in my throat and I wash it down with the chocolate milkshake.

"Well, my friend. I guess this is where we part company." Tom appears behind my right shoulder. This is the first time in twenty years that he has disturbed me.

Tom has represented that part of my psyche that was so fragmented due to the trauma that it broke away from the real me. He was an avenue or outlet for me to use. A way of venting my frustrations on the evil world around me. I have spent uncountable hours in his company debating the rights and wrongs of my actions. I cannot use him as an excuse, what is done is done. I must pay for the crimes that I have committed.

"Indeed, it is time, my friend. I wish you well and I will see you on the other side." I turn to face him, but he has already vanished.

The sound of hard-soled shoes on the linoleum floor of corridor outside my cell, heralds the arrival of what will be my final visitor. I drop to my knees and clasp my hands in front of me, in supplication before the throne of grace. The turning of the key in the lock and a sudden draught tells me that the door is open. I raise my head, just a little, and open my eyes. The first thing that meets my gaze, is the hem of a black robe, from which a pair of shiny black shoes protrude. I lift my head higher and the large crucifix suspended around the priest's neck, is my next reference point. I continue to lift up my head and reach a face that is weathered and wrinkled. It has seen many years in God's service and his features are kind. Who knows what secrets lie behind those sparkling blue eyes? Our priests carry not only the full weight of our burdens, but their own as well. Please pray for them.

"Good evening, my son. I am Father Aiden Kilpatrick. I am here to administer the last rites for you."

"Thank you, Father." I lower my head once more, as he begins with the sign of the cross.

He then goes on to lead me through the Sacrament of Confession. Once this has been dispensed, he takes me through the Apostle's Creed and I renew all of my baptismal promises. Such a pointless thing to do really I know, but I go along with the game. Perhaps if there is a God, he will look favourably on me. Once this is complete, the priest steps forward towards me. From his left-hand side, another pair of feet appears. These are quite petite but also peek out from underneath a long, black robe. I raise my head and as it explores the figure in front of me, I can tell that even the loose fitting garment cannot conceal the body of a woman. Her face is framed with a white wimple, but those features are unmistakable. Her eyes are cloudy as she holds out the golden bowl she is carrying.

"Thank you, Sister." Magdalene steps forward and the priest dips two fingers into the receptacle, covering them with oil.

"In the name of the Father, Son and Holy Spirit. You will say with us the Lord's Prayer." He anoints my forehead with the sign of the cross.

The cell is filled with sounds of our conjoined voices as we recite the Lord's Prayer. Magdalene stares at me with a love that I remember from when we first met. Perhaps if things had been different, we could have become something. Instead, she has cut herself off from the world and devoted herself to the church. That is such a shame, as she would make someone a perfect wife. For the first time in my life, I feel some form of regret as the prayer comes to an end.

"It is time, my son." The priest's words have a finality about them and I stand.

Both he and Magdalene turn their backs on me and depart the cell. I follow on behind them. As I step outside of the cell, two guards who I have never seen before, take up a position behind me. Prison Officer Squires who has been on the block for most of my time here, is stood facing me.

"Are you ready?" He steps forward so that he is only two paces away.

"I am." I swallow hard and try to coat my mouth, which has quickly become dry. Oh how I would love to taste another milkshake.

"Follow me." Squires rotates on his heel and with Father Kilpatrick and Magdalene leading the way, we step off in unison.

They say when Death comes to you, your whole life flashes in front of your eyes. I am not sure if that was true, but for every step I take, a memory invades my mind. Some are pleasant, while others are not. It is a map of life's journey from beginning to end. I am ready to take that final step of my own particular journey, with no regrets and definitely no remorse.

I am led into a room that is almost clinical in nature. The walls and floor are a gleaming white and I have to squint my eyes against the glare. In the centre of the space, is a blue leather reclined chair, with restraints attached to it. Squires takes me by the hand and helps me onto the place from where I will not rise again. I shuffle backwards until I am comfortable and he places his hand on my head and gently pushes me back until my shoulders touch the leather. With experienced hands, he quickly fastens the restraints around my legs and arms. A guy in a white coat inserts two needles in each of my arms, securing them with some tape. Once he has finished, he nods to the Warden of the penitentiary, who was waiting for us in the room. Without hesitation, he begins to speak.

"Curtis Stewart, you have been sentenced to death by lethal injection, by a jury of your peers, in the great State of California. It is my duty to carry out that sentence on their behalf. Have you any last words to say?" He looks at me without a flicker of emotion. Not even a little pity.

"I have not, Warden. They got what they deserved." I will not lie, even on pain of death. I am not sorry for what I have done. They made me who I am. God will judge me soon enough.

"Very well. Officer Squires, carry out the sentence." He looks to the Officer, who presses a button on a panel in front of him.

I watch as the plunger descends on the glass cylinder and the coldness enters my veins. So many times have I felt that sensation and the euphoric high it brings. Although this time, the high will never be repeated. I look through the single window, which looks out onto the gallery of people who have come to watch my demise. My mother and grandmother are in the front row and my mother appears almost inconsolable. My grandmother looks at me with those loving eyes that tried to teach me right from wrong. Her love was unconditional, even after everything I have done has been revealed. As my consciousness slowly begins to wane, I catch sight of a group of three people. Two males and one female. The older male has short, well-trimmed hair, which is turning grey at the sides. His features are so familiar, and then it hits me. It is Peter, or as I later found out, Special Agent Patrick Devlin of the FBI. I should feel anger towards him, but I do not. I tried to take his life, that night in the catacombs, but I am glad that I failed. The woman and young man sat with him, seem to be very close. It is then, in that brief moment before death, that I remember the photograph I found in his Bible. These are his family and I would have deprived them of many happy years together. I would have denied them something that I craved for myself all of these years. I turn my head away and look towards Magdalene. Tears stream down both cheeks and her shoulders quiver and shake. My heart is filled with sadness, but an overwhelming sense of joy, as I step towards the brightest of lights. The darkness takes me, and I am at peace.

The End

The Author

I am a British born author. I have written in a number of genres under various names. I began writing seriously in around 2015 and in about 2016 I tried my hand at writing erotica. I was influenced by reading a number of books by Dark Romance authors and I knew from that moment that it was the direction I wanted to take.

Favourite Authors:

I love English Classics like, Shakespeare, Dickens, and anything historical. I did however love horror writers like Stephen King and James Herbert when I was younger. I read a book by Charlotte E Hart recently, and it piqued my interest in the BDSM lifestyle. She writes so descriptively it makes you invest in her characters.

Influences:

I love human nature and how we all interact with one another. When I see someone, I always wonder what is going on in their heads. What secrets lie behind those eyes? We all have secrets buried deep down, those things we don't want others to know. It is this thought process and the complexities of the human mind that fascinates me.

How do I relax?

I love the outdoors and taking long walks in the mountains which are only an hour's drive from where I live. I also like to read, watch TV and socialise with friends.

Hopes and aspirations:

I hope any books that I publish will be enjoyed by those reading them. I enjoy creating a world that others may or may not have entered before. It is either familiar to some but also interesting to others. The ability to take a reader on a journey that due to their own personal circumstances they ordinarily would not have been able to take.

Other books by the author

I have written a number of books under the pen name of Zak Hardacre. They are of the same style and content as this release and do contain adult content and challenging subjects.

Explosive Chemistry

Undercover Liaisons

The Principal's Daughter

Male Escort Book 1 "Innocence"

Male Escort Book 2 "Discovery"

Male Escort Book 3 "The Professional"

Alters

Salvation

Hemispheres

Coma